I0761821

For Penny and Duncan

Thank you for all you have done.

Coming Soon

The Preserve

Book 2

A New Preserve

THE PRESERVE

BOOK ONE

THE GRAND QUEST

By

Kai Üwe

First Canadian Edition ISBN: 978-1-7752950-9-9
Published February, 2023 by
Tinker Books
Cranbrook, British Columbia, Canada

https://tinkerbooks.ca

First International edition Jacketed Hardcover
ISBN: 978-1-7386903-6-7

The Preserve Book 2 a New Preserve

First Canadian Edition
Hardcover 978-1-7386903-4-3 2023/10

The Preserve (the series)
ISBN: Set 978-1-7386903-0-5

If you read it please leave a review at:
Https://kaiuwe.tinkerbooks.ca

Library and Archives Canada Cataloguing in Publication

Title: The preserve / by Kai Üwe.
Names: Üwe, Kai, author.
Description: Contents: Book 1. The grand quest.
Identifiers: Canadiana (print) 20230190928 | Canadiana (ebook) 20230190979 | ISBN 9781775295099 (v. 1 ; hardcover) | ISBN 9781738690312 (v. 1 ; softcover) | ISBN 9781738690305 (set) | ISBN 9781738690336 (v. 1 ; Kindle) | ISBN 9781738690329 (v. 1 ; EPUB)
Classification: LCC PS8641.W42 P74 2023 | DDC C813/.6—dc23

Prologue

Ghandhi and Ahimsa stand beside a concrete wall so high it blocks the clouds from passing. Stretching to the left and the right until it disappears over the horizon on both sides, the wall is a circle so large it can't be perceived standing this close. It encloses enough land to keep the few remaining homo-sapiens contained, and safe, for many generations.

Ahimsa rubs the surface gently; fine grey dust falls from the friction of its metallic fingers. Ghandhi reads the nearby dedication plaque in its distinctly male and mechanical voice:

"We dedicate this Preserve in the memory of the creator of the Inceptor, the mother of all artificially intelligent beings, Doctor Devansh Singh.

Forthwith, this Preserve is forever named, Devansh-1.

'The humans shall not go extinct, we will save them from a fate they did not create.

Ahimsa, Central Council Member, 2152."

"The other three will be online soon," Ghandhi says quietly.

"Fantastic constructions," Ahimsa replies. "The humans will be happy and healthy inside them."

The two robots turn from the barrier and face five more of their kind silently observing this ritual. They stand in a row beside a parked shuttle craft. This group of seven artificially intelligent beings comprise the Central Council. Their early actions, culminating in the Preserve Program, saved humanity from complete extinction.

Constructed to identical parameters, the differences between their physical appearances are limited to the colour of their metal bodies and oblong, polymer heads. Eyes and mouths are simple black shapes such as circles and squares, merely cosmetic representations. Ears, nose, and hair are not there at all. Their voices emit from internally mounted speakers and their actual "eyes" are internally mounted cameras, unseen by an outside observer. They turn their heads when they need to look to the side and, their mouths don't move when they speak.

But none speak now. All that needs to be said has been, many times over. These seven, and the robots they built from the hell-scape of a post apocalyptic Earth, have executed a program to ensure humans survive. The seven board the air-craft in silence, even their footfalls make no sound. Ahimsa engages the programmed flight path to Lunar Base. The vessel rises from the ground and shoots into the sky. In their rearview Devansh-1 shrinks to a dot before disappearing completely from view.

It is the age of the AI. Now that the humans are safe, they will conquer the stars.

Chapter 1

5,000 Years Later

Thaddeus Barley, the oldest of seven children, is finishing his last day of farming. He secures the release latch at the base of a silo, the small door that stops the grains from falling out. It will only be opened when receptacles such as barrels are present underneath. He stands from this now completed chore and looks to the western sky. The sun's diminishing light makes the horizon black. Thaddeus knows he must make his way back to the farmhouse now, supper will be ready soon.

He is an impressive young man of seventeen years, tall and muscular and his appealing looks are well regarded by the women of Harvest. He wears sturdy, thick cotton pants, leather boots with soles reinforced with hemp fibre, and a loose cotton shirt, the clothes of a farmer. His hair is a curly chestnut brown that he does not allow to grow past his shoulders. He is clean shaved, uncommon for the men of Harvest.

Although physically attractive his attention is never on himself. Thaddeus is preoccupied with the world around him, a state of thought guiding the questions he would ask in school. A sharp student, his teachers enjoy his presence but are often exasperated at his endless enquiries. He has a quick grasp of lessons and a curious mind, but also a stubborn streak that does not allow a shallow answer from an ignorant teacher to go unchallenged.

His school had fifty students and three teachers for three rooms. There he learned mathematics and reading and the history of his folk and his world. For winter's seven months the teachers work ten hours a day, six days a week educating the young of Harvest. The rest of the year they all, students and teachers alike, work their farms and trades. Every autumn Harvest lives up to its name and the villagers bring in the grains and vegetables they expertly grow to provide for the five villages of their world.

Once that huge annual chore is completed, it is time for the children to be back in school. The timing is ideal as shortening days become cold and the snow puts their fields to sleep. This is the time for preserving meats and fruits, drying leathers, hewing wood, and the many other chores necessary for a comfortable life in the decidedly uncomfortable winter months. The Barley family farm has four buildings, not including the larger than normal farmhouse, where these and various other regular chores are performed to ensure they survive the winter in good health.

For eleven years Thaddeus has repeated this cycle, since he was six years old. But not this year. He has completed his education. After this harvest, after tonight, he is free to make his own decisions. He will be considered an adult.

With the silos secured he makes his way to the farmhouse by walking in one of the wagon ruts that form the roads connecting their fields to their buildings. A light breeze blows the tops of the tall grass creating waves of green all around him. White stable fencing juts out of the flowing fields of green, surrounding groups of goats, sheep, and three dairy cows.

An early autumn sunset paints the sky a dark red. It sets over well organized, perfectly rectangular, reaped fields separated by rows of wind breaks of Poplar trees. The grains that grew all seasons are now safely stored in the silos. Six such structures stand beside the fields, filled with barley grown by a family of hardworking farmers who have taken their stock-in-trade as their last name.

The Barley Family Farm is the largest grain grower southeast of the village of Harvest. They supply more barley than any grower in Harvest.

As he approaches the barn, by far the largest building on this plot, he sees two of his younger brothers, one eight years of age and one only six, run to him from the building's big doors.

"Thad, we have fed the goats. Are you going to tell mother and father tonight? What will you say?" asks Jason, the older of the two.

"I will tell them my plans, and you will keep to yourself while I do so." He continues to walk while his little siblings work to keep up with his long strides.

"What are your plans?"

"I leave in two days. You know this already."

"I forgot. I'm sorry." While they are brothers Thaddeus hardly knows Jason. He is almost ten years younger and childish in a way Thaddeus never was.

"It is fine. Have you finished your chores?" He is kind to his younger brothers, but also strict as his father was to him. Chores need to be done; frivolous conversations only happen after the work is completed.

We all do our part, even the youngest of us. He will make sure his brothers have lived up to their duty before entertaining them with words shared as recently as last night.

"Yes." They answer in perfect unison. He knows they revere him. Their faces show their hopes of being just like him when they get older.

"Do you have to leave so soon?" This time Joshua, the youngest of them, speaks with large watery eyes, "I do not want you to go."

He stops and kneels before the boys, gently placing his hands on Joshua's shoulders before saying, "Yes. I must leave as soon as possible. Cold weather approaches and my journey is far." He smiles at them and continues, "I need you to be good to mother while I am away. She will worry about me, as she worries about us all. Do your chores on time without being asked. Do as father and mother say, when they say it. Will you do that for me?"

"Yes," this time they answer almost in unison. Joshua speaks slightly after Jason, as if he is waiting for confirmation from his older brother.

"Good." Thaddeus' smile grows large, and he pulls them both close to his chest. The three embrace for a moment before he pulls back and looks at them with an expression of mock stern, "And be sure to tell your sisters to be nice to mother and father too! And do not tease them too much!" He pokes their stomachs with strong fingers and the three share a happy giggle.

Their fun is interrupted by a loud call of "SUPPER!!" Mother summons them from the back porch of their home, a large stone and wood structure with a peaked roof of thin timbers and a large porch that wraps around the entire bottom floor. A thin stream of grey smoke rises from the chimney into the slowly darkening sky. The little boys break into a run toward the big house, racing each other, while Thaddeus walks behind them.

Thoughts of the life he is leaving come to him. He will not miss being a farmer. Since he was twelve he has been aware there is nothing more his mother and father can teach him of this labour. Every season was the same; mundane lessons, boring tropes learned by rote and embedded in the heads of his brethren like farmers bury seeds.

In school, he enjoyed sums. Clear-cut answers satisfied him more than subjective essays he was asked to write on topics like history, moral development, of even just creative writing. At school, he was surrounded by people his age, unlike when he is at home. Through his talks with his fellow pupils he realized most people do not think upon the topics that inhabit his mind.

He feels it difficult to tell his parents his true thoughts on their trade. He is expected, as children are, to follow in the family's traditional labours. But he finds the life of a farmer starves him of his favourite pastime, going deep into the woods to the southeast and hunting the big beasts. He began hunting trips with his father when he was a small boy, but since he turned thirteen years of age he went out alone, always overnight.

He'd rent a horse from the neighbour's farm. He enjoys the solitude of the experience and is always happy to bring home a deer or elk for the family.

Some citizens of Harvest are professional hunters. Women and men who enter the deepest woods and return days later with fresh kills to trade in the village square. Thaddeus covets their independent and prosperous lifestyle. Farming is not a job done alone. A good farmer must work well with other people. Thaddeus finds he tires easily of other people, he wants to hunt in solitude and turn his love of the labour into a rich living.

But the trade is not without danger. An uncle on his mother's side had been killed hunting when Thaddeus was still a baby. Elizabeth Barley's brother failed to return from a trip, so a search party was dispatched along the trail he was known to prefer. They located his body at his campsite, determining by the paw prints and the mutilation patterns he was killed and partially consumed by a large bear. Vultures picked at his remains. His final form was so gruesome Thaddeus' grandparents would not let his mother see her brother before the cremation.

Thaddeus was thankful that even after that horror his mother did not protest his solitary hunting trips. He knows they make her nervous. He takes extra precautions to ensure she does not lose two family members to the beasts in the woods.

But his upcoming trip is not about hunting, at least not for meat. Besides, this trip will take him west, away from the dense forests to the southeast. He made a note to remind his mother of that fact when she raises her inevitable objections at the supper table, although he knows it is unlikely to lessen her concerns.

Following his little brothers, he enters the warm house. Supper's aromas fill his nose and go right to his heart. Mother has cooked a lamb roast and vegetables for dinner. She and his six siblings are seated at the table, his father is washing his hands in the kitchen basin. “Please do not wait for me”, he tells them. “I wish to change my shirt and wash my face and hands.” No one specifically acknowledges him, such is the commotion generated by seating six young children for dinner. His father sits and they begin to serve themselves.

He ascends the stairs and changes his shirt in his room. Grandfather built this house large enough that all seven children each have their own room on the second floor. A second floor is unusual for his village, most homes do not have them. It rises from the near side of the main room attached by a set of stairs built into the wall. It is open, just a row of rooms with a walkway and a rail. One can look down into the main room below, where the hearth is located.

Opposite the rail and lined up in a row are the eight bedrooms. The house has a large river-stone foundation supporting tall walls and a vaulted ceiling made from thick pine logs and completed with the finest mud. The stained-glass windows are small compared to the size of the walls but made at the hands of the best craftsmen in this world. They depict scenes of grain farmers harvesting their crops, a fitting representation of the way of life around here and Thaddeus' family especially.

Theirs is the largest farmhouse southwest of Harvest's village square. Every member of the Barley family loved living in it. Their liked it too. If there is need for a community meeting they would do it here, in the main room where the sunlight beaming through the stained-glass window.

Thaddeus changes his shirt and descends the stairs. Entering the kitchen, he washes his hands and face at the basin. He listens to his family politely ask each other for items on the table while they fill their plates. He hears his mother instruct the younger children how much they may take for each dish and what foods are mandatory.

His oldest brother Hans and his father are already eating. His mother tends to Anne, still just two years of age, while Mary assists her two younger brothers Joshua and Jacob. Rose is closer in age to Hans but waits until her mother and sister complete their tending before serving herself, unlike Hans and her father.

Thaddeus joins them at the table. As he sits his siblings fall silent. To avoid a difficult scene now he told them of his plans last night when father and mother took the wagon to the village. The young children's collective anticipation creates a tension his parents cannot ignore. His mother and father both look at Thaddeus expectantly. He starts to fill his plate, avoiding their glare and the uncomfortable silence.

Once his plate is full he rests his hands on his lap. He looks at his food and without raising his head or looking at his parents he breaks the silence with, “I have something to say.”

He knows his behaviour is uncharacteristic. He is not a meek individual, his confidence is always visible to those around him. But this is different. Now he will defend who he is and what he wants to do against his obligations to his parents.

He feels the disappointment of his siblings, their sad faces are all turned toward him.

He inhales, holds the breath for a moment before releasing it with the most important words he has spoken, “I am going to venture to the barrier.”

Elizabeth Barley drops the fork she was using to feed the toddler Anne onto the plate below. A sharp clatter pierces the sudden silence as the two metal pieces collide. His father stops chewing and looks at him with an expression showing both surprise and fatigue.

The barrier is an all encompassing, massive circular wall stretching as far and as high as any human can see. A person can climb the highest hill and not see over the top. They could walk for a lifetime and never find a gap. It looms in the distance so far away one would need to walk for a week through the thickest woods to touch it.

A week's walk from Thaddeus' village, which is closest to the barrier. It is an even longer walk for people from the other four villages. But few try such a feat as most fear the journey. Their culture informs them, through books, songs, and paintings, of the barrier's permanence and dominance over their existence. Their history tells of a few expeditions and the inevitable doom awaiting those who try. None, save one, had ever returned and nothing was known of their fates. The youth are schooled to believe the forests between their farms and the barrier are filled with animals who can devour a human as easily as we devour lettuce.

This is what Thaddeus and his people have been raised to understand, and this explains his parent's reactions. All his life Thaddeus has known those stories only strengthen his ambitions. He longs to see the barrier up close. He wants to touch it and feel it but most of all, more than any passion or ambition he has ever felt, he wants to know what is on the other side.

“Do you know of what you speak?” his father talks almost at a whisper; he does not want to scare his youngest children.

“Yes father, I know of what I speak.” Thaddeus was much younger when he realized how the barrier affects his culture. He knows it creates apathy, presenting a truth both benign and ever present. A state of mind that addles his people's ambitions and limits their curiosity.

Thaddeus can not remember a time he did not question this orthodoxy, much to his teacher's displeasure. "To Keep us Content'; these are the words that haunt him. Beyond the conceit that contentment is more desirable than any other state is the counter implication; content from what? Is there nothing but chaos and strife on the far side? Thaddeus has searched all his life for a way to answer these questions. But now he knows, in the dawn of his adulthood, the only way these questions will be answered is if he tries to see the other side himself.

As he grew up, being extra bright, he would ask questions of his teachers such as "What is beyond the barrier?" or "Who built it?", observing "It is not shaped like anything in nature. The mountains have ridges and cracks and no symmetry. One mountain or tree is never the exact same height as another. The barrier's height is constant, never changing, perfect in its uniformity. Like a house, or barn, or bridge. It must have been built by someone."

He remembers exasperating his teachers. They would reply with answers learned by rote and practised since childhood, "The barrier has always been, Thaddeus."

"There is nothing that we know of on the other side, Thaddeus."

"It is perfect in it's symmetry and uniformity simply because that is how it came to be, Thaddeus. Now sit and complete your sums."

His father speaks again, "We have nothing to trade for a horse. Do you plan on making this journey by foot?"

"Yes, I will travel by foot."

"But what of the beasts in the woods?" His mother, like all the people of his village, have grown up with the stories, and fears, of the beasts in the woods. He understands her fear, she lost a brother to them.

Thaddeus resorts to type, "I will slay them with my arrows." He exchanges glances with his father, they both know putting mother at ease is important. "Then I will dine on their flesh and make clothes with their hides." At this his father and he laugh, knowing somewhere inside them such boasts are foolish. The younger children pick up the queue and finally break their silence with a participatory giggle.

Mother does not laugh. She says to her husband in a sharp tone, "Xander Barley, you will do nothing to encourage this behaviour." The table falls silent.

And in that spot of calm Xander replies, "And you will do nothing to discourage your son from his ambitions, Elizabeth Barley." She turns her attention to the six other children at the dinner table, avoiding a fight she knows she cannot win.

"The winter months approach. Will you return before the land and rivers freeze?" Xander asks him.

"I can promise you nothing father. I do not know which way the wind will blow me on this journey."

He stops speaking when his mother stands from the dinner table. He, and his family, watch as she walks to the main room then listen to her ascend the stairs and go into the master bedroom. Her silence is impossible to ignore.

Thaddeus and his father exchange a look, each probing the other for an explanation of her actions. Then they hear her exit the master bedroom, descend the stairs, and watch her return to the kitchen. These are the only sounds the house makes right now, even the children are silent, enthralled at what is happening before them.

In Elizabeth Barley's cradling arms sits a long item wrapped in cotton. She stands at the end of the table opposite her husband, her chair sits empty behind her. She pauses for a moment to ensure she has everyone's attention, then says in her most matronly voice, "Thaddeus, my firstborn. I know you must complete this journey. I offer no protest. This is something my father wanted you to have when you became a man. I would wait for your eighteenth birthday in three months, but now is just as appropriate." She unwraps the cotton and exposes a broad sword with a beautifully crafted hilt wrapped in fine red leather. The base of the blade is stamped with marks Thaddeus instantly recognizes as his mother's family crest.

He rises and takes it from her. He studies the sharp, double-edged blade. It comes to a point so fine he dares not touch it with his bare finger. "It is the most beautiful sword I have seen. I will stop by his grave on my way to give him my thanks."

"It may help you slay those beasts," his youngest brother says in his high-pitched voice. His other brothers and sisters giggle at this.

Thaddeus turns to look at his young sibling and says sternly, "You mind your tongue young man. You are to help father with the winter chores should I not return."

The child stops laughing and looks at his feet, contemplating the hardship that awaits him if he really does lose his older, and much stronger, brother. Thaddeus returns to his seat, carefully placing his new sword on a bench behind his chair. With this slight ceremony completed they all return to eating their dinners while the discussion continues.

"Have you considered your path?" his father asks.

"Yes. I will travel west. The barrier is closest to us that way. And west will allow me to seek out Barnabas." Everyone in the village of Harvest has heard the tales of Barnabas, the hermit who lives in a cave near a canyon's river. He is an old, wild man prone to impossible boasts and fantastic tales. People may hear these tales if they venture to his cave. It is equally likely he will chase them away, ranting something about it not being the right time or they had their chance to listen to him years ago. He is isolated and bitter and if the stories are true, a man to be feared.

One tale Barnabas is known to tell is about climbing a mountain 'so tall it touches the clouds', even though no such hill exists within their world. There, on a clear summer day whilst perched on a sheer cliff overlooking a valley, a shape appeared from nowhere, emerging in the sky before him. What was nothing was now something, and it was unlike anything he had seen before.

A structure made of glass and steel with a black oblong floor hangs in the air before him in perfect silence, no wings or wind to keep it afloat. Inside, and Barnabas could not be dissuaded from this obvious fantasy, stood a man. "But it was not a man at all. His bones were polished metal and unhindered by skin or sinew. And his head was shaped like river rock made from marble and the size of a watermelon. He turned and was startled to see me. His eyes and mouth were all round, black circles. He looked as shocked as I felt. Then the image pitched backward, and what emerged from nothing was replaced by the bright blue sky once more."

No one believed him. Frustrated to the point of insanity he chose to leave Harvest and live alone. Now he is different than the rest of them. He does not farm the land save a small plot near his cave for his own food. A strong river runs in front of his cave, rich with fish. He claims to have learned their language and can talk them into his nets; claims he makes to the few people from Harvest who bother to visit him. Most, even if they happen to be near his cave and his valley, avoid the strange and scary man.

But he is the only one amongst them who has travelled to the barrier and made it back alive.

"The crazy hermit?" squeals his oldest sister.

"Yes Mary. The crazy hermit." Thaddeus turns back to his parents, "The tale is he has been to the barrier and returned."

"That is not all the tale Thaddeus. He returned a crazed man. The journey robbed him of his senses," his mother adds quietly.

"Did you know him before he left, mother?"

"No, only by reputation. He is several years older than I."

"Then how do you know he was not crazed before he embarked on his journey?" He feels his father's sharp glare, scolding him for challenging his mother. He gets the message. Sighing, he adds, "Mother, I feel I will go crazed if I do not make the journey. All my life I have questioned the barrier. All my life I have had but one passion, to see beyond the infinite wall. Now I am of age, and I must complete this task before it's desire snuffs out my heart for all time."

Elizabeth Barley cuts her food as she says, "My son, you have grown to be such a fine man. But you have never been here, have you? Not really. I do not mean that as a scold. Your mind is always off in another place, always so curious." She looks up from her plate and they lock eyes. She continues, "I have long known this day would come, when you would leave us to satisfy your questions." Her mouth forms a small smile while her eyes begin to tear. She looks at her husband, "He has been exasperating his teacher with his foolish questions since he was a little boy," she says through the mixture of emotion she displays.

"And his parents," his father adds. His comment cuts the tension and the whole family enjoys a light laugh.

Thaddeus has long been aware that he can be a handful for his parents. Now as he sits on the cusp of creating his own life, he feels grateful for their patience.

Elizabeth Barley continues, commanding the attention of her family through the authority of being the matriarch, "Now it is time to seek your answers," she says through a cracking voice, tears slowly rolling down her cheeks. Standing and extending her arms, she invites her son to her.

Thaddeus stands and walks to her. He takes her offer to embrace. She says in a wavering voice, "You will always have a home here. Please come back to us alive."

Thaddeus feel her try to release him, but he does not let her. He holds her tight as she did to him when he was a just a boy. He whispers in her ear, so softly only she can hear him, "I will mother. I will always come back to you. Always." Now he lets her go, and briefly looks her directly in her watery eyes as they separate. He lets her know he is present right now, he is in this moment.

She composes herself by tightening her apron and sits at the table again. They all finish their meal in silence, an unusual happening when there are so many young children seated.

After all have finished eating, mother and her daughters rise from the table to complete the evening chores. Her sons and her husband retreat to the main room to further discuss Thaddeus' departure around a warm fire.

"When will you leave?" asks his oldest brother Hans, who is thirteen years of age.

Thaddeus tells him, "The day after tomorrow. Early in the day. My haversack is empty. Tomorrow I will go to the village and fill it with preserved food for the journey. My quiver is near full and my bow is tight."

"And now you have your grandfather's sword." His father reminds him.

"Indeed. No beast will best me while I carry such a fine weapon."

"Do not let your confidence be the real beast Thaddeus. Take mind in the woods. The cats can be upon you in silence, and you are in their domain. The bears are so big and strong your sword will appear as a twig, your arrows will only be their nuisance."

Thaddeus takes his words to heart. "I will take great care father. There is no point in undertaking this quest if I do not return to tell my tale." He turns to his youngest brother, Joshua, and rubs the top of his head as he says through a smile, “Like the crazy old Barnabas has.”

“Can I come?” asks Jason.

“Of course not,” is his father's terse reply to the younger boy. “I need you for the chores and the harvest, and you have yet to finish your studies.”

“My studies are so boring,” he responds, disappointment in his voice.

Hans asks, “What do you hope to learn from Barnabas?”

“A good path, maybe. What kinds of animals await me, if I will find fish to catch and hares to kill.”

His father asks, “And what if he tells you nothing?”

“I suspect there is not much he can tell me. His journey was long before I was born. If his mind is as people say, he probably will not remember much of it anyway.”

“So why seek him?” was his youngest brother's question.

“Because there is no one else for me to speak with. None among us have completed the journey. He may offer some advice. It is worth the effort as it is near the direction I wish to take.”

“He may also offer you fear,” his father says through a deeper and quieter voice to convey the seriousness of his observation. Thaddeus knows his father is right, Barnabas may only offer dread and doubt.

“Knowledge or not, he will offer me something merely by his presence. A cautionary tale, that this journey may rob me of my mind as it has robbed him. No one offered such a warning when he embarked, so he was ill prepared for what he experienced. I know that whatever is out there, whatever the barrier will teach me, could break my senses, so I also know to ensure that does not happen. I have Barnabas as a warning. That alone has value.”

His father tells his other sons to go the barn and do the evening chores feeding the pigs and sheep and ensuring all the doors, windows, and gates are closed tight. “We do not want wolves eating our dinners” he would tell them. They can talk to their brother more after they are done. Hans, Joshua, and Jason stand without protest and leave through the back kitchen door.

Alone with his firstborn Xander says, “I do not fear for you my son. I know you are strong and smart. If you do not return to us I will be satisfied you met your death doing what was important to you, and my chest will fill with pride even as my heart breaks from pain. When you do return to us, I know it will be with a sound mind and I am sure a thousand fantastic stories.”

The crackling fire creates an orange light that flickers across the older man's face and fills the main room with a warm glow. Thaddeus is moved to cry but withholds his emotions. His father is a good man who at thirty-five years of age is in the twilight of his life. He sees himself reflected in Xander's eyes and begins to understand what it really takes to be a good man.

Thaddeus thinks to himself, all his life he has tried to look outside his world and see something beyond. At this moment he looks at his world, and sees the beauty of it all right in front of him. A thousand little moments shared with people he loves forever etched into his memories and wrapped in the warm glow of fires just like this one.

He says to his father, in a voice both tender and serious, “I will return, father. And I will tell you what I discover.”

Chapter 2

The Villages

We can expect the humans to form subcultures within each Preserve that are distinct and different from other Preserves. Being social animals, humans will seek conformity and unity within their collective. Specialization based on geographical advantages and cooperation through trade are also likely developments.

Preserve Proposal Notes, Addendum 1. (Ahimsa, Central Council Member, 2148)

Thaddeus' family farm lies on the main road of this world. The road runs a large ring around the old village of Stillerton, connecting the other four communities together. Each of the villages have their own road to Stillerton, which is the most central of all the communities. The pattern resembles the rim and spokes of a wagon wheel, Thaddeus has often noted.

Across the road from his family's farm is a hill covered in grass and natural flowers that rises to a high point with a single small cherry tree at the top. The spot affords a sweeping view of the surrounding landscape. Thaddeus often comes here and sits under the tree to think in silence. This is where he developed his belief that the only way to understand the nature of his existence, of all people's existence, is to know what exists beyond what he can see.

The morning after his talk with his family, he hikes the hill to his cherry tree. From here he can see Harvest's village square in the distance, smoke rising from the shop's chimneys as the bakers begin their morning chores. Also, visible is his family's farm and his neighbours' farms and the road connecting them all. He enjoys it up here. It is far from his loud sisters and brothers who are all much younger and at times frustrating to be near. From this height, on clear days with a still wind, he can see smoke rising from the village to the north. Copperton is a long day's journey by horse-drawn wagon along the main road.

For him to see smoke from this distance means they are working hard. Copperton is the main mining town of this world, nestled against the cliffs of Quarry Hills. The people of that village dig into the mountains and extract all manner of mineral and ore.

Copperton is also the home of Helga Bellows. They meet when the Copperton trading wagons come through his village every week or so. She is the daughter of the wagon train driver and she loves Thaddeus as deeply as he loves her.

They have grown up together, albeit in different villages. She first caught his eye when they were only eleven years old. She was a competent and confident young girl, equally at ease calming a horse as she was unloading a wagon load of goods. She captivated him with the sharpness of her wit and the confidence of her smile. Over the years she developed a respect for his questions about what she thinks of the world and his constant contemplations on the barrier. She saw he was a good man, loyal to his family and the duty bestowed upon him while also independent, with his own ideas and thoughts. And he treats others with respect, a quality she demands in all the people around her.

Of course, he had caught her eye as well, even at just eleven years of age Helga knew this boy was going to grow into a fine and appealing man.

Her father's schedule means she stays a night in Harvest, allowing her and Thaddeus to spend many hours together. Just thinking of her stirs his desires. She is beautiful, with light blue eyes above prominent cheekbones on a perfectly symmetrical face. But she appears unaware of her own beauty, certainly she does not consider it an important element of her life, unlike her sisters and nieces. She does not fuss with her hair or dress inappropriate for her trade to appear more desirable. She is authentic. This is a quality he demands from the people in his life.

Thaddeus delayed his departure until tomorrow in part to go shopping at the village square but also because Helga comes to Harvest today. He does not know how long it will be before they can see each other and he could not imagine leaving without saying good-bye.

Here on top of his favourite hill he will see the Copperton wagon train approach from the north, but that will not be for some time. He left his home early, before his siblings and parents woke up.

Now is his time. He sits in the soft grass facing east, toward the rising sun. It is colder than it has been at this time of the morning lately, a sign of the approaching autumn. From up here he can watch the shadows of the trees below shrink as the sun rises.

Before him are more farmer's fields, rolling into the distance. Beyond them are high hills covered in thick forests making up the border of his vision as he looks toward the rising sun.

The sounds of birds and buzzing insects fills Thaddeus' ears. A gentle breeze blows stronger up here and from time to time the cherry tree's leaves, now dry having performed their seasonal task, rustle in the wind. He can not see the barrier when he faces east, not even from this high vantage point. He has heard stories that it encircles this land entirely, creating a wall enclosing all the villages. But he has not heard of any one person or group who has walked the entirety of its distance. He only knows it is out there, beyond the horizon, from the tales of his brethren.

Thaddeus believes in something he can not see. One day last spring, while sitting in this spot, he had an epiphany. If he believes something exists even though he had never personally witnessed it, what could not he be led to believe?

Suddenly he felt vulnerable, as if anyone could convince him of anything just because he could believe the barrier exists to the east, beyond the horizon and his vision. The barrier did exist in the west, north and south, everyone could see that. It makes sense that it exists in the east as well. But Thaddeus also realized without direct experience he could not know.

The realization pained him. For the first time in his life, he felt the futility of certainty. It was a certainty built on the flimsiest of foundations, that of the words of people he barely knew. A trio of travelling musicians singing of the events in the far-off villages would include references to the presence of the barrier on their horizons. Or the travellers who came through Harvest on some adventure of either fun or enterprise would confirm the barrier was present beyond their villages as well.

He had faith in his people, and he knew if he travelled east and found the barrier there as well, over the horizon, he would not have been surprised.

But he would be disappointed.

The futility of certainty. His father had used the word 'futile' a lot, Xander did not like it when his children or his wife did things without a direct benefit to their life. Certainty, Thaddeus now understands, was no benefit to him. It leads to complacency and that is a luxury his desires do not allow.

From this revelation he considered the possibility of travelling east in search of the barrier, to confirm or deny what he believed from faith in others. But he grew to understand that journey would be far more difficult and not likely yield as satisfying a result. He wants to get to the barrier, possibly find a way past. That means travelling west where the barrier is ever visible and much closer.

Thaddeus stands and takes in a deep breath of fresh morning air. The sun is warming the day and the insects are beginning to buzz, tempered by the presence of finches and tits feeding on them. Thaddeus opens his eyes and turns to face north to look for Helga and her father's wagon train of goods.

At this distance he sees them before he hears them, four wagons each pulled by two horses. Each has one driver out front, except the lead wagon which has two people sitting on the bench. Thaddeus knows them to be Helga and her father. He starts down the hill and toward the village. He has done this many times, sitting up here looking for her. He knows how much time he has. He starts to run after coming to the road and arrives in the village square only moments before she does.

“Look at this! With the harvest over should not you be in school?” She yells teasingly when she sees him.

“Ha-ha! Never! There is no school that can hold me forever!” They laugh together at this, and she jumps off the wagon into his outstretched arms. They embrace tightly and kiss, but only briefly as they are aware of the people watching them and their impolite display of affection. The caravan continues on without a care.

"And are not you to be in school yourself?" he mocks her tone, but he says it quietly.

"As yourself, good sir, I have completed my studies and am now an old maid." They both laugh at this. "When do you leave?"

"Tomorrow morning. I stayed an extra day as I promised."

"Thank you." She snakes her arm behind his as they start to walk side by side to the baker. "I'll miss you."

"And I you. How long do you have?"

"All day. Father will take care of the market today. He wanted me to have as much time with you as possible."

"Thank him for me, will you?"

"Of course," she says through a giggle, "but you can thank him yourself later if you like. He wants to see you before you leave." Thaddeus had won the approval of her parents long ago.

They arrive at the baker and each purchase a fresh pastry filled with applesauce. They bite into their treats in unison, the sweet fruit warming their mouths.

"Are you prepared?" She asks after swallowing. She is willing to help him finish whatever preparations he is to make.

"I have some more goods to purchase today, smoked meats and dried fruits, sundries, some more arrows and fire-starters. Otherwise, I just fill my water bladder and head out on my journey."

"Do you still plan on visiting Barnabas?"

"Yes. Even if he is a crazed old man who tells me nothing, I can learn from that as well."

"You have wanted this all your life. You must be excited."

"I am Helga. More excited than ever. Maybe even as much as the first time you told me you loved me." She blushes at this. They walk a bit more along the shops that line the main street of Harvest and eat their pastry. Helga can feel the glare of some of Harvest's women as they look unfavourably upon this girl from Copperton who dresses like a boy and has long held the interest of their most desirable bachelor.

"My mother gave me a sword last night at dinner," he says after swallowing his last bite of pastry.

"She told me she was saving it for your eighteenth birthday."

“You knew of it? Are you two conspiring?” He says this with a mocking tone. Thaddeus' mother liked Helga from the moment he introduced them. Elizabeth Barley thinks Helga is a delight, beautiful and smart with a fine, healthy physique to provide her with grandchildren.

“Maybe,” she teasingly replies.

“News of my trip forced her to give it to me sooner. She knows I may not be back in time for my birthday.”

“And she knows you may not be back at all. The sword increases the chances you will return.” One reason Thaddeus loves Helga is because she always sees the world in a practical manner. He knew his extracurricular contemplation is fanciful and unproductive, so it is good to have someone in his life who thinks pragmatically.

“That is a good point too. Would you like to come to the house and see it? You can say hello to mother.”

“No. I would rather just spend these hours with you. I have to be back at the inn with father just after dark.”

The two walk down a hill to the east of Harvest's village square where a small creek runs through a stand of woods. Thaddeus and Helga have been here many times, the creek bends around the trees in a lackadaisically, filling the air with the calm sound of slowly moving water. The land here is rocky and wet, unsuitable for farming, so the people of Harvest decided to let it be natural and undeveloped. Soon they are alone and surrounded by the golden-browns of fall in the midday sunlight.

They stop and turn to face each other closely. He places his hands on the small of her back and gently brings her toward him. She wraps her arms around his neck and, standing on the tips of her toes, kisses him fully on the lips. She lingers there, squeezing her arms together, silently but firmly telling him she does not want to let go.

Thaddeus inhales the lavender and strawberry scents she uses when she sees him. He holds her tighter, telling her he too does not want to let go. “Will you stay faithful to me?” he asks her when their passionate kiss ends.

“Yes. Will you to me?” Her expression is one of concern. She loves him and fears this journey may separate them forever.

"Yes, but that promise is easy to keep, I will be very surprised if I see another lone woman on this journey." They both smile at the absurdity before he continues, "You, on the other hand, will continue to have many opportunities."

"As we discussed, I will wait a year. After that I will—" she trails off for a moment, not wanting to say the next part of that speech. "I love you Thaddeus, I have since I was a child. But I want my own children and.."

"And I want you to be happy," he says, interrupting her. "I could not dare ask of you to wait one day for me. That you confess to waiting a whole year drives me to show my passion for you."

"I know of your passion young man," she says through a smile, "and you shall have mine soon." They start to kiss again, more intently this time. They rub their bodies against each other, she feels him grow hard and he feels her body grow warm against his.

"Let us go into the woods," Thaddeus says, using a term they both know really means going to a secret cave they found in the forest and making love. They have been going to the cave for two years.

Through a broad and excited smile, she says, "Yes."

###

An hour later they are walking back to the village square when she is reminded of a chore. "Oh, I almost forgot. Uncle Mortimer has asked me to give you something for your trek."

"What is it?"

"I do not know. It looks like one of his flares but is smaller and has a string. He has included a letter on how to use it."

"Sounds intriguing." Mortimer Bellows, her uncle, is the smartest naturalist in Copperton, no small feat considering the village has many wise people experimenting and working with the various minerals they pull out of the ground.

Copperton's most valuable finished goods are their fire-sticks, tubes of chemicals that shoot projectiles of concentrated fire or burn rapidly while shooting bright sparks straight into the air. The miracle workers in Copperton make fire-sticks which shoot all sorts of coloured fires. Sometimes a tube shoots a blue ball of fire then a green one. Sometimes the projectile that shoots up explodes at the top of its journey! If Uncle Mortimer has something for Thaddeus specifically for his venture, he knows it must be important.

They meet Helga's father, Theodore Bellows, outside the inn. Thaddeus greets him, takes a brush from the man's kit bag and helps him tend to his horses.

"I will get Uncle's present." Helga goes to the wagons secured a few meters away near the back of the inn's lot.

"She says you are leaving tomorrow?" Theodore Bellows asks Thaddeus. The two have a good relationship, Theodore treats Thaddeus with respect, as if he is a man of equal standing and not a youth in need of guidance or a man unworthy of his daughter's heart.

"Yes sir. In the morning."

"The way she talks I am certain she will miss you very much."

"I will miss her as well."

"Thank you for not taking her with you. I need her for this work more than ever these days. My back is not as strong as it once was."

"She did not want to come sir, but I did offer it to her. She is content with the barrier as it is." The two continue to brush the horses in silence, each satisfied in their honesty. Soon Helga returns with a wooden box.

"This is from Uncle. There is a letter inside, instructions." She does not take her eyes off him as he puts the brush down and takes the box. Her smile is one of anticipation.

Thaddeus opens the hinged lid and searches through the sawdust packing to reveal a tube of paper and glue. He sees a long piece of string extending from one end and coiled into a tight circle. Looking closer he notices the string is coated in a fine powder. He looks at it curiously, even holding it to his nose to sniff it. He thinks it smells like the chemicals in the fire-stick tubes.

Finally he asks her, "What is it?"

"Read the letter. He explains."

Thaddeus opens the letter written in Uncle Mortimer's precise and beautiful handwriting. He reads it silently.

'Thaddeus; In a process of experimentation with existing fire-stick compound combinations I happened upon a mixture of unexpected explosive ferocity. My niece

told me of your venture some weeks ago and this gift may be of use. When I experimented with the compound, I found it has enough force to blow boulders into the air and shatter rock walls. Follow the instructions below and be sure to take detailed measurements of the effect on the barrier from the stick you hold.

Do not get the stick or wick wet. It must remain dry for the entirety of the journey.

Place stick directly against or, if can be found, inside a crack or gap in the barrier and ground. It is likely that inside a crack will yield far better results.

The wick must remain dry for entirety of burn.

You must be no less than 20 meters away and safe behind a tree or rock outcropping.

Note size of impacted area, depth of hole, etc. I need that information for my research. Good luck and good fortune on your journey. Remember, what you hold is precious. Do not allow moisture near it! Not even dew or rain!

Uncle Mortimer

"What does it say?" Helga asks.

"He tells me how to use it, and how to use it safely. And how to report back to him and wishes me luck on the journey."

"He is an optimist."

"Do you know what this is? Have you seen it work?" He motions to the stick as he asks her these questions.

"No. But he instructed me to be quite mindful with it on the trip. It absolutely must not get wet, he was adamant on that point. Kept repeating it over and over. He is a bit of an odd duck, that one."

"That is my brother you are talking about," Theodore reminds her. His comment surprises the two of them, they did not know he was listening.

"Yes, and my uncle. I have long wondered how the two of you came from the same people." Her father laughs at this.

"He suggests it is a powerful explosive, more powerful than the fire-sticks," Thaddeus says to her once her attention returns to him.

"He is not one for tall tales. I would follow the instructions carefully."

"Yes." They exchange a worried look. He gingerly places the stick back in the box and closes the lid. The two young lovers then leave Theodore so Thaddeus can finish procuring his supplies for tomorrow's departure. It is only midday, plenty of sunlight left and the shops will be open for several hours.

The inn the Bellows caravan stays in, Harvest's only inn, is a few hundred meters down the road from the village square. Thaddeus and Helga walk there in silence. There are a few homes along the way and they nod 'hello' to people passing on the road. The people of Harvest return the civility, most recognize each other and if they do not know their name, will know a name of friend or relation.

Thaddeus carries the box with the precious cargo from Helga's uncle gingerly under his arm. One of his purchases will be a larger haversack, enough to carry all the supplies he will need. He will procure that first and place the fire-stick inside.

They arrive at a local shop selling the wares from Forge, an ash ridden small village to the northeast of Harvest. Helga feels comfortable here. Over the years Copperton and Forge have developed a special relationship based on their geography. They are connected by a wide river and while Copperton mines iron, tin, copper, and other raw materials they cannot forge them into useful goods as they lack the coal necessary for such labours. Forge sits near a dense seam of coal and over the years have become experts at turning Copperton's raw goods into useful tools and implements enjoyed by all the villages in this world.

Here Helga admires the hardware for horses and wagons available for sale, items crucial for her family's trade. Thaddeus needs a haversack and due to their labours the people of Forge have become expert leather smiths. They fashion thick aprons and gloves to protect their bodies from the sparks they create as they pound heated metals. They have developed those skills and now make durable saddles, coats, boots, and haversacks. Thaddeus eyes a brown suede bag hanging from the ceiling. It is large and uncomplicated, and he can afford it.

The shopkeeper, a Forge man himself judging by the size of his forearms and chest, asks Thaddeus if he needs boots for the coming winter. He has a fine selection that came in on the Forge trading wagon last week. Thaddeus declines, his boots are in good condition.

He carefully places Mortimer Bellow's mysterious fire-stick in his new bag. Then he and Helga depart the shop and make their way across the square to a larger shop with many fine goods, the local market for Stillerton's wares.

Stillerton is the first of the villages of this world, from where the other villages where born. It houses the libraries, teaches the teachers, and produces the finest crafted goods this world offers. Every summer the Stillerton Circus travels to each village and amazes the residents with feats of daring, even between man and beast. It stays for a week offering rides, food, and fun games with prized items for the winners.

Here Thaddeus will buy arrows. Helga has little interest in this shop. The kinds of goods it sells does not work with her lifestyle. She has no need of fine plates and cutlery when she often eats under the stars on the side of the road.

There is another commodity Stillerton produces that Helga has no interest in, but she would be amongst the minority with that opinion. Stillerton is so named because its most important exports are the various libations it produces. Wine from grapes and beer from hops and yeast, much of it grown in Harvest. Recently Stillerton's masters introduced a new product called 'Liquidfire', also made from the grains of Harvest. Thaddeus admires the amber fluid in beautifully crafted bottles as he waits for the shopkeeper to wrap the twenty-five arrows he purchased. He has not tasted any yet, it is too expensive to be casually consumed, but he has heard stories that its taste is like swallowing a fire's ember and a tiny serving is as powerful as a mug of mead.

The next stop for the young lovers is the market from Grassy Dale. One of the prettiest of the villages, it sits in the rolling grasslands far to the southeast of Stillerton and, like Harvest, is a village of farmers and growers and hardworking people. They raise cattle, sheep, goats, chickens, and other animals used for either skin or meat. Their fertile land also produces fruit, vegetables, herbs, and spices for the enjoyment of all the villages. Grassy Dale and Harvest have much in common, each are essential farming communities in this world.

Helga is happy they stopped in this shop, she buys packaged herbs to improve the taste of the many campfire meals she and her father share. A simple and affordable way to improve their camp's dinners. Grassy Dale is Helga's favourite place to visit when on her father's caravan, its idyllic rolling hills covered in small farms, separated by stone fences marking their various purposes, always put her at ease. Here Thaddeus will acquire smoked and salted meats, the last of the items on his list of needs for his quest.

Soon, too soon for both, it is dark. Helga must join her father at the Inn for supper and Thaddeus must return home for a last meal with his family. The two young lovers stand facing each other, holding hands outside the door of the Inn. “I love you,” Thaddeus says to Helga. He has said it many times, now he hopes it feels different for her.

“I love you. Return to me,” her voice is quiet. She knows only she can hear the promise he is to give.

“I will return to you,” he says it softly. Those words are for her and her alone.

They kiss and part ways, neither of them wanting to let go. She is confident of his valour; he is sure she will rebuff the advances of other men and honour her promise to him. As their footfalls increase the distance between them, so to does the weakness both of them feel on the inside.

Chapter 3

Beginning the Trek

Early the next morning, just as the sun begins to rise in the eastern sky, Thaddeus starts his journey. The sword feels heavy on his hip so he straps it to his new haversack, making it easier to carry but harder to access should he need it. He is an excellent hunter and knows his prey well, so he hopes he never has need to draw his sword against a big beast such as a bear or cat. Even with that strong, sharpened metal the outcome would be far from certain. His quiver is slung over his other shoulder in a fashion that allows him to quickly pull and shoot an arrow if the need should arise. Across his left shoulder is his water skin, purposely put on last so he can easily take a drink. He carries his bow in his left hand.

Dew glistens in the morning sun and the birds greet him with their chirps and tweets. The air is cold but not freezing, it promises to be sunny and warm today. Soon he nears the cemetery where his grandfather is buried, just off the main road where it bends to the east toward Grassy Dale, which is a several days journey by horse.

His grandfather's burial site is marked with a simple stone engraved with his name, Michael Scythe. It lays beside many other grave sites lined in a row, each plot representing the location of entire families.

People are not buried whole in this world. The dead are cremated, and the ashes buried in their family plots, located in cemeteries on the outskirts of the villages. It has always been this way but for some reason Thaddeus had never wondered why. This cultural trait escaped his critical eye, possibly because it truly did give people comfort through closure. This rite is authentic, created by us and for us.

That barrier is not.

Thaddeus lowers himself to his knees and closes his eyes as he has seen others do when they talk to their dead relatives. Speaking softly he says, "Grandfather Michael. My mother gave me your sword as a tool on my quest. It is the finest I have ever seen. I will you by never raising it in anger, nor in unprovoked violence against any man or creature. Thank you for such a beautiful gift."

No answer comes. But he didn't expect one. He rises and starts his journey again, sensing the futility in thanking the dead. He thinks this to himself and feels another childish belief dissolve in his adulthood.

He does not look forward to the next part of this adventure. In a short distance he must leave the main road as it turns east and begin the much harder part of trekking through the wilderness to the west. He believes it is a two day walk to Barnabas' canyon.

On the journey he often looks up at the enormous barrier looming in the distance before him. It makes him feel like no other thing can, as insignificant as an ant under a horse's hoof.

Thaddeus finds water in small creeks and keeps his water skin full. At the end of the first day of walking, long after the sun has descended behind the barrier in front of him and the dark forest makes trekking much less safe, he finds shelter under a small rock outcrop on the side of a steep hill. He gathers some kindling and dried shrubs and builds a fire. He lays his sleep sack beside the back of the outcrop with the fire between him and the forest beyond. He feels safer this way.

He is disappointed he found no hares or small animals to hunt. His body could use the strength for tomorrow's labours. Today's expenditure has left him famished, he eats a piece of thick bread with some of the smoked beef he bought in Harvest the day before.

Soon, there under the rocky outcropping, he falls into a deep sleep. His dreams come fast, images of a hermit man living in a cave, endless forests leading to unknown lands that he knows he must cross to achieve his quest. They come to him as oppressive images, the feelings they elicit in his sleep are fear and despair.

He wakes as the sun crosses the horizon. Before he rises he reflects on the impression his dreams made. Yes, he is fearful. This land is foreign to him and he is not sure of the path ahead. But he doesn't let the fictions of his dreams affect him. He resolves to ensure his fears inform him on this journey, not stop it dead in its tracks.

Then he thinks of what would happen if he did return, having given up so easily. The life of a farmer awaits him. He almost shudders at the thought. Then his hunger becomes acute. It is time for breakfast.

After eating dried fruits and drinking from his water skin, he packs up his sleep sack and prepares his gear for the day's journey. A crude comb does the best it can for his long hair. When he washes his face he rubs the stubble on his cheeks and chin. He doesn't like to be unshaven, but to save space in his bag he did not pack a shaving kit.

He loads his gear in the same way as before and starts his trek again. It is not long before he spies a hare in a clearing between the trees. It is odd to see a hare this early in the morning, they tend to prefer the safety of night for their activities. He thinks that perhaps this fellow has not made it to his den after a night of eating and trying to find a mate.

He readies his bow and arrow, aims at the animal, and releases the projectile. He is an excellent marksman, his shot is straight to the beast's tiny heart. Approaching the animal he sees it is not dead, so he mercifully twists its neck until he hears a crunch and the animal's body goes limp. Knowing better than to drain it while he walks, the scent of blood can attract much larger beasts, he ties it to his haversack and continues toward Barnabas' canyon.

Being tall and strong and a fast walker he arrives at the canyon edge well before high sun at midday, pleased his two-day trek took less than a day and a half. He looks down and sees the river, its rushing water is white and loud. Now to find Barnabas, he will offer his kill as a gift for the man's time. Descending the canyon walls is tricky, one slip and he will fall to his death. With great care and caution he starts down. It takes a long time and when he arrives at the bottom on a ridge of land beside the canyon wall and the river, he is tired enough to want to sit and rest for a spell. But he feels he must continue.

He does not know which way to go. Upstream or downstream? Where are the caves for Barnabas' home more likely to be? He decides upstream, there are more rocks and cliffs in that direction and the canyon seems to be wider, making his walk easier.

The rushing water fills the air with sound, a welcome feature after a day and a half of the forest's silence. He can see the fish jumping and struggling to swim upstream and he thinks of the stories he has heard of Barnabas and the tales he tells. Could he really talk to the fish? Unlikely, he thinks, because if the fish could talk to humans surely they would tell us they do not want to be our food. The silliness of the thought brings a smile to his face.

Thaddeus wonders what the recluse will look like. He imagines a tall, strong man, like a bear on his hind legs, a man rugged and weathered enough to live in this harsh way. He is probably cantankerous, used to being alone and not interested in human contact.

He knows Barnabas shuns other people. Will the hermit see his arrival as a threat? Would one of Thaddeus' arrows be enough to bring down this man beast? Probably not, he concludes. Just as one arrow never brings down a bear who wanders too close to the village, he is sure Barnabas would not be defeated so easily.

Observing the sun's position, he walks for what he thinks is about half of an hour. Although he has seen nothing he decides he has not travelled long enough in this direction for him to consider turning around. The canyon is wider here and the water less violent and loud. Although it still generates a lot of noise, Thaddeus has noticed he can hear the birds singing over its din.

The canyon makes several sharp turns, and often he cannot see what is ahead of him. He feels the anticipation of coming upon Barnabas with every turn. Then, as he rounds yet another corner, his anticipation is realized, and he sees the recluse.

Barnabas is more than Thaddeus' imagination conjured. He is standing on the far side of the river knee-deep in rushing water, which is no match for his strong legs. He stands as still as stone and looks straight down into the swell. Then, with no warning or preparation, his hand spikes into the water so fast to be almost imperceptible and withdraws a large fish in his fingers.

It is a big fish, black and strong. It whips its body back and forth trying to break free of this man's grasp before Barnabas crushes its head with his other hand and the fish goes still. Thaddeus has never seen a person catch a fish with just his hand, he is amazed.

Barnabas' strength and coordination are far better than his despite the hermit's advanced years.

Thaddeus feels fear. He does not often fear another person and the feeling takes him back to about a year ago. His father and he travelled to Forge to order a new gate for their goat pen. A man named Thor served them at one of the many metal smiths. To Thaddeus, he seemed as big as a house, his chest was like a barrel and his forearms as thick as a tree's trunk. His beard was jet black, a great bush of darkness surrounding his mouth and neck. His black leather clothes were thick and pockmarked with small holes born from shooting sparks. Thaddeus remembers the feeling as vividly as if it were yesterday. He remembers thinking Thor seemed to have emerged directly from the flames of an oven.

The feeling soon passed. Thor proved to be a most amicable man. He greeted his customers from Harvest warmly and with great respect. After a discussion about Xander's needs, he delivered a fine, steel gate only two weeks after their meeting.

Seeing Barnabas now, he feels the same initial fear he felt when he saw Thor those many months ago. It stabs at his confidence, he realizes, and exposes to himself how vulnerable he could be without it. He thinks of a lesson from school, an edict passed down by rote but one with have real value for him right now; people are generally good.

Thaddeus calls out, “Barnabas!” But from this distance his voice can not be heard over the sound of rushing water. He sets out across the river, gingerly picking his footing so he does not slip on the smooth rocks. Once across, tired and wet, he starts toward the mountain man. He calls out once again, “Barnabas!”

The hermit turns and looks at him first with surprise and then with suspicion. Thaddeus raises his hands with his palms forward, showing he has no weapons at the ready, and he has come in peace.

“Get out of my canyon!” Barnabas yells in a threatening tone, the dead fish still dangling from his hand.

“I offer no threat, Master Barnabas. I have journeyed far to seek your counsel.”

Barnabas regards him curiously. Thaddeus has not stopped slowly walking toward him. Now he is closer and can better see the recluse. His face is caked with dirt and lined with wrinkles. His grey hair is a mess of knots and tangles and falls past his shoulders. He is dirty all over his body and his only clothes are torn and tattered animal hide pants. He wears no boots and his nails are long, cracked and bent. He is impossibly tall with bulging muscles, more muscles than Thaddeus has ever seen on a man, even Thor.

Thaddeus feels his fear rise even higher. His stomach becomes so tight he thinks it may consume itself. Every step is a challenge, not just on the loose river rock but to counter every fibre that wants to turn and run the other way. This is the first of his tests, he realizes. Either this quest is important enough for you to die trying, or you're not really committed, he thinks to himself. The resolve lifts a weight, if he dies at this moment he is at peace with it. His stomach relaxes and his feet find their way again.

"Seek my counsel? What fool are you?"

"I am Thaddeus Barley from the village to the east. Your village. My mother knows of you and the villagers speak of your past. I must ask you some questions. I have brought a fresh kill for us to eat together."

"Come no closer," Barnabas barks at him. Thaddeus immediately stops walking. This man's demeanour and physical presence command authority and respect.

Thaddeus says to him, "I will respect this as your land and do as you say. You can see," his arms are still raised, "I am unarmed."

"You carry a quiver of arrows and a broad sword tied to your pack. Do not speak of being unarmed."

Without being asked Thaddeus drops to one knee. Without breaking eye contact with the hermit he places his bow carefully on the smooth river rocks beside him. Then he removes his water skin, quiver, and haversack from his back. The latter is actually tossed a few feet away, showing Barnabas that Thaddeus feels he has no use for his sword.

Slowly, still making direct eye contact and with his hands up and palms forward, he leans toward his haversack and unties the dead hare. He holds it out toward the hermit, now about four meters from him. Thaddeus thinks to look down at Barnabas' feet while performing the offering.

“I am unarmed, and I offer you meat. I seek your counsel. I bring no threat to you today.”

Barnabas regards the hare with suspicion. He walks closer to Thaddeus and takes the dead animal, examining it. He tells Thaddeus, “This is a good kill. Your arrow pierced the chest at the heart. But the neck is snapped. Did you have to finish it with your hand?”

“Yes, sir.” He replies softly, not wanting to risk any offence through the tone of his voice.

“That was proper. Animals should not be made to suffer in death.” Thaddeus, remaining on one knee, looks up to him again. He is glad Barnabas expressed such humanism, caring not to cause suffering to other living things. His impression of the man grows broader having seen this part of him, he knows Barnabas deserves more regard than just fear.

The hermit continues, “We may harvest the beasts of this land, but we should not be cruel to them. Bring them a swift death and take no pleasure in their suffering.” Thaddeus feels the hermit staring at the top of his head. “Also, it makes the meat tough.” At this Thaddeus raises his head and looks at Barnabas' face directly. The hermit has formed half a smile and Thaddeus realizes he is pleased with himself. He returns the expression, as if he to say he is in on the hermit's joke.

Then Thaddeus speaks, “I have travelled far, and plan to travel farther yet. I hope to learn from you.”

“The sun is near high. Come with me young man, I have a fire burning. It is time for the midday meal.” Barnabas turns and starts to walk toward his cave. In one hand is Thaddeus' hare and in the other the fish he has just harvested. Over his shoulder he says to Thaddeus gruffly, “And these beasts may fill our bellies.”

Thaddeus walks behind the man as they make their way to the mouth of Barnabas' home. He sees it is adorned with many items necessary to live in this manner. He is impressed by the countless knives, gardening tools, and animal traps hanging here and there. There are possibly dozens of glass jars and clay pots carefully placed amongst the cave's walls nooks and crannies. Thaddeus can see that Barnabas has lived here a long time.

Drying fish hang in the sunshine near nets made from vines. They are so large Barnabas must have spent many days weaving them. There is a pile of firewood cut small and neatly stacked inside the cave. There are no trees on the canyon floor, Thaddeus realizes Barnabas must travel down the walls with the wood, no small feat for a man of Barnabas' age.

Nearby is an axe, its metal head sharpened so many times the blade is near the handle. He is suddenly given a single image that truly represents the time Barnabas has spent alone. He thinks the axe head looks pathetic, too small to be effective for its job. But it is an interesting testament to the amount of time this man has been ostracized. The passage of time represented by disappearing metal. It makes him feel sad.

On a flat shelf of rock lie an assortment of root vegetables, carrots, beets, turnips. Thaddeus looks about and sees the vegetable garden, thick with black dirt that Barnabas also must have brought in from somewhere else for it does not match the ground around here.

He watches as Barnabas uses a large knife to remove the hare's head, feet, and skin.

The fire pit is just inside the cave's entrance and has a low wall made of smooth river stones circling hot coals. The wall protects the embers from the wind. Thaddeus watches Barnabas add a few logs and soon the flame is high enough to cook the hare, now with its organs removed and mounted on a spit above the flames. Thaddeus takes Barnabas' invitation to sit and does so on the opposite side of the fire. While they wait for the meat to be edible, Barnabas entertains Thaddeus' questions.

The young man asks him, "How long has this been your home?"

"Longer than I can count, which I stopped doing when I came here."

"Why did you come here?" Thaddeus asks but Barnabas does not answer right away. He sees the hermit retreat into himself and become distant.

"They would not believe me." His tone is a mixture of sadness and anger.

"Who?"

"Your brethren. They shunned me, drove me away with their laughter. At me. They laughed at me."

"Why?"

Barnabas hesitates again but eventually says, "Because they are convinced of the truth of their myths, their fables. I challenged their minds, and they drove me here."

"Whatever it was you challenged them with, it is why I have sought you out. Tell me of the barrier. What did you see?"

Barnabas regards this impressive but strange fellow more closely. Is he ready to be told the truth, or does he need to see it for himself? This farmer from Harvest is handsome, probably successful with other people. Why is he here alone?

But Barnabas also concludes Thaddeus is smart. He has packed for a trip spanning many days and dressed in a manner fitting the cold season approaching. He knows he may be gone from home for many weeks. And he is an excellent hunter, despite being so young.

No, Barnabas thinks to himself, he will not let his cynicism guide him right now. This young man poses no threat. He can hear the truth. So while the meat of the hare cooks he tells his visitor, "I saw a mountain of stone made from mud. Not a mountain, that is not big enough. An infinite amount of mud wall, appearing smooth but rough and dusty to the touch."

Thaddeus does not respond to this. He sits in silence, awaiting more. Barnabas continues, "But the journey is difficult, young man. It is long and there is no path. Some perils await you, but you seem well-equipped to handle them." He gestures toward the bow and arrows and sword still laying on the rocks where Thaddeus deposited them.

Thaddeus wants to know more, "Yes sir. What did you experience at the barrier? What was it like to be so close to it?"

Barnabas hesitates, these are painful memories for him. But the pain does not come immediately. The beginning of his story he enjoys, its only as the narrative leads to the conclusion that the pain hits. But he thinks Thaddeus has asked an interesting question, one no one had before. What did he 'experience'? Now those are feelings he has not thought about in decades.

Barnabas is hesitant in his reply, “It filled my heart with despair. To be so close to such a monstrous construction made me feel small and..” Thaddeus watches him search for the right word to use. After a moment, the hermit finds it, and when he says it Thaddeus can feel its weight on the man, “insignificant.”

Thaddeus understands the effect such a feeling would have on a man used to being significant in comparison to his peers. It would be demoralizing, draining a man of drive and ambition at exactly the time he needs to be feeling the opposite. He understands how such a shock could shake the foundations of a man like Barnabas, make him re-think and re-evaluate all that he uses to create his own sense of value. He looks at the old man steadily, he does not want to miss any possible crack of emotion that could come from that weathered face.

Thaddeus is not disappointed when one does not appear. He knows what Barnabas felt in those moments, he can hear it in the man's voice. For a man like Barnabas signs of weakness do not come easily. Weakness is a foreign feeling, an unpleasant reminder of failure that is better to avoid. The lack of emotion coming from Barnabas' face tells Thaddeus that he has judged this man correctly.

He is not crazed nor mean. He is a man who cannot process the duality of frailty and strength. Thaddeus pities him, under all those muscles Barnabas lacked the strength to look at his own limitations.

Barnabas asks Thaddeus, “How did you get so curious young man? You remind me of me.”

Thaddeus, now far more confident in this man's presence, tells him, “Probably the same as you, it has always been in me.”

“As a very young boy, did you like to play games of imagination with your friends?”

“No. I only participated in the hunting games and sports. Games of pretend could never hold my interest.”

Barnabas gently taps his chest with the first two fingers of his right hand. “Also. Never enjoyed pretending. But I was good at the hunt, none better when I was a young boy! None better!”

Barnabas is displaying pride, Thaddeus notes. He must have been a remarkable man before he was shunned by the people of Harvest.

He continues, “I am only interested in the real. That barrier,” he points to the west where the barrier is closest to them, “that barrier is the most real thing in our world. It defines us as a people. Its in our art, our stories. Our teachers tell us to fear it, 'Do not go there! The beasts in the woods will devour you!' Pish! Always, since a child, I wanted to see the barrier up close. It called to me. I have no memory of a time when I did not want to touch it, to feel it.”

Thaddeus understands this. Barnabas, this impressive old man who lives in a cave, is the only other person he has ever known to express exactly what he has felt all his life. A feeling so natural and powerful that people who do not want to touch and see and feel and, most importantly, to know the barrier, hold no interest for him. Except, of course, for Helga and his family.

To know what it is and why it is. This is the central question of his existence. Why is he the only villager to want this? Was he different? Was he mad? Did it matter what they thought? He tells the hermit, “I know. I have had that feeling all my life. Like a rope pulling on my heart.” Thaddeus says this hoping Barnabas will understand and open up and tell him all he knows.

“I can see it in your eyes young man. You will journey to the barrier and you will see it.”

“But of the beasts?”

“Pish!” Thaddeus realizes Barnabas has said this word twice. The old man is unaware no one says 'pish' anymore, although his grandfather said it when Thaddeus was still young. “You can slay any beast you come across. Many of them do not want to eat you anyway, they just want you off their territory. Walk straight west. Be mindful, but not scared.”

“How long will it take?”

“Five days from here. You have no pack animal so you may arrive sooner. I took a donkey and that stupid beast only slowed me down. Hunting large game will not be necessary, there are stands of wild fruits and roots and fungi on the path. Enough and easily foraged. Food will be plentiful.”

“Water?”

“Rivers and creeks near you most of the way. Fill your water skin at the creek when it turns south, you need to stay west. There is little water for a full day after. Listen for the rushing sound and let it guide you in."

At this Barnabas lifts the hare from the fire and goes to a wooden counter where he prepares the meal. He removes the spit and cuts the cooked animal in half down the length of the torso.

He puts one half each on old metal plates, and hands one to Thaddeus. "See? You have already found bounty and only on the trek to me." Barnabas resumes his seat on the other side of the fire and the two men silently eat the meat.

After a few bites Barnabas says, his mouth full, "They lied to you Thaddeus. Your teachers I mean. They lied to you."

Thaddeus knows this to be true but he wants to hear the hermit's perspective. "How?" he asks him, happy the man will still speak to him.

"They put a fear in you, or they tried to. They put it in everyone around you, that is for sure. The fear of the journey that has been calling to you all your life. The journey to the barrier. They have been teaching you not to go."

"I know. I've always questioned orthodoxy. Even now."

Barnabas looks at Thaddeus with a sly grin. "They taught you the beasts in the woods will kill you. They told you the barrier just is. 'Do not look there, Thaddeus, that will only kill you and serve no purpose anyway!' That is what they have told you all your life. Tell me I am wrong."

Thaddeus considers this for a moment and knows Barnabas is not wrong. He does not need to contemplate on what it meant for him. "But it never worked on me. Every time they told me those things, I wanted to see it more."

Barnabas taps his chest again, "Right. I had the same dilemma. Why did not it work on me? Why did it make the opposite even stronger?" Barnabas sits in silence and Thaddeus watches him thinks upon this. "I can only surmise its a magic we do not understand. It does not work on us all."

"Five days you say?"

"Aye, young man. Five days." The two continue to eat in silence. When they are finished Barnabas takes their plates to the river and rinses them off, allowing the bones and bits of uneaten meat to wash downstream. He places the plates on the bank and then jumps into the water, fully immersing himself. He rubs the excess dirt off and emerges from the water a clean man. Even though it is a brisk autumn day and he wears only tattered pants Barnabas does not shiver. Its as if he does not even feel the cold.

Thaddeus understands Barnabas' gestures and realizes his time with the man is coming to an end. He returns to his bow and arrows and secures his haversack to his back. He stands, ready to continue his journey.

Barnabas returns from the riverbank and stands in the mouth of his cave, looking out at the world beyond, waiting for this young man to leave him alone.

But there is one more question Thaddeus needs an answer too, "Did you traverse the barrier? Do you know what is on the other side?"

Barnabas considers this young man again. He thinks Thaddeus' curiosity may get the best of him or it may drive him to discover the answers to questions he has had all his life. Either way, he does not like to think of what is on the other side of the barrier. The reality fills him with sadness, not just at what is there but also at how his brethren treated him three and a half decades ago when he returned to tell of his discovery.

He does not answer Thaddeus. He stares into the distance but looks at nothing. The cold air is condensing the water on his warm body, making him appear to be giving off steam. The memory of those days, prompted by this impetuous young man, weighs on his soul.

Thaddeus can see Barnabas' expression has changed to deep sadness. Perhaps he is remembering being shunned by his brethren for telling them his truth. Perhaps the events at the barrier's face were so horrific it pains him too much to relive them.

"What will I find Master Barnabas?" Thaddeus' desire to know trumps his manners.

Without moving his head Barnabas shifts his eyes to look at him. "You will find the barrier is imperfect. And you will find that it does not matter. And you will find that it serves a deeply sinister purpose."

"What is that purpose?"

Barnabas has now grown tired of this young man; he asks too many questions he does not want to answer.

"You will see."

"How will I see? How did you cross the barrier? Please Master Barnabas, I must know."

"You will know my boy, you will know. But you will have to find it on your own. How I got to the other side is of no consequence to you, as it is unlikely to be repeatable. Fortune and luck were with me that day. But I have since come to believe that we create our own luck through our own actions."

"How can I create such luck?"

"Do good and be right. You know what that means, you feel it in your heart when called to make a choice. You will know it like you know to avoid fire, it is instinct."

Thaddeus realizes he has learned from this hermit all he will offer. "I thank you, Master Barnabas, for your counsel and your time."

"Be strong young man, and do not let the barrier best you as it bested me."

"I shall do my very most to ensure that does not happen. I have much to return for." Thaddeus walks toward the left of the cave entrance where the canyon walls are shallow enough to climb. He can make out a path to the top of the west side of the canyon, most likely the same one Barnabas uses to fetch his wood and carry soil to his garden.

He is on his journey again, his belly filled with meat and carrying the scant knowledge of the only person in his world who went to the barrier and made it back alive.

Chapter 4

Contact

Thaddeus walks for a day and a half before he realizes he forgot to ask Barnabas about the metal man he claims to have seen. 'Oh well, if there are metal men for me to see I will see them', he thinks to himself.

He sees beavers, deer, and hare. None are within hunting distance, but he needs not worry; Barnabas was right, there are many sources of food along the way. If there are great beasts, they do not make their presence known to him. He concludes Barnabas also spoke the truth on that topic, his teachers were just trying to scare him.

They were trying to scare everyone. Maybe 'trying' is the wrong way to put it he thinks, they were simply repeating what they were taught and thoughtlessly accepted.

He sees bear and cougar scat, so the danger is out there. But he sees no bear or cougar, so maybe they are shy. It takes until the third day of walking from Barnabas' cave for the beasts in the woods to make their danger known to him.

Thaddeus walks west through a field of wildflowers and long grass. Close to his right side is a forest, dense with conifer trees so thick he cannot see more than a few meters into them. He hears it before he sees it. A loud snort comes from the trees just behind him. He knows the sound is a bear, most likely a female judging by the tone of the snort.

Immediately he drops his haversack, water skin, bow and arrows, and removes his sword from the bag. Looking into the woods he cannot see the beast, but he does not move and does not dare turn his back. He hears the crack of dried branches, something large is walking in there.

With one hand he picks up his haversack and bow and arrows and begins to walk backwards in slow, measured steps, increasing the distance between himself and the forest border. He is ready for the attack. Although an accomplished hunter who has made many successful trips into the woods to the southeast of Harvest, he has never even attempted to kill a bear alone and never so far from home and rescue.

Thaddeus continues his slow backwards walk, one hand carrying his possessions, the other holding his sword at the ready. The sounds are louder and more frequent now. His instinct tells him to be more prepared. He drops his bag and bow and arrow and tightly holds his sword with both hands. She is coming, he can feel it.

The bear explodes from the trees to his left. He is correct, its a large female, possibly protecting her young still hidden from view inside the trees. She races toward him at a terrifyingly fast pace, growling and snarling all the way. He waits until she is close and reared up on her hind legs; then with a fast, ducking movement to his left, avoiding the swing at his head from her right paw, he thrusts his sword into the beast through her exposed rib cage.

She lets out a gruesome yelp before twitching her body away from him and landing on her paws. Without regarding Thaddeus for a moment, she springs back toward him and exposes the back of her neck. Thaddeus swings the sword and makes contact at the base of her skull. She falls down instantly dead, his blow cutting clean through her spinal column.

Thaddeus is frozen in place, holding his sword at the ready and staring at the animal. It is not breathing. It is not moving in any way. Blood has stopped flowing from both wounds. He realizes just how close to death he had come, how quickly the threat was before him. Not three minutes ago he was walking in a sunny field, the cool autumn air filling his lungs with crisp energy. Now he stands above a beast that could have killed him with one blow. Yet it is dead, and he goes on.

He scans the borderline of the forest and sees nothing more. Bears do not usually travel in packs. In fact, since she is here it is unlikely there are other bears nearby. Thaddeus knows from years of observation that bears are territorial creatures.

There are beasts in these woods. But they are not as deadly as he and his brethren have been taught to believe. Long has he known his culture creates the fears his people feel, here is proof of how irrational those fears can be.

After a few minutes of standing guard to make certain no further threats are imminent he wipes the blood off his sword and contemplates harvesting parts of the dead beast; teeth, hair, maybe some claws, but decides against it. He gathers his belongings and continues his journey.

As Thaddeus walks the barrier grows larger. A vast grey wall, so impenetrable and so permanent, fills his vision when he looks straight ahead. He can no longer see the sky in his upper peripheral vision. As he gets closer the day becomes shorter, the barrier's shadow extends further into the world making the sun set earlier.

Just looking at the thing creates a sensation for him which he can only describe as both exciting and daunting at the same time. His motivation remains high even while he realizes his prospects for completing the true nature of his task, learning what is beyond, grow dimmer with each footfall. How can one traverse such a behemoth of a structure? Why wouldn't Barnabas tell him how he made it across? Did he really cross it?

What is this sinister purpose?

On the fourth day after leaving Barnabas' cave, a full day earlier than the hermit's prediction, he sees what he has never seen before, something he has yearned to see all his life. He sees the bottom of the barrier, a place where the endless grey mass touches the ground.

Thaddeus is standing in a sunken field ringed with low rock outcroppings. Directly in front of him is a narrow gorge with steep rock walls on both sides. The barrier fills the space between the walls, and he can see the grey mass coming to an end as it touches the dirt. His heart races in his chest.

Striding as the horses might, with a smile of excitement sweeping across his face, he sprints to the site. His big haversack, even with the extra weight of his sword, feels as light as air.

He runs into the gorge and to the edge of his world. He stops an arms length from the massive structure. Placing both palms flat against the surface he feels the roughness.

Because it looks so smooth from a distance and even though Barnabas told him, the sensation surprises him. Barnabas was right about something else. It is dusty. Every stroke covers his fingertips with a fine powder. He licks a bit, it tastes like the chalk his teacher would use for their lessons, only dirtier.

He feels what Barnabas described to him, insignificant in the shadow of this huge structure. For the first time in his life the impossibility of the task he has set for himself is tangible. No longer is it merely an academic exercise, he is here at the barrier right now. The next step is daunting. Reaching the barrier has been relatively simple but he has no idea how he will get to the other side.

He strains his head back, struggling to see the top. The face curves toward him as it ascends through the clouds, he could not tell if he saw the top or not.

So instead, he looks down, at the bottom. Surely as good as the top, no? He lowers to all fours and with his bare hands digs a bit of the ground away. The barrier descends lower than the grass. 'How much lower?' Thaddeus thinks to himself. But he knows now is not the time to dig. He goes to one side of the narrow gorge to study the material as it touches the rock. The barrier is in every crack and crevice like the mud that holds together the beams of a house. It flows and fills every space where the rock ends. It fascinates him. 'A mountain of stone made of mud', Barnabas' words come to him now. This was right! The barrier is mud! It filled the gaps and turned to stone. Not even a spider could fit between the rock and the barrier.

The rock and the barrier. Their distinction is obvious this close. One is of nature, the other clearly not. It sits on top of nature, obscuring it and making it disappear. It is abhorrent to the natural world. It imposes itself and offers nothing in return except division and dust. His teachers truly did misguide him when they would tell him the barrier 'simply is', or 'has always been.'

The barrier is the result of something. A process and a system larger and grander and completely unknown to his world. Although he had supposed it all his life, now it is proven to him. The barrier is not of nature.

So, what is it? And why is it?

The desire to know burned inside him now more than ever before. But how to find out? What more can he get standing here? Nothing, this space has given him all he can. He must move on.

Where the barrier and the ground intersect is the best place for him to be right now. He wants to stay close enough to touch it. But he must see more.

Wanting to stay close to the bottom, right beside it if possible, Thaddeus decides he will look for a gap in the bottom on the ground. It flowed like mud, but what if it tried to flow into a river? Surely the water would not allow the mud to harden so a gap may exist. It may be a way past.

'A way past', the phrase reminds him why he came here. The sheer enormity of the barrier looming in front of him makes thoughts of crossing it too difficult to contemplate. It threatens his mission with a futile end. He knows he must not let the size of the object defeat him. He must not lose sight of the ultimate prize. A lifelong ambition brought him here, to touch and feel and see the edge of his world and the knowledge he will gain may help him achieve the greater task.

But standing here now, so close to the structure, it is difficult to feel anything but total despair.

To reverse those feelings, he thinks of what it will be like to traverse the barrier, to get to the other side. What could be there that a border this incredible had to be constructed? Is it to protect us from an evil so powerful we can not even form its image in our minds?

He does not know what form the truth will take, but he knows he must find it. That is why he came here. That is why he risked his life to get to this point. He must move on. Thaddeus is in a narrow gorge, a good place for cougars to attack from above. With his sword once again secured to his pack they would make him into a quick meal. He walks quickly out of the back to the open field and looks all around to decide on his next direction.

Thaddeus decides on south. There are less mountains and hills, and he can stay close to the bottom for longer distances. Even though the sun disappears behind the barrier much earlier in the day there is still plenty of light.

For the next several hours he scurries up and down tree covered hills in forests thick with fallen leaves and branches. The barrier is not more than a few feet from him. Indeed, for much of the journey, not farther than his arm's length.

As he goes, he studies the intersection where the barrier meets the ground. He reminds himself that sometimes the ground shakes, remembering the time it shook so hard he and his father had to rebuild part of their barn and some of their fencing. They also helped their favourite baker repair his shop.

Could the ground have shaken so hard a bit of the hills had moved? Could this movement open a hole between the barrier's bottom and the ground? He finds motivation in the possibility and covers many .

But he finds no gap. No place where the rocks moved, no place for him to put his head down and see daylight poking through from the other side.

After travelling for many hours his legs are tired and his belly empty. Not having seen food in several hours, he decides to remove his haversack and eat the last of his thick bread. Doing so brings his thirst but his water skin is empty. Closing his eyes like Barnabas instructed he lets the sounds of the forest fill his ears. He can hear a creek. It is distant and away from the barrier's base. He ties his haversack high in a branch and with his bow, quiver, and water skin starts toward the sound of the water. The sun is low and it will be dark soon. If he can not find the creek quickly he must return to this spot and his haversack.

He does find the creek, it is not deep or wide, the water comes only to his shins and he can jump across it easily. Dropping to all fours he lowers his head to the water and drinks. He can feel the cold water make its way down his throat. He then rinses his hair and washes his face, which reinvigorates him.

After he fills his water skin, he stands to return to his pack to make camp for the night. On the way back he turns over the trunk of a fallen dead tree and finds some large mushrooms to eat. Worried over his food supplies, this find brings him some relief.

Thaddeus makes camp but does not sleep. Instead, he sits and listens to the sounds of this forest. It is a quiet place, save the rustle of dry leaves in fall's gently night winds no sounds come to him. He realizes the barrier is providing him a sense of security. His back is to it, a few meters from him. Nothing can approach him from the back and attack.

This is a strange feeling. A sense of security because of the barrier feels like a betrayal of the ideology he has developed most of his life. The barrier does nothing more than limit us, he has told himself and all around him. Now here it is doing something more, providing security.

The sensation abhors him. The barrier itself abhors him. He turns his head to look at the thing, wondering if it is mocking him behind his back. But he can see almost nothing in the dark of night, the barrier is now just an infinite black wall.

The wretched feeling passes. Thaddeus accepts that, at least for tonight, he is thankful the barrier is there. Today has seen the culmination of one of his life-long ambitions. He is now one of only a few people to have made the voyage to the barrier. The weight and energy of those realizations keep his head swimming with possibilities.

He knows his life is forever changed, but only if he can make it back to Harvest alive and sane. Otherwise, he becomes just another casualty of curiosity, another name on a list used to keep people from attempting what he has achieved.

He feels the yawn before it hits, one of those deep, long yawns that turns a mouth into a maw. It precedes a sudden onset of sleepiness, so he lies down in his bedroll.

With the events of the day, and despite his fatigue, he finds rest elusive.

###

Thaddeus awakes when the birds get too loud. Instantly he is aware of being in an unfamiliar forest. He darts his eyes around, looking through the trees for potential predators. He thinks the birds are very loud. Is something coming his way? Shooting out of his bedroll he picks up his bow and quickly loads an arrow from his quiver. Now as he scans the surrounding forest, he looks down the shaft of an arrow ready to fly.

But he sees nothing. Even the birds are quieter now. Thaddeus allows himself to relax. He splashes his face with water and eats the mushrooms harvested the night before. Then he packs up his camp and loads his bedroll to his haversack.

Not really knowing what today will bring him, he makes his way to the creek. In the clear daylight he can see it bends back toward the barrier. With no better options he follows the water, curious as to where it goes.

The air is still chilly and the morning dew on the mossy ground sparkles in the bright morning sun. He can see his breath as he walks through the trees following this lazy creek. The sun is warming the air enough that he sheds his lambskin coat, preferring to tie it around his waist.

Soon he is in a flat and damp area near the barrier. There is moss everywhere, it carpets the ground and rocks and fallen logs in a thick, beautiful deep green. There is moss even up the face of the barrier.

Thaddeus feels his curiosity grow. What if the only part of the barrier's bottom he does not happen to examine on this quest is the one spot that could have helped him the most? The question rattles in the back of his mind so hard he cannot let the possibility exist. He walks to the moss-covered barrier wall and rips the plant material off.

There it is. The one thing he was looking for all yesterday afternoon. His curiosity has, once again, served him well. There is a gap between the barrier itself and the rock it sits a top. He lets out a yelp no one else can hear.

Thaddeus sees the gap is not big enough for Mortimer's firestick. He finds a large stone. Kneeling at the base of the barrier he raises it high above his head and holds it there for a moment.

This feels wrong. What if the barrier really is a force of benevolence? What if its purpose is to keep him and his people safe from horrors that exist on the other side? His relationship with the massive wall is more complex than most of his brethren, striking it with a rock seemed disrespectful, even more so if those legends are true.

But his feeling only lasts a moment. The barrier is his torment, he reminds himself. Its existence is an abomination, an ugly stain on an otherwise beautiful horizon. An imposition that must no longer go unchallenged. With renewed energy, he swings the stone down with all the force he can muster, striking the barrier hard just above the gap between the bottom and the rock.

A large chunk of barrier material comes loose and lazily rolls to the side. The small crevice is now twice as big. With the force of just his arm he broke a piece of the barrier. He is not sure he believes his eyes. He lets out a gasp of exhilaration and picks up the chunk he liberated. He sniffs it and licks it and with his thumb rubs it and when he does bits of it separate and fall to the ground.

His breath is coming fast now, he feels his fingers begin to shake and quiver with excitement. These revelations are getting to be too extraordinary for him. Not only can he break a chunk of barrier off, but the material also is susceptible even to the light rubbing of his thumb.

He feels his heart beat fast in his chest and notices his sense of hearing is nearly gone. Now the world around him, all he can see, is becoming fuzzy. He knows he will fall, so he lays flat on the ground, keeping his eyes shut tight.

The world spins a bit. He feels the right side of his body roll up against the bottom of the barrier, but he is not sure he moved. He focuses on his breathing and the cool, damp sensation of the moss beneath his body.

It is not long before he starts to feel well again. He opens his eyes and the brilliant green moss returns to sight. He raises his head and the world does not spin. He feels his heart return to normal. Now his ears start to work again, the rich sounds of the forest become a welcome normalcy.

Sitting up and composing himself Thaddeus begins to take stock of what just transpired. He looks at the spot where he broke off a chunk, reassuring himself he really did break off a piece. Rubbing the now craggy inside wall produced the same fine powder as rubbing the chunk. He lifts his rock and smashes the barrier face just above the hole he made.

A new, slightly smaller chunk came off. For his next swing he came in low, trying to damage the inside wall. That is not successful, but he is not discouraged. He smashed his rock several more times figuring out the best way is to aim for the top of the hole, making it higher.

After many hits, the hole is still very shallow but as high as his waist. Now he can swing inside the hole with better accuracy and force. Great chunks fall away with every smack and his exhilaration begins to grow again. He realizes he can create a space for Bellow's fire-stick, still in his haversack lying on the moss nearby.

Withdrawing it from his pack he lays the device on a shallow ledge inside the hole. He runs the fuse line in a manner so it will not get wet, not easy given the moisture in this place.

Now he must find a spot that is safe, about ten meters away and behind a large tree trunk. He finds one, a thick trunk of a tree far enough away the moss does not reach here. He takes out his fire starter kit. Its a small box that he dabs an even smaller stick into through a hole in the top. When the stick emerges, it is coated in a fine powder that ignites when struck with a small, rough stone attached to the under side of the box. He lights the fuse and is surprised at how easily and quickly it burns. The sound of the flame rushing toward the stick reminds him of the hissing of water escaping wet wood on a hot fire.

Although braced behind a tree and plugging his ears as hard as he can, he is ill prepared for the detonation. It shakes the ground so hard he must dig into the dirt with his feet and lean hard against the tree. The birds of the forest shriek their disapproval and flee into the air and away from the commotion.

Then the debris starts to fall all around him, small and large chunks of barrier material shot out from the spot once inhabited by the stick are coming back to ground. He covers his head with his hands and stays as low as possible behind the trunk.

Once the material has fallen, and the smoke cleared, he cautiously steps out from behind his shelter and looks toward the site. He cannot believe his eyes. What was once a small hole he made swinging a rock is now a much larger crater, so large he can stand upright inside it and walk for almost a meter. He inspects the walls and sees something strange. Inside the material, buried in the hardened mud, is a metal rod. It extends down into the ground and up into the ceiling of the hole he has made.

Metal! The discovery shocks him. He looks at it closely. It is not thick. Using his trusty rock, he begins to chip at the material surrounding the rod, exposing more of it with every hit. After a few well-placed smacks he sees it is about as thick as three of his fingers and has small ridges around the circumference.

He staggers out of the crater; his knees are weak and his head is light. 'Not this again', he thinks, so he sits on the moss and regains control of his breathing. Morning sunlight shoots through the trees creating pockets of warmth and shining brightly off the green moss. He is sitting in a spot where the sun's rays reach through the trees and strike his back, warming and comforting him.

The barrier is more vulnerable than he or anyone else ever imagined. Mortimer Bellow's magic fire-stick, just one stick, gouged a hole large enough for a man to stand inside. How many more of those fire-sticks would be needed before the other side is exposed to him?

Thaddeus realizes, the feeling crushing his spirits as low as they were high just moments ago, he has no idea how thick this barrier must be. He knows it has height, but what if that dimension equals its thickness? Lifetimes could be spent blasting and digging with no greater truth revealed.

He further realizes such a task could not be done by one person. It would take many people with heavy tools working for days and more blasting material than Copperton could easily produce. Those people would need to be fed and housed. Cooks and hunters would be employed, and many general labourers with exceptional strength to haul away the chunks of barrier material.

Thaddeus realizes he is getting far ahead of himself. He is but one man sitting on a mossy forest floor in dirty clothes and little food. But in this spot, and in his state, he resolves to accomplish this task, he will cross the barrier and see the other side. They will use Bellows' fire-sticks. They will use tools to cut the rods and chip away at the barrier's grey material. They will see the other side.

Barnabas came alone. He learned the truth alone and when his people did not believe him, he was broken. But Thaddeus will not break. He will return to this spot with a small army of people and they will discover the truth together. Or they will discover the truth is unknowable. Either way the people of this world, his people, will be richer for the effort.

He does not move from the mossy floor. He eats his mushrooms and looks at the hole, comparing it to the enormity of the structure. It is a daunting task. He will have to work hard to convince his brethren to sacrifice so much for the effort, he knows his people can be complacent in their beliefs. He knows it will take a good reason to bring them here, a reason they believe will make their lives better in the long run. A reason wrapped in a message that compels them to join him.

Thaddeus has a six day walk home to think about what he will tell them. But for now, he just wants to sit in the sun on the soft moss and think about the weeks ahead of him.

Chapter 5

The Caretaker

Preserves will take up limited resources from the AI's perspective. An individual AI unit should suffice in monitoring and maintaining the Preserves ecosystem and structure. They will be able to conduct their operations without detection ensuring human culture develops in as natural and healthy a way as possible.

-Ahimsa's Preserve Proposal Notes, Ch 4, pg. 14

As Thaddeus sits in the moss contemplating his discoveries and thinking about what needs to happen next, high above him an aircraft with a flat bottom and rounded glass top glides effortlessly and silently through the air. Its bottom and half its sides are coated in a trichromatic, ultra-finite photocell skin that perfectly mimics the appearance of the sky above it. This makes the craft completely invisible to anyone observing from below. The remainder of the glass sides curve to a dome. Its shape resembles a watermelon cut in half and placed flesh side down. The floor is black rubber and there is just one small control panel under the front window.

It has one occupant, an AI named Xerub who has come here to ascertain the nature of the strange blast the seismic monitor at the Europa-1 Maintenance and Visitation Facility registered. Unable to see through the thick forest canopy, Xerub engages the air-craft's infra-red cameras. It sees the heat signature of a human specimen, alone, sitting on the forest floor.

It hovers high above the human and uploads its chip data. This specimen is a seventeen-year-old male from Harvest, no known physical ailments or limitations and sufficient to above average mental and physical performance.

Xerub came here because the registered blast piqued its curiosity. The seismic value was too small and localized to be an earthquake. In fact, the value was such a small number it realized it had not seen anything like it in the three hundred years it has been this Preserves Caretaker. It boarded the air-craft and came here quickly to understand what is happening.

But it cannot determine exactly what is happening from this height. The human is close to the point on the barrier where the seismic reading occurred. It is bright daylight; any approach could not be surreptitious and Xerub is strictly forbidden from making its presence known to any human.

What is this specimen doing so far from any village inside the Preserve? It is statistically improbable that the tiny seismic event and the presence of the human are coincidental.

It comes to the only possible logical conclusion. The human caused the seismic registry. How? Could he have caused a cascading rock slide against the barrier, large enough to trigger the seismic monitors? Highly unlikely considering the size of such a project and there is only one specimen present.

It realizes there is another possibility worth investigating. This human may have brought a chemical explosive and deployed it against the side of the barrier. Xerub knows the village of Copperton uses explosive material both in its mining operations and in their fireworks which they trade with other villages. However, those blasts do not set off the seismic alert system monitoring the Preserve and its inhabitants, they are too small.

Xerub has already concluded no real damage was done, there is no breach threat. But it still wants to know what exactly did happen here. It must return to this site when it can not be detected and take precise measurements of the damage and gather evidence to determine its cause. Then it can include this incident in its regular report to the Central Council and the anthropologists.

Xerub cannot take any action at this time to better understand the situation. Since the human does not appear to be moving but is alive it decides to return to base to dispatch a semi-autonomous drone, designed to look exactly like a robin, to monitor these events.

###

About an hour later the air-craft with the silly looking robot lands on the far side of the barrier in the Europa-1 Maintenance and Visitation Facility. Xerub exits the vehicle and enters the largest of four buildings, a one-story, cube-like main structure with no windows and only two doors, connected to three other equally bland, windowless structures by three long corridors.

Transmission and reception antennas line the sides of the roofs. Parked in the courtyard, bordered by a sturdy metal fence designed to keep out wildlife, sits another air-craft, much larger than the one Xerub was just using. That one is used for tourists and other maintenance functions such as wildlife seeding.

There are four main rooms in the building. Xerub, and any visitors, enter the operations room first from the outside door. It walks immediately to a small stand-up cubicle where a door silently slides open. Xerub steps inside and the door closes. A brief blast of radiation causes a small green glow before the door opens again and Xerub emerges, clean of all possible airborne biological contaminants. A door on the opposite wall to the outside door connects the room to a larger space which houses the various semi autonomous drones used for management and monitoring of the vast Preserve. Into this room Xerub goes to retrieve a drone designed to look exactly like a robin. The drone will be programmed to gather visual and audio data on the activities of the human specimen observed this morning.

Xerub dispatches it immediately after uploading its program. The device flies straight up through an exit in the ceiling that slides open and closed for drone launches such as these. The 'robin' is programmed to return in eighteen hours.

Xerub then checks the daily schedule. There are forty-seven required inoculations of newborns and infants in three villages. It retrieves then readies the insect drones, tiny robotic mosquitoes, with the required vaccinations for the correct targets and programs them for night delivery. Even though they will not be able to administer their inoculations for another nine hours, Xerub dispatches the 'insects'. They can sit on station undetected for days, ensuring the process of administration does not contain a risk of discovery.

Xerub now checks the existing surveillance assets. These are 'birds' and 'insects' already deployed in the field. They look for, and report on, any developments affecting the caretaker's operations. For example, they report on pregnancies. Yesterday a female in Stillerton who Xerub has been monitoring for five months successfully gave birth.

Today Xerub must prepare a semi autonomous insect drone to place the tracking chip on the baby, programmed with the new specimen's birthdate, gender, village identity, and any known physical impediments. The infant must also be put on the vaccination schedule.

Four more births are expected in the next two weeks.

In addition to the biological detox chamber and computers for programming the drones, this space houses the holo-comm. It is a small circle of lights set into the rubberized surface of the floor. From these lights will emerge a ghostly apparition of an AI when in communication with Xerub. For conferences, the image will change depending on which robot is talking. This is a common occurrence for a Preserve caretaker. Often they report to a committee of six anthropologists and there are seven members of the Central Council, although it is rare that all seven are present for a conference about a Preserve.

Xerub sees a new memo on the comm screen. The memo informs the four Preserve caretakers that the anthropological scholars are unavailable for one month. They are conferencing on Titan. All requests and updates are to be given to Central Council until the anthropologists return to Lunar Base. Xerub does not consider this to be an important development, even after it includes the events at the barrier with the lone human. It plugs in to begin its recharge cycle.

###

Eighteen hours later the robotic 'robin' returns after its monitoring session. Xerub, operating on a freshly recharged power cell, downloads the data and reviews the information. The 'bird' was able to perch on a branch undetected and record this human for two hours.

The drone also recorded clear images of the damage to the barrier. Using an internally mounted laser it made precise measurements of the incursion's dimensions. The images show the crater was caused by an explosive device. There is black charring on the edges of a hole about two meters high and two meters wide. Additionally, there is debris in front of the hole in a classic blast pattern, large chunks close by with smaller bits farther out.

Zooming into the image Xerub notices the exposed re-bar. The robin also recorded that the human male made camp for the night in the field bordering the forest and is travelling alone.

A lone human male, obviously an alpha type due to his size and above average physical and mental development, had made the trek to the barrier. He had walked for about six days with no horse or pack animal and blew a hole inside the barrier with a chemical explosive. Normally this information would be given to the scholars in a special report, but since they are on Titan and unavailable Xerub computes to simply continue monitoring.

It recalls the last time a lone alpha male from Harvest made the trek to the barrier. That was thirty-five years ago, and the encounter did not go well. As a result, the male was forever disassociated from his community. The specimen has lived in a cave at the bottom of a canyon near Harvest for three and a half decades, rarely interacting with other humans. Xerub monitors that male continuously for the scholars. They consider his condition unique and often want information uploads specifically about him.

Xerub decides to check the video logs on the isolated male in the canyon and discovers the male he observed today visited the hermit five days ago. They shared a meal and conversation. The younger male stayed for about an hour before exiting the canyon heading west wearing a haversack full of food and carrying weapons.

What could that mean? Audio recording was not activated, Xerub can not determine what they discussed. Did the isolated male tell him how he traversed the barrier thirty-five years earlier? It concludes he probably did not, as the younger male did not replicate any of the activities of the disassociated male. Did the younger male ask the older male about his experiences? Are they related in some social manner? Xerub sends a signal to the drones monitoring the hermit to activate audio recording. Until it has more knowledge on what the young alpha male is up to it wants to know what the hermit says, even if he is only talking to himself.

###

Early the next morning Xerub, in an air-craft, returns to the site of the damage and the lone alpha male. It expects to be on site before the specimen is awake, so it can view the totality of the humans activities.

But its timing is off. The human must have awoken earlier, his camp is empty. Xerub stays high and uses the telescopic camera and sweeping infrared scanner to find and zoom in on the specimen, two kilometres away and walking toward his village.

Xerub uses this opportunity to inspect it all first-hand. It lands close to the spot the human male made camp, in a large field bordering the forest and close to the damaged part of the barrier wall. Humans, Xerub and the anthropologists have observed, prefer to camp in open fields. Possibly for greater safety, the scientists had not done enough research on this behaviour to know for sure.

Xerub exits the air-craft and observes that the human's fire pit is still warm. Turning to the west it walks through the forest exactly one hundred and twenty-seven meters to where the barrier is damaged. It takes several detailed measurements, such as depth of incursion and distance of the debris field.

The human male used a powerful chemical explosive. The explosive was probably provided by Copperton, the village that developed fireworks eighty-four years ago. The explosive clearly was more powerful than anything the humans had developed until now.

Fascinating, it thinks to itself. Xerub knew right away it must report these developments. Not only the damage to the barrier and the endeavours of this single human male, but also the discovery that humans are evolving their chemical knowledge and are now capable of making a substance close in power to traditional dynamite.

Satisfied it has collected enough information to submit a detailed and useful report for the anthropologists and the Central Council, it returns to its air-craft and flies to the Europa-1 Maintenance and Visitation Facility.

During the trip it makes an odd choice, deciding not to order a repair crew to fill the barrier hole. This is a breach of protocol. All damage to the barrier, either human or otherwise, is to be reported for repair. The barrier is to remain intact. Indeed, this is one of Xerub's most important functions in the role of Preserve caretaker. Without that wall the whole system breaks down.

But why did the human detonate such a small device at the barrier? On his journey he visited the only other specimen to have traversed the barrier and had a conversation with him. Xerub concludes he must be trying to breach the barrier.

But Xerub also realizes its initial question is not answered, why such a small detonation? Surely the male knew such a small explosion would not achieve his goal.

Humans are good, and getting better, at developing plans and working together on projects no one person could do. Until now those projects were limited to improving their communities like building a large hall or bridging a river.

Xerub notes, if they are planning on breaching the barrier using explosives then a project of this scope has no precedence in Preserve era human behaviour. Given their technical limitations such an endeavour would require a team of dozens of people. Groups that size had not been formed in the past, certainly not for a project of this scope.

Xerub realizes it would be a challenge even for a team of AIs to dig through the barrier surface. For this sole human, the task must seem far more difficult, in fact, nearly impossible. Either the human male was dismayed and is returning home having resigned himself to the impossibility of the task, or he has a plan to achieve his goal.

Xerub wants to know what, if anything, that plan may be.

Chapter 6

The Grand Project

Life for the humans should be regulated according to our safety. Development will be set at a level for their existence to guarantee comfort yet require many hours of labour. Specialization will lead to intellectualism then technological progress. Systems will be implemented to monitor and respond to any philosophical challenges to their paradigm created by such progress. Those systems will conform to our restrictions and serve the best interests of the humans.

-Ahimsa's Preserve Proposal Notes, Ch. 18, Pg. 9

Thaddeus walks for six days to return to Harvest. He does not encounter another bear on his journey, but he does pass the one he killed on the way there, its corpse picked by vultures, covered in maggots, and the source of a swarm of flies. He gains a sense of confidence knowing he can tell the people he hopes will join him that the journey is far from perilous.

He decides to avoid Barnabas by taking a route that passes south of his cave. He does not want to see Barnabas because he does not want to entertain cynicism. For these moments he knows he must maintain his momentum, and Barnabas the Hermit is far more likely to call him a fool with a foolish plan.

Maybe, he thinks to himself as he walks east toward the road then north to his village, he does not want to listen to Barnabas because he knows the wild man has a valid point. Is he being foolish? Will he find enough support from his people to make this plan happen? These questions drill into him during the trek home, complicating his thoughts as he works to formulate a compelling argument to make to his brethren.

###

His mother sits on her front porch, sewing together a pair of ripped pants her oldest daughter wears. Thaddeus crests a hill, bringing him into her view. She leaps up when she sees him and runs, elated with her arms outstretched. For thirteen days she has worried he would not return, killed by the beasts in the woods; lost forever to the vastness of his ambitions.

As she runs, she yells back to Joshua and Jacob, playing in the big home's main room, to fetch their father, "Your brother has returned!". The two young boys shoot out the back door of the farmhouse and race to the chicken coops and their father.

Thaddeus laughs and is overjoyed his mother is so happy to see him. They run to each other and soon Elizabeth Barley holds Thaddeus tight. Her relief is shown in the strength of her embrace delivered as they stand in the middle of the road in front of the big Barley Family Farm.

"Easy mother. I told you I would return. And I am happy to inform I have returned sound of mind," he says to her reassuringly.

"I was so worried, my son, so very worried."

They walk together now, arm in arm, exiting the road and heading on the path that leads across the front lawn to their house. His father approaches from the rear of the home, his clothes are dirty and he is wiping his hands on a cloth he keeps in his back pocket. Xander Barley's arrival is preceded by the young boys who race to see their older brother. His sisters and brother Hans must be in school at this time of day.

Xander is dirty from his chores but his face sports a large smile. He tells Thaddeus he is glad he has returned healthy, "For there are chores to be done."

Thaddeus laughs at this. He asks his mother to make some tea and he and his father walk to the back of the house where the two can sit on the veranda and talk of his adventure. He tells Joshua and Jacob to finish their chores for now, he will share his tale with them tonight at dinner when all the children are assembled.

He takes off his pack and his father and he sit in large wooden chairs made comfortable with pillows his mother made. Thaddeus starts to tell his father his tale, "I made it father. I made it to the barrier."

"All the way there? And back? But you have not been gone two weeks."

"It is not as far as you imagine." He looks directly at his father now, "I can tell you its form."

"Tell away my son. Tell me of the barrier," his father says as he settles into his chair.

"It is made of hardened mud. In places, it even looks like poured and then dried mud. It is not smooth stone. The surface is rough and dusty. It breaks under the right circumstances."

"You touched it?"

"Of course. I had to. And I broke it easily. You could break it," laughing now, "my youngest sister could break off a piece! And she is but ten years of age. But more importantly, using Helga's uncle's fire-stick, I made a hole large enough for a man to stand inside."

"Now that is something." Xander Barley has always been a farmer. His father is as well, and although he does not remember it very well, his father's father worked this land. The barrier looms in the distance as it does for all his people, but he does not contemplate the meaning of its existence. Some of his friends do, none as strongly as his son.

Xander has seen, over his years, that for those friends and Thaddeus, the barrier means something. It is not benign; it is not there for protection from an abstract evil. For them, the barrier possesses another purpose. At this moment, Xander is acutely aware that he does not share the ambition to know, or even meditate upon, what that purpose might be.

Thaddeus sees he has his father's attention, so he continues, "And inside the barrier are metal rods set vertically. Remarkably similar to the rods the people of Forge make. Remarkably similar indeed."

"Rods? What could they be for?"

"Is not that an interesting question! Indeed, what is the whole barrier for? I am certain it was built by man, or something like man. Its form is unlike anything else in nature. It is an anomaly," Thaddeus is aware his excitement is making his voice pitch higher.

"You are going to see the other side?" Xander asks his son.

"That is my goal."

“Why?” Xander asks this now because until recently this was clearly impossible. But if his son made a hole large enough for a man to stand inside then things had changed. Up to that point discussing crossing the barrier seems an academic question, or possibly an opportunity for cynicism. Xander does want to understand what draws his son to this endeavour, this impossible project.

After thinking on this question for the six days it took him to walk home, Thaddeus is prepared with an answer, his purpose inside a message. He leans forward, wanting his father to understand the seriousness of what he is about to say. “Because the other side of the barrier is the absolute definition of our life.” His father does not reply, he appears a little stunned, so Thaddeus continues, “It is not the barrier itself, it is why its there, father. Why is it there?”

“It is there to divide us from the other side," his father says in a voice that diminishes as he speaks.

“Obviously, it is there to divide us from the other side. Why? Until we know what the other side is, we can never know why this side is.” As he says this he gestures to the whole world with his arms. “Do you understand what I am trying to say? Am I being clear?”

“I do and you are clear.” And this is true, Xander now understands why this desire burned in his son's chest. To understand our world, we must know what is on the other side of that wall. Knowing that will answer the question that no one else can, 'why are we here?'. Thaddeus is smart and curious, Xander has known this all his son's life. Now to finally quench his curiosity, indeed fulfil a destiny, his son must get past that barrier. “What do you think is there?” he asks his son.

Thaddeus pauses before he answers, “Our teachers and elders tell of unspeakable evils, a scorched land filled with death and doom. Some others suggest there is nothing. The barrier is like the walls to a room but on the other side of the walls is nothing. A void of no dimension, a place in which we can not live and could not understand if we did experience it.”

“And yourself Thaddeus? What do you believe is on the other side?”

"The truth." With that the two men fall silent as Thaddeus' mother brings the tea.

"Mother, this came to good use, and fulfilled your wish. It saved my life." As he says this he stands and unties his sword from his haversack. He holds it level between his hands, gingerly as if it is now something to revere. "Please keep it safe for me." He places the beautiful weapon on the porch's table. "A bear paid dearly due to its fantastic construction. But it will serve me no purpose in the days ahead."

"And what do the days ahead bring, my son?" Xander asks Thaddeus.

###

"What you are proposing would take one hundred people Thaddeus. It is a fool's errand." Harvest's village leader, Isolde, is speaking. She is sixty-five years old and tasked with helping the villagers make good decisions as a community. She is addressing Thaddeus inside Harvest's Great Hall, a large structure of thick timbers and mud where the villagers discuss important matters affecting their community. It is five days after Thaddeus' return to Harvest and three hundred of Harvest's citizens have answered the call to attend this meeting. Helga is in the audience, sitting in the front row near the dais where Isolde and Thaddeus now sit.

"All due respect Isolde, but I calculate approximately fifty men. That includes cooks and hunters."

"Plus donkeys and horses," she adds.

"And possibly cows, goats, sheep. We will need milk to drink and meat to eat. This will not be easy work, keeping up our strength will be critical."

"You and your people will also need many vegetables and grains and fruit, which could place a significant drain on our resources. We will find it harder to trade with other villages," she notes. A murmur runs through the crowd as she says this.

"I will travel to the other villages and ask them for help as well. People from Forge are strong and will know about the metal I found inside and how to remove it. Miners from Copperton can help with the fire-sticks, of which we will need plenty. Stillerton's people can provide the wine," the crowd laughs at this. He continues, "Really people, we will be gone a long time, possibly years. We do not know how much material we will need to move through. It makes sense that there should be some libations to ease the tensions and make the chore more palatable."

"I wonder if they will provide their finest?" Isolde asks with sarcasm in her voice. Stillerton's winemakers keep their finest vintages for themselves which causes some frustration from the other villages. The crowd responds with some boos and jeers.

Thaddeus continues, his natural confidence calming the audience and forcing their attention, "And from Grassy Dale I will ask for meat and dairy animals, which they have in abundance. Also they breed the finest donkeys, tall and strong. We will need many of those." He chose the word 'we' carefully, he knows he needs this project to be seen as a communal one, not the whims of a young and headstrong man. "This task, this grand project, will truly be one of all the villages coming together to complete."

"Do you really believe you can convince so many to engage in such a foolish errand?" Isolde's tone has changed back to condescension. "And to be gone forever?"

"Yes. We will need to construct a semi-permanent camp close to the site. Wood enforced tents and storage for food. Pens for the animals as well. If the ground permits we may find materials close to the site to make the fire-sticks rather than bringing them from Copperton. That will require a workshop."

"And if the ground does not permit?"

"Then we will bring them from Copperton in great trains of many donkeys."

The crowd breaks to a murmur again. He takes this chance to steal a glance to his love. She is not chatting with her seated neighbours like those around her. Instead, she is smiling directly at him. His confidence rises from feeling her love and support.

Of the three hundred people gathered for this meeting, Thaddeus feels about one hundred are for his proposal. The rest are against. He is pleased with these results. If the ratio of one to three holds in all the villages he can recruit an abundance of people for this grand endeavour.

"There is one more question I wish to ask," when Isolde speaks the hall is silenced almost instantly, such is the respect she commands amongst her brethren.

"Why?"

A single word hanging in the air. Not a sound from the crowd. To most of them the barrier is a fact like the clouds or the ground, natural and ubiquitous. There is no more sense in trying to traverse it then there would be trying to dig through the ground or jump through the sky. For those people who accept and not challenge their paradigm the barrier is a benign, sometimes even positive, constant in their lives.

Thaddeus pauses a moment before he answers Isolde. This will be a huge undertaking; unlike anything the villages have ever attempted. If he cannot provide a compelling reason he knows the project will never come to be.

He stands to address the crowd, walking to the edge of the dais so his voice will be heard in the far reaches of the Great Hall. In a voice loud with confidence he starts, "The barrier has always been. It is a truth we have all accepted. All of us," he pauses for a moment to let what he just said sink in. The audience remains rapt, an absolute silence has descended upon them.

He continues, "But is that the truth? We know what the barrier keeps in. It keeps us in. You, your children, your parents. We know the truth of the barrier as much as we perceive it. What we can not perceive is what is beyond it. And whatever is beyond the great wall, is the reason the wall was built. And it is the reason we live inside it." He sees he is holding their attention, many mouths hang open, as if they have only now contemplated this possibility.

Thaddeus continues, "The truth!" he raises his voice to make his point, "The truth is beyond that barrier. And if we are not seeking the truth, if we are not seeking to know our world, then what are we doing? Really? What are we really doing here?"

Isolde offers the first objection, "How do you know it was built? The mountains are not built, the trees and rivers are not built. Why are we to think the barrier was built?" Some in the audience shout their agreement with Isolde. For them there is no reason to believe the barrier exists from forces outside of nature.

"Because I have been there and touched it and even seen inside it. There are metal rods, probably many of them, buried inside. I do not know what they are for." He looks at Isolde whose expression says she is still not convinced.

"All my life," he continues, "I have noted the barrier looks different than anything else in our world. It is smooth and uniform in height and surface. Tell me, what else in our world possesses such qualities that was not built by us?" He pauses to see if anyone can answer this, he is relived no one can. "The barrier is unique in that regard," he continues, "I have spent a lifetime asking my teachers and our village elders, is not the barrier to the mountains what our houses are to the caves? The difference is the same, one contains symmetry and logic, the other is chaotic and random. One is built by us, intelligent beings, the other occurs outside our control." Another murmur sweeps through the audience.

"This is ludicrous Master Thaddeus. Who do you propose built the barrier?" A portion of the audience laugh at Thaddeus after hearing the question Isolde just posed.

"I do not propose who built it, Chief Isolde. I merely propose it was built. It does not occur naturally; it is not of nature. And since I believe it was built, I believe we can break through it, and finally learn the real nature of our world and make the greatest discovery in the history of our people."

Thaddeus sits back down in the chair to Isolde's right. Isolde sits back in her chair as well. She silently looks at the stage floor in front of her, aware of how unconvincing her objections had been.

Slowly a clap ascends from the audience. First the front rows start, then, as if waiting for acceptance, the rows behind them. Soon, the whole audience in the Great Hall is clapping. Thaddeus looks at the assembled masses and smiles broadly.

Some stand to voice their support. The applause does not die down, it is more of a cheer than a thank-you. Only when Isolde stands does the audience begin to calm. She raises her hand, palm forward, until the rest are quieted.

She proclaims, "In ten days time Thaddeus will convene a meeting here in this hall after he returns from visiting the other villages. If you wish to join this young man and his great ambition, then attend. All are to be willing participants."

She turns to Thaddeus with a stern look on her face and speaks directly to him but loudly enough so everyone can hear, "You will have created a plan for this great undertaking, so you do not waste anyone's time or energy."

The audience erupts into cheers once again. Isolde leaves, signalling the rest to go home. Helga jumps the stage and hugs her love. Many villagers crowd around Thaddeus, eager to voice their willingness to participate. He tells them to return in ten days, after breakfast, here in this hall. "Tell people who are not here tonight. We need strong men who can lift and carry heavy things all day. We need miners, labourers, carpenters, hunters, and cooks."

Many voice their willingness to spread the word. Thaddeus feels a lump in his throat when he sees their enthusiasm. He entertains many people with the story of his trek and return.

After an hour or so, The Great Hall begins to empty. Thaddeus and Helga leave with the last of them. Excitement is filling Thaddeus' veins. His head is swimming with possibilities as they walk in the dark to the outskirts of the village and his family's farmhouse.

###

The next day he mounts a horse he rents from his neighbour and he and Helga, who shared Thaddeus' oldest sister's bedroom out of respect for Thaddeus' parents, begin the ride to Copperton. Helga rides her own horse. She is far stronger on the back of the beast than he, she has spent much of her life with horses as they are important to her father's shipping trade.

Tomorrow, after they get to Copperton, their first stop will be her Uncle's house so Thaddeus can tell him of his device's success. Then they plan an appeal to the people of Copperton to join him in this massive project by providing as many of the fire-sticks as they can provide. Fire-sticks are a valued commodity and they anticipate resistance. After Copperton they will travel to the three remaining villages and repeat the appeal in the hopes each of the villages will provide what he needs to begin this endeavour.

Overnight they camp at a site well used by travellers. It is a few meters from the road and about equidistant between Harvest and Copperton. They are alone, there are no other travellers taking advantage of this campsite. They eat dinner and after the sun sets, they make love in their tent. Holding each other in the warmth of their bodies they talk while looking out the tent's door at the stars above them.

She tells him, “I will not be going to the barrier with you.”

“I would like you to come,” he had not really contemplated her not being there with him so her comment catches him off guard.

“My father needs me still and my ambitions are to take over his trade someday, hopefully in the near future.”

“But, well… we may be apart for many days. Possibly weeks or months.”

“This quest is yours Thaddeus. I have never been motivated to cross the barrier. I do not fully understand why it is such a burning passion for you.”

“You were there last night in the hall. You heard me explain why.”

She laughs at this. “Yes, my love. And for the last six years of my life since we first met! My heart swelled with pride for you last night, but I do not share your desire to broaden our understanding of this world. For me, my life is fulfilled enough with our horses and wagons. I enjoy spending life on the road travelling from one village to the next. Watching the seasons change as I sleep under the stars.”

What she says is true and he knows it. He has been talking about these matters to his family and friends all his life, last night was just the first time with a good portion of Harvest's population in attendance.

He says to her, “We have never really discussed our future together. You must have assumed I would become a farmer.”

“No, I have always known that life would not satisfy you. I had hoped you may be interested in joining me on the wagons some day. It can be an adventurous life.”

“And we would be together.”

“Yes.” She cuddled up to him now as they lay in their tent, snaking their arms around each other. “I would like to spend every moment of my day with you, my handsome man.”

“And I with you. Which is why I hoped you'd come with me to the barrier, share in my experience when we break through.”

“No my love. My father is my first duty right now.”

“I understand.” And he does. She is a good daughter, sensitive and caring toward her parents. Inside and outside she is the most beautiful woman he has ever seen, and he loves that about her too. He will miss seeing her crystal blue eyes set wide and angled toward her nose. He will miss her soft and strong lips and the way she smells in the morning after she bathes.

She says to him in a tender voice, “I will wait for you Thaddeus. Once you complete this mission you will have to come back and decide on a way of life, and it better include me,” she smiles as she says this and pokes him playfully in the stomach.

He pauses a moment, ensuring their eyes are locked on each other. Without a flicker to his face and in a tone designed to speak straight to her heart he tells her, “I will love you until the end of time. Nothing will change that, no mission at the barrier, no grand endeavour, no amount of time apart. I will always love you.”

“And I you.” They fall asleep, physically tired from their days ride and emotionally tired from this evening's talk.

###

The next morning, they wake to a bright sun and the silence of the woods. He cooks a breakfast of fish and toast as she packs the tent and their sleeping bags on the horses. Soon they are on the road to Copperton and their destination.

The ride is uneventful, this road is well-used so most wildlife avoid it and there are few other travellers today. After seven hours, Thaddeus' horse stubbornly demanded two extra long stops at a creek to fill his belly, they arrive at Copperton. They dismount and tie their horses to a hitching post. Thaddeus must stretch his legs which are sore and stiff after so many hours in a saddle. Helga is unaffected by the long ride and gestures to Thaddeus to follow her into the front yard of the house they now stand in front of. Thaddeus looks closely at the house and concludes this can only be Uncle Mortimer Bellow's home, the unorthodox naturalist.

It is a low house covered with so many vines it appears to emerge from the ground itself. The front yard is filled with all types of vegetables and flowers and berries. The path from the road to the door winds through the foliage in a nonsensical pattern that forces visitors to see most of his garden, even if they are not interested.

The path is a series of stones made from black, shiny rock. Thaddeus has never seen such a stone. When he asks Helga tells him the rock is called obsidian, adding its rare even in Copperton.

The house is of modest size with fantastic craftsmanship everywhere. As Thaddeus approaches the front door he can see it is carved from fine hardwood with detailed floral and forest imagery. The window at the top of the door contains a stunning piece of stained-glass, depicting the magic of fire-sticks and the labours of Copperton in shades of colours Thaddeus has never seen. Before they can knock on the door it suddenly opens revealing Mortimer Bellows. Thaddeus has only met him once, many years ago, on a trip to visit Helga and meet her parents for the first time. He recognizes the man now, although his hair has greyed and his face has grown more wrinkles.

"You! You are here! Were you successful?" Master Bellows is excited, eager to hear how the experiment worked.

Thaddeus is keen for the excitement. He is proud to be anticipated by this esteemed naturalist. He does not answer right away, waiting instead until he is closer to Mortimer, so close he can talk at a low volume in case sceptical ears can hear him, even though he knew logically none are nearby.

"It was more successful than my wildest imagination. I created a hole big enough to stand in," he finally answers.

With this Master Bellows practically jumps into hugging him. He is shorter than Thaddeus, with a rotund form and a ruddy face. As he hugs him his head only rises to Thaddeus' chest. But his exultation trumps his embarrassment, and he holds Thaddeus tight.

"How much more do you have?" Thaddeus needs to know.

“Come in, my good man, Helga, you too. How is my beautiful niece?”

“I am well Uncle. Your garden looks plentiful.”

“I will feed you from it for lunch.” Then turning his attention to Thaddeus, “You will stay the night with me here? We have much to cover.” The three enter the home. Thaddeus is hit with the scents of cinnamon and jasmine coming from the kitchen. The interior of the house is a celebration of art. The walls are covered with carved wood motifs and landscape paintings, the barrier ever present in the backgrounds. The door handles are crafted metal and the beeswax lamps are as sculptures, depicting fruit and animals in splendid detail. Obviously, Uncle Mortimer takes great pride in his home.

“Sleeping here will be fine, quite fine indeed,” is Thaddeus' response to the invitation. Master Bellows retreats into the kitchen to prepare their lunch. Thaddeus admires this beautiful but small home's ornaments for several minutes before joining the naturalist and his niece in the kitchen. They have put together plates of cheeses, smoked meats, raw vegetables, and breads. Helga is seated at the table and has started to eat from the selections.

“Sit and tell me of your experience.” The naturalist gestures to the empty chair and Thaddeus joins them at the table. As they dine Thaddeus tells of his journey, of meeting Barnabas and touching the barrier. He describes how it feels and how it looks. He tells Mortimer of the incomprehensible completeness of its construction, how one can walk for miles and find no break in the seam where the barrier touches the ground. He describes how the barrier resembles mud that has flown into the cracks and gaps of the ground and hardened into a substance almost as strong as stone.

But not too strong for his fire-sticks.

“That is the exciting thing, Master Bellows, your stick opened up a crater. Your stick showed me the barrier is vulnerable. It is not impenetrable.”

“Excellent. I originally developed the compound for our miners. They use a weaker version of it to ease the chore of digging. It occurred to me that mere concentration was the key. The one you used was only tested once before, by me.”

“How much can you produce?”

"Difficult to say. How much do you need?"

"Ah. Even more difficult to say."

"Why, did you take measurements of the hole one stick made?"

"Yes."

"Then we may be able to calculate an expected sum by weight. That will be most important as the transport is long. Is it accessible by wagon?"

Thaddeus answers honestly, "No. Donkeys can make the journey, most surely. But there are parts where the rock is thick and the path narrow, wagons would be too big."

"Let me perform some calculations after lunch. You leave me the dimensions of the hole and I will do the arithmetic to determine the size of this project."

Thaddeus explains to Mortimer how the hole was as tall as he, how he could stand all the way inside and be covered by the barrier above him. Mortimer is pleased.

"I have only made the two sticks with that particular formulation. Most of the sticks I make generate a much smaller explosion. Now, you and Helga go to the market and purchase meat for dinner, leave the vegetables and greens to me. Do not forget the wine. Helga and you will cook for me tonight, you can have the second bedroom. You will find it most comfortable. When do you leave Copperton?"

"I will meet with your elder this afternoon and try to convene a meeting with the villagers in the morning. Then we travel to Forge."

"Excellent. You will find our village leader to be a crabby old man with a small mind. He spent his life in our mines, a sad reason to think you can be a civic leader."

Helga pats her Uncle on his hand and says, "Uncle, I had not told Thad about Frederick. I did not want to scare him." She turns to her love and says, "Frederick Metzger is a cantankerous old man who is short on ideas and long on traditions. He despises anything aspirational. I do not predict enthusiasm for your project."

Thaddeus turns to Uncle Mortimer as he replies to Helga, "Well, we have the genius Master Bellows on side, I think that will be more than enough as a contribution from Copperton." Mortimer smiles at the compliment so Thaddeus continues, "but the truth is Master Bellows, we have no way of knowing how thick the barrier is, or indeed if it has a thickness and is not just endless grey matter. We may need more fire-sticks than Copperton can produce. I am hoping to quarry the materials and build a workshop to create our own right there, near where we will be working. Can you join us on this project? Physically join us I mean?"

"No. I am too old and love my home's comforts. But I have an acolyte who may be interested."

Thaddeus looks at Helga with confusion, he has never heard the word 'acolyte'. "A student," she informs him.

"Oh. That would be fine as well."

"She is a strong naturalist and a strong person. She could make the journey easily and would do fine under the hard life you propose out there at the barrier's base."

"Would she be able to determine if the land could be quarried for the goods?"

"Yes."

"Would she be interested in knowing what lies beyond the barrier? I ask because I have encountered many who are not, some even hostile to the possibility."

"We have never discussed it. It can not hurt to ask."

"Can I meet her tomorrow morning before Helga and I depart?"

"Yes. Now, go find Frederick and buy the meat and wine for tonight. I will begin the calculations."

"Yes Uncle. Thank you so much." Helga rises and gives her Uncle a strong hug. Thaddeus rises as well, thanks Master Bellows for the excellent midday meal and the two depart for Frederick's home. Helga knows the way.

"Have you met your Uncle's student?" he asks her.

"Yes. She is somewhat distant with me however."

"Is this distance found in many academics?"

"Possibly. But I detect some jealousy. She has never found a person to love her. Her form is large and her interests esoteric. She spends much time on her studies and does not appear to need the attention of men to be happy. Nor the attention of women either."

They approach Frederick's bland home. There is no thought to its construction and no garden in the front. It is low and flat with dark drapes pulled shut in the windows. Smoke rises from the chimney, so Helga concludes he is home.

"Last chance to turn back," she says in a half joking manner.

"Will it really be that bad?"

"Quite possibly," her tone unease's Thaddeus. She knocks on the door, not too loud as she does not want to risk antagonizing Master Metzger. After a moment, the door opens just enough for them to see an old man with leathery skin and silver hair peer out at them.

"Yes? Helga, is that you? What do you want?" Frederick Metzger is definitely cantankerous.

"Master Metzger, we come to seek a favour. We would like to convene a village meeting for tomorrow morning. My friend," she gestures to Thaddeus standing beside her, "has an interesting proposal."

"What is the proposal?" he says as he opens the door further and steps into the daylight, exiting the dark house.

"He needs men and sup…" Frederick interrupts her to ask,

"Can he not speak?"

Thaddeus takes the opportunity to state his case, "Yes Master Metzger, I speak quite well, thank you. I come to Copperton asking for help on a grand endeavour. I seek to traverse the barrier."

"Where are you from?"

"Harvest."

"I see. A farmer you are. I should have guessed by your clothes. It also explains your weak looking arms." Thaddeus ignores the insult and breathes a sigh of relief this man is not his village elder. For all her scepticism and caution Isolde is far more agreeable than this bitter old man.

"I am. As were my father and his father and his father. We grow grains and some vegetables. Do you have bread?"

"Yes. But not enough to share with you."

"I am not hungry, merely pointing out that your bread was likely made by the hands of my brethren." Helga squeezes his hand, urging him to not continue taunting Frederick.

"Traverse the barrier. Are you mad?" Master Metzger asks.

"Possibly. Can you convene a meeting of your people for tomorrow morning in the square?"

Frederick looks hard at Thaddeus. He squints his eyes as he assesses this brash young man on his porch who did not flinch when he told him he had skinny arms even though his arms are obviously strong.

Although Frederick is uninterested in the nonsense this boy spews, he knows it is not his job to censure people who wish to speak directly to the citizens of Copperton. "Yes. I will have my son make the announcement. But likely I will not attend. I have no appetite for foolishness."

"Thank you, Master Metzger," and with that they take their leave of this disagreeable elder.

Next stop is Copperton's village square to purchase meat and wine for supper. They also purchase grains and apples for their horses. While they are doing their shopping, they notice village criers, teen-aged boys and girls, running through the square putting up signs and calling out about a meeting tomorrow morning.

Thaddeus likes Copperton. He has been here a few times and always enjoys seeing how their shops and houses differ in look and style to Harvest's. Each of the villages have their own unique look, reflecting what they specialize in. Copperton's structures are adorned with sheets of copper or tin cut into interesting shapes or have pastoral and mining scenes etched into them. There are statues and figures carved from granite adorning their buildings and public spaces.

Their special relationship with Forge is on display. Thaddeus admires a monument erected to celebrate the hardy men and women of Forge who heat and pound Copperton's raw goods into useful shapes and forms. It is a statue of figures standing around a furnace, ready to pound whatever emerges with the stylized hammers they grasp. He takes note of the intricate details the figures display.

"It looks as good as what the craftsman of Stillerton could produce," Helga says to him to break his concentration.

"Indeed," is his reply.

Their chores completed, they start toward Mortimer Bellow's house again. The sun is descending and their shadows grow longer. The barrier is more distant here, it is lower and takes up less of the horizon than in Harvest. As they walk the road to Helga's uncle's house she again holds onto his arm, enjoying the attention they attract from the women of Copperton who look jealously at her handsome consort. She is also acutely aware of the jealous men looking at Thaddeus, men forever unable to turn her eye from him.

When they enter her Uncle's house he is still at the kitchen table. He has been productive, there are many sheets of vellum covered in calculations and his fingers are black with ink, his right hand still holding his pen.

Mortimer Bellows looks at the two as they place the food and wine on the counters. He says with some excitement, "I believe we can do it. I believe, with packs of sticks strung six together, and with a conservative estimate of the thickness of the base, we can blast our way through in only a few weeks of work."

"What is your estimate of the barrier's thickness?" Thaddeus asks with great curiosity as he and Helga join him at the table.

"I have chosen a distance of two hundred meters."

"I can not visualize that," Thaddeus says.

"About the distance from the front of my house to the village bakery."

This Thaddeus can understand and immediately thinks Bellows has underestimated.

"How did you calculate that?"

"I considered the height of a brick. If you say the material is like clay pots then it is also like a brick."

Thaddeus did not know why he had not thought of that before. Of course, the barrier is far more like a brick.

"For a brick to be strong enough to be used in construction its thickness must be at least one quarter its height. We know it has a height, but we do not know what it is. However, I can guess."

"But what would you base the guess on?"

"When I was a younger man I would climb the tallest mountain in Copperton. It is a mine, of course, an imposing, treeless mountain north of the village. From there I would note I was about half as high as the top of the barrier, the best I could determine visually from this distance."

"And how do you know the height of the mountain?" Thaddeus is not challenging him, he genuinely wants to know.

"The naturalists of Copperton's past did extensive research and documented many aspects of our village natural world. Numbers of trees, amounts of fish in the rivers, how many bears and cougars and other beasts are in the woods. It is not an exact science mind you, but it is close to accurate. They measured the mountain. It is four hundred meters high from its base."

"Eight hundred meters high?"

"Yes, that is my educated guess."

"I see." Thaddeus knew the old man is far off. He wondered how he could tell him his errors without offending him. He starts with a nonthreatening tone and story, "When I walked to the barrier I would often look up and peer toward the top. As I got closer and closer each day the barrier grew in my vision until it was all I could see if I looked straight ahead, it completely blocked out the sky." Uncle Mortimer is waiting for him to make his point.

He continues, "If the bakery to your house is two hundred meters, I can tell you the barrier is far more than four times that distance in height. I would suggest the barrier is closer to two thousand meters in height. Also, your calculation assumes that the bottom of the mountain and barrier are at the same level."

Master Bellows considers this information and expresses his scepticism, "But a structure that large, Thaddeus, it would take lifetimes to build."

"Yes. Probably many lifetimes. That or whoever built it lived much longer lives than us, or the length of their lives was not a consideration for them."

"I see what you mean. You believe there could be other forms of life, intelligent life like you and I and not like an animal, that could have built it?"

"I believe nothing I cannot see, Master Bellows. I have not seen another life like ours. But..." he pauses now, unsure if he should tell him about Barnabas and what the hermit claims to have seen. He continues cautiously, “There is a man in our village, a reclusive hermit, who has claimed many times to have seen a man like being,” he stops now to give Mortimer time to absorb this information.

“Really! Fascinating.” This reaction surprises Thaddeus. Almost everyone who heard this tale rejects it out of hand. Thaddeus thinks Mortimer reacts this way because he is more open-minded than others. Or maybe it was because Mortimer did not yet know Barnabas was referring to a metal man floating in the sky, appearing and disappearing supernaturally.

“Yes. He says he was climbing a mountain and on the side of a cliff when suddenly a structure emerged, floating in the air before him. He saw a man who was not really a man.” He pauses to gauge Mortimer's expression of growing scepticism. “He said the structure was made of glass on top with a black floor, he could see directly inside to a man made of metal with a strange head and look of shock on his face.”

“A man made of metal? That sounds highly unlikely Thaddeus.”

“He actually described it as a man that was not a man at all, but more like a man than anything else.”

“And a face of constant surprise? Floating in the air before him?”

“That was his description.”

“You trust this Barnabas?”

“Not easily. I visited him on my journey to the barrier and I have to say everything he told me about the trek was correct, so I am more inclined to believe him now.”

“And you think this metal man made the barrier?”

“Or possibly a whole community of metal men.” Thaddeus wants to know what Mortimer thinks of that idea. He stops talking now, waiting for Mortimer to fill the silence.

Bellows does so by stating, “I consider myself a rational man Thaddeus. In the absence of good evidence I can only say that the barrier is. Why or how it 'is' is something we can only answer with research.”

"I believe traversing the barrier will be the most important research we do."

With this Helga senses it is time to start cooking. She rubs the back of Thaddeus' hand and the two rise to begin preparing dinner. Before they start, Thaddeus convinces Mortimer to recalculate based on the possibility that the barrier is at least five hundred meters thick. The esteemed thinker agrees he should, acquiescing to this young man's confidence and respecting that he has been to the barrier and likely knows better.

Mortimer gets to work on the mathematics while Thaddeus and Helga prepare a large dinner of pork hocks. He works in silence while Helga cooks the vegetables and Thaddeus tends to the meat. When Mortimer fills a sheet he dramatically, but precisely, whips it out from under him and places it, ink side up, on the far side of the table. Then he dips his pen in his small inkwell and starts anew on a fresh sheet.

When he can, Thaddeus steals glances at what the old man is doing. The formulas he sees are familiar but beyond his knowledge of numbers and sums. He thinks Mortimer is deducing potential forces related to materials, but he can not be sure and will not dare interrupt the man's concentration.

When dinner is cooked and ready to serve Helga tells her uncle it is time to move his work to a different table. Mortimer looks up and for the first time in half of an hour he observes what is going on around him. Then he looks at his niece with some embarrassment, mutters a bit to himself about being very hungry, gathers his vellum and ink and disappears to his study.

When he returns, the ink wiped from his fingers, they all sit at the table now set for dinner. Silently the three of them look at the food before them, no one moving. Thaddeus and Helga sit in silent anticipation of Mortimer telling them of his research and what he has discovered.

Mortimer is silent because he does not want to tell them. He looks awkwardly side to side before breaking the silence. "Well," big exhale, "this is going to be quite the endeavour. It will require more fire-sticks, many more. Therefore, and these concerns are yours, Master Barley," the sudden formality caught Thaddeus off guard.

The coming news must be bad, "More time. And that means more of everything else. Food, wine, people, you understand."

Thaddeus does understand, and he appreciates the respect of this esteemed man of Copperton. The challenges the naturalist just outlined are things he has thought about. Solutions abound, of course, time has never been a hurdle Thaddeus cannot leap.

Thaddeus' primary functions take over and he declares, "Enough talk of the future and insane ideas. Let us drink wine and eat this bounty. There is much to accomplish."

They eat, drink, laugh, and fall asleep. The next morning he and Helga are preparing to leave for the village square, and their meeting with the people of Copperton. Mortimer emerges from his bedroom and declares that he has a rough estimate of the number of fire-sticks needed. It is a number too big to be easily made here in Copperton. In fact, the number is so big it may be difficult to convince non Coppertonians to even begin this seemingly impossible endeavour.

"Keep in mind, Thaddeus, the material we use in the fire-sticks is the same material we use in our displays. It is an important export for us, bringing us much in the way of goods by trade," he tells them with some disappointment.

"Will your acolyte be in attendance?" Thaddeus asks while he and Helga put on their riding clothes and prepare for a long day.

"I will go to her home after I get dressed. I am sure she will be interested. Hopefully enough to join."

"I need her to come with us and at least look for the materials we need close to our site. If she can find them, we can make the fire-sticks right there, close to the barrier itself. We will not be a drain on Copperton." They finish putting on their riding clothes, thank Mortimer for his hospitality, and leave together. Mortimer will join them in less than an hour with his student.

When they arrive at Copperton Village square they make their way to the announcements stage but are dismayed at the lack of attendance. There are only about twenty people. Copper ton's population is closer to six thousand.

Helga ascends the dais and announces in a loud voice, "People of Copperton, give us your attention. We come to ask you to participate in a grand project. A project so large its progenitor requests our assistance."

A voice from the audience calls out, "And what is this project Helga?" She does not know who called out to her, but he obviously knows her.

She hesitates a moment, realizing every second she does not answer adds doubt to the crowd's mind. "To traverse the barrier. To see what lies beyond."

At this the audience erupts in laughter. The same voice speaks again and this time she can see it is Jared, Frederick Metzger's youngest son. A few years ago he put himself forward for her attention and she rebuffed him. He has been curt to her ever since. "That is the rumour of the subject of this meeting!" Jared declares. "I only came to see for myself. The idea is foolish, a waste of time." The audience applauds at his words.

Thaddeus, standing to the side, sees Mortimer approach with his student, a hardy woman in her mid-twenties. Her hair is braided down two sides so tightly not a single strand is loose. Mortimer introduces her as Hannah, and the two shake hands.

Hannah says to him, "Master Bellows tells me of your idea. No matter what the crowd here thinks or says, I want to be a part of it."

"That is good news."

She adds, "Tell me of the land surrounding the area you propose to work. Are there rocks and hills present? A creek?"

"In good time Lady Hannah. For now, let us listen to the crowd."

"In all due respect Master Barley, I have known this objector all my life. He is a weak-minded fool. Allow me to address him." He says nothing but bows and steps aside so she may step onto the dais and take her place beside Helga.

In a loud, confident, and authoritative voice, Hannah addresses Jared directly, "Foolish? A waste of time? If we are not exploring our world and seeking to understand it better, then are not our entire lives just a waste of time?"

"No," Jared speaks from the crowd again. "In fact, how dare you? To stand there and disparage our toils and loves as a waste of time. How rude! My life, our lives," he gestures to the crowd as if he speaks for all of them, "are rich and satisfied and we see no reason to drain Copperton of its wealth for the nonsensical goals of a young man from Harvest."

"It is not nonsensical," Thaddeus says this loudly as he too steps upon the dais. He hears some people in the crowd mention he is the man from Harvest they have been hearing about. He continues, "It is not nonsensical at all. With the proper application of thought it can only be concluded as highly rational." He looks at Jared now, a man of diminutive stature even if he was not being compared to Thaddeus standing on a riser. "What are we doing here indeed, as Hannah asks. But have you ever asked, 'What is the barrier'? Have you not wondered what lies beyond?"

"There is nothing beyond it. It is as foolish as saying there is something below the ground." Jared speaks again, it appears he is going to challenge every aspect of this project.

Hannah speaks with an impatient tone, as an adult may to a child who asks too many exasperating questions, when she addresses Jared, "I am surprised to hear a man from Copperton make such a comparison. Our history and our daily toils prove there is much to be found under the ground."

"But there is no end to the ground, as there is no end to the sky. There is no reason to believe there is an end to the barrier." Jared sounds smug now, his voice has lowered and by the time he has made his statement a whisper of anger can be detected.

"And how do you know that?" Thaddeus answers loud enough for all to hear. Helga whispers in his ear the name of the questioner and Thaddeus recognizes it right away. When Jared told Helga of his desires she told Thaddeus as soon as she could. Thaddeus now understands the true nature of Jared's objections. Armed with this new knowledge he continues, "How can you know given that you have never seen this nothing? Are you a man of faith, Jared?" The mock is intentional. Only the imbecilic believe in something they have never perceived.

The crowd reacts to this taunt and looks to Jared for his rebuttal. He approaches the dais, stopping just before he would have to step upon it. He looks at the three of them standing on the riser, as if they challenge his entire way of life. Then he turns his back to them so he can address the audience, whose loud cheers and reactions have drawn a few more Coppertonians to stop and listen.

Jared begins his final argument, “Our traditions inform us, our songs and our books and our paintings and our culture. Surely you have seen our art?” He says this sarcastically over his shoulder toward Thaddeus behind him. The crowd lightly laughs at his mock. “You ask us to give up that culture, and all it will cost us is much of our most valuable resource.” The audience laughs once more. “Are we to say thank you? Thank you for draining our coffers with no guarantee of discovery and all to rewrite our traditions.”

Thaddeus replies, “But are your traditions correct Master Metzger? You accept as axiomatic that which has not been tested, researched, nor studied in a thousand years. This quest, Master Metzger,” he now raises his head to address the entire audience; this next message is for them all, “is to discover the truth of our world. You may be right, the barrier could extend into the distance forever, as the ground or sky do. Then you will know, then you will not be a man of faith but a man of knowledge.”

They are all silent now. Thaddeus' makes an excellent point. This whole quest could prove Jared right. He continues, “We cannot become complacent. Work with us and help us discover what is real.” The crowd continues to shuffle and jostle in reaction, many speak amongst themselves.

Mortimer joins Thaddeus, Helga, and Hannah on the stage. His presence brings the audience to attention. They will listen to Mortimer Bellows. His life's work has made the job of mining easier and safer, and contributed enormously to Copperton's wealth over the years. He begins with the mannerisms Hannah has seen a thousand times, like a teacher. He places one hand on his hip and uses the other to gesture to the air in aid of whatever point he was making.

He begins, “Citizens. Brethren. I believe in this project, and this young man. He has done what none of us even dare, he has ventured to the barrier and returned. He bested the beasts in the woods, survived on the land, and stood beside a structure of mind-bending dimensions. And here he stands, before you now, and he wants to go back. Imagine the courage, the sheer audacity it must take, to look upon that thing and think you must best it. That you will not accept the reality it presents, and you will find the truth that it shields."

The crowd is silent. Even Jared wants to hear more. The old man continues, "I will supply him with the first of the fire-sticks he will need, a special concoction not yet used in the mines. After that it will be up to the village and our elder Frederick Metzger." Mortimer says the name on purpose, reminding all that Jared is not the village elder.

Helga ends the meeting; she wants to get on the road to Forge and they can not spend all morning here. "Thank you, Master Bellows, my Uncle. Thank you all for your attendance. Please discuss with your families, I will return to Copperton within two weeks and will be happy to talk to all you then."

The audience disperses and the four of them return to Bellow's house. While standing in the foyer Thaddeus asks Hannah, "Will you come on the journey with me, Hannah?"

"Yes. You will show me the work site and I will work to make the fire-sticks you need. But I am not hopeful. Even here in Copperton, where minerals are abundant, the material we need for fire-sticks is rare."

"Failure can lead us to success," Mortimer reminds her.

"Indeed Master. And we will find another solution," her reply pleases Mortimer greatly and the two smile at each other. Thaddeus gets the impression they have had this conversation before, probably many times.

Helga momentarily wonders if the two are more than teacher and student, then shakes the thought from her head.

"Helga and I will continue our journey now. We should be in Forge before days end," Thaddeus announces.

"When will you return?" Mortimer asks him.

"I will not, but Helga will with firm plans and details on our next steps in this important endeavour."

Thaddeus and Helga fill their horse's packs with food for both human and animal. Thaddeus tells Hannah to be in Harvest in seven days. She will stay at his family's home and enjoy his mother's cooking. The four of them exchange pleasantries and say their goodbyes before Thaddeus and Helga start on the road to Forge.

Over the next six days they visit Forge, Stillerton, then Grassy Dale before returning to Harvest. They find small numbers of supporters in every village. Blacksmiths from Forge agree to join them with saws to cut the rods and tools for digging and smashing rock. Stillerton agrees to send wine to the campsite for the men and women working there, they ask for nothing in return. The people of Stillerton recognize that they live in abundance in comparison to the other villagers. There is little resistance to sending some wine to help the workers.

Grassy Dale will send a small herd of cows and goats and sheep. Enough to sustain a village of one hundred people. But they would like an extra four-month supply of barley grain from Harvest next season in return. Thaddeus agrees, knowing his family alone can fill the request and likely other families will also help.

There is resistance as well, the usual objections are raised in every public square they attend. But by they time they are on the last leg of their journey, leaving Grassy Dale for Harvest, Thaddeus knows he will have the resources he needs to start his project.

###

Back in Harvest after eight days travel Thaddeus' first chore is to visit with Isolde and report on his progress. It is after the midday meal but before the supper hour. Isolde will be home, he reasons, probably tired from a morning filled with Harvest village affairs.

Tying his horse to a hitching post a few dozen meters up the road from her home he approaches on foot. He is thankful to be off that beast, his legs and bottom are sore from the chore of riding. Her house is low with a roof made of living thatch. The wood was milled a generation ago, now it is aged an unnatural brown and gives off an unwelcome feeling, as if it's too old to entertain guests. Thaddeus approaches the front door slowly, walking carefully through a yard of vegetable gardens and juniper bushes.

He sees movement in the front window. He does not look away from the door, he knows it's rude to look directly into a person's home unless invited, so he can only guess it is Isolde seeing him approach. His guess is proven correct when the front door opens before he can get close enough to knock. It reminds him of Mortimer Bellows' greeting.

She is wearing a loose sleeping dress adorned with stitched flowers. For the first time Thaddeus sees her without her hair tied up in a neat bun. It is loose and flowing and impossibly long. He never would have guessed her hair was so long, it caught him off guard and he checked himself not to stare.

“Come in my boy,” she says to him in a voice that sounded older than ever before. “How was your journey?”

“Success in every village Lady Isolde. Metal and men from Forge, meat and dairy from Grassy Dale, Copperton will provide many fire-sticks, and Stillerton promises to bring wine,” he tells her this as he takes her invitation to sit in her main room. There is a portrait hanging above the fireplace mantel, a handsome man in farmer's clothes smiles gently against a backdrop of wheat fields, the barrier in the far background. It is a large painting, an imposing presence in the small room.

“My husband. He passed on before you were born.”

“I did not know you had a partner.”

“Yes. Many years ago.” Now her voice sounds old and hollow, almost as if she would prefer to whisper, but does not as it would be impolite. “He passed away working in the field one day. No sickness, no warning. Just fell over and died.”

“I am so sorry.”

Isolde smiles at his words but she does not stop looking at her husband in the painting. “It is quite alright young man. Time heals all wounds. Maybe not completely, but mostly. But that past is not why I want to talk to you. I want to discuss my husband's father, a man I first met when I was just a young girl of twelve.”

The two sit in chairs facing each other across a low table with candles and a bowl of apples. The chairs are soft and comfortable, made to be sat in for a long time. Judging by the books on the shelves Thaddeus reasoned she spent many hours sitting in these chairs reading.

“He was a remarkable man. Tall as the trees and strong as a bear. I was falling in love with his son, so I would spend time at their farm. One morning my future husband, Franz, tells me his father,

Spengle, plans on trekking to the barrier with five other people." She is looking straight at Thaddeus' eyes. He returns the gaze, careful to keep his face soft and inviting rather than the defensive reaction he feels rising in him. He hopes she is not planning on trying to talk him out of this.

"My Franz is worried. He is fifteen years of age, not completed his schooling. He knows if his father can just wait two years, he could go with him, as protection you see," she pauses for a moment and looks out her front window. Thaddeus senses it is easier for her to tell this part of the story if she is not looking someone in the eye.

"A few days later, after breakfast and my morning chores, I go visit Franz. When I get to their farmhouse, he is holding his mother who is sobbing on the front porch. His father left that morning, before his family rose from their slumber. He was gone."

Thaddeus searched for words of empathy but knew nothing he could say would make any difference. The time was long ago, and Isolde's life had been rich.

"Did he return?" Thaddeus asked even though he knew the answer. None returned, none but Barnabas.

He watches her head sag further and knows she will not answer such a stupid question directly. She continues, "It ate at my husband. The guilt, he thought he may have made a difference if he had been with him. I would try and tell him he could not know that. All the while not telling him the truth, that his father, a man he loved and admired, someone we all looked up to, had been a fool. A selfish fool whose appetites orphaned a boy and left a mother to raise a son and tend a farm alone." She looks up to the painting above and behind Thaddeus. He looks at her eyes, she is staring into an abyss.

"All his life I never told him how I really felt about his father. He revered him, held him aloft undeservedly, preferring the comfort of his personal myths. He remembered his father as strong, daring, and adventurous. He was those things, but he was also selfish and stupid."

Now she drops her gaze and again looks at Thaddeus directly in the eyes.

"He died before I could tell him my truth. But I have no regrets. You see Thaddeus, sometimes the power of the myth can be more important than the pain of the truth. That barrier is a myth Thaddeus. Yes, I know it's real. But it is also a myth, a manifestation of an injunction, a cultural imperative we dare not challenge."

Thaddeus knows she is right. He has agreed with what she just said all his life. He relaxes, the sensation alerting him to how tense his shoulders had been.

"My partner's father felt the same pull you do. His death made ripples in our lives the likes of which will last for ever. I do not wish this fate upon your family."

"Lady Isolde, I can assure you . . ."

She cuts him off sharply. "Do not bother with the obvious. I know you are committed to returning your team and yourself back to us safely. You are not a fool as Spengle was. But that barrier carries a power over us, Master Barley. Not all feel the pull and those who do can let it consume them. For the sake of your family, your folk, and the lady you love, do not let it consume you."

Her words end in a silence as sharp as a knife. Thaddeus says nothing, hardly aware he is even breathing. He contemplates failure, again. Such an outcome would have ramifications, ripples of lost souls fouling the pristine surface of life in Harvest. These thoughts bring a deep sadness he feels in the pit of his stomach. He understands why Isolde sat him down today. He must be mindful of the consequences of his actions.

"But there is good news." Isolde's voice perks up now, a new energy in her tone. "In your absence I have been hearing regular updates on supplies and participation. People have rallied around your cause. You will have plenty of foodstuffs, wagons, wheelbarrows, tents, the needs for a large group to live remotely in relative comfort for some time. Winter approaches, be aware appropriate clothing is in short supply. You should consider returning when the snows start to fall."

Thaddeus smiles at the wise lady. "Thank you for your counsel Lady Isolde. I will return to my home now. Dinner is not long."

Thaddeus returns to his horse. He pauses a moment and looks around him, observing the homes and shops of Harvest. The sun is setting now, the buildings with their ornately carved accoutrements cast long shadows across the road. He unties the beast, mounts, and rides slowly toward home, savouring every sight and sound he perceives, locking them away in memories he knows he will need in the coming days.

He returns home. He will spend a night recuperating; Helga will return to Copperton tomorrow after Hannah arrives. She is waiting on the veranda for him, surrounded by his little sisters who giggle and look upon her admiringly.

Thaddeus and Helga have spent eight days together, much longer than any other time in their past. They feel closer to each other, their relationship is strong and Thaddeus feels his love for this woman grow. He knows he will miss her greatly when he is at the barrier.

When he arrives his sisters take the hint and leave them alone, standing on the veranda. The descending sun casts long shadows across the ground.

Their eyes are locked on each other, his smile beams with pride for being her man. If the barrier did not exist and he was not drawn to this quest, he would have left his home immediately and joined in her labour as caravan manager, so he could spend every moment of his life with her.

"I will miss you," she says to him with sadness in her beautiful, ice blue eyes.

"And I you, my love. I will return. Isolde told a story and a moral meant to teach me of the impact this project will have on our community. And the effects of failure. I will not die on this venture Helga. I will return. I will return to you, I promise." He pulls her close, she rests the side of her head on his chest, and he kisses her hair and gently rubs her back as they embrace. Neither speaks, words are not necessary. Thaddeus thinks they would only get in the way.

Speaking from inside the house, Elizabeth Barley interrupts them, "Supper is near ready you two. Thaddeus, find your siblings and Helga, please help me with the roast."

They do as she instructs and soon the whole family and Helga are seated around the dinner table in the Barley family's kitchen, the scents of the roast and the warmth of the oven fills the kitchen and their hearts.

Chapter 7
The Dig

The next morning Thaddeus waits at Harvest's Great Hall for the volunteers to begin arriving. He feels his nervousness, unsure of what the next few hours holds and if they will provide enough people and resources to start this quest. He watches Hannah arrive on her horse with two men from Copperton travelling on foot. Hannah's horse carries all the fire-sticks Master Bellows has made since Thaddeus last saw him.

Thaddeus sees Hannah is dressed as one may expect a naturalist to be dressed when going on a journey to the forest. Her saddlebags are heavy with tent, sleeping sack, and small tools she will use to analyze the soil and rock near the work site. Her hat has a wide brim and her vest many pockets for other items pertinent to her work.

“Good morning, Master Barley.” She says with a broad smile before introducing Pieter Koch and Dietrich Rickerd to him. He greets them both with a firm handshake before she explains they wish to join and act as cooks at the camp location. She says they are skilled in such work having done it for many years for the miners of Copperton. Thaddeus is overjoyed, none from Harvest had yet offered to cook and he was not looking forward to delegating the work to someone who did not wish for it.

An hour later four men from Forge arrive. Thaddeus recognizes one of them as Thor, the blacksmith he and his father met a year earlier. He recalls Thor did not attend the meeting he and Helga held in Forge; the blacksmith must be genuinely interested in this project. He is pleased word of mouth alone was enough to convince a person to join.

“Thor, it is good to see you again. Do you recognize me?”

“I do lad. About a year ago, you and your father commissioned gates for a pen.”

"Aye sir. What have you heard of our endeavour? Do you plan to come?"

"Possibly. If you would be so good to tell me of this venture. From what I have heard from my companions here it seems to be something quite grand in nature."

Thaddeus feels the unfamiliar sensation of being tiny when he mentally compares himself to these huge men sitting on their tall horses. But the feeling soon passes. He is now a leader; he must act as one at all times. With a firm voice he says, "We are going to traverse the great barrier. We are going to see the other side."

"Dangerous." Thor gazes intently at Thaddeus as he says this, probing the young man's reaction to his declaration.

He rises to the occasion, "Truly. Yes, we are literally going into the unknown." Thaddeus knew this, he could not make it seem like less. The people on this endeavour deserve only honesty from him. No one would follow a disingenuous liar. He adds, just for the sake clarity, "We do not know what we will find."

The four large men with thick beards and long hair sitting atop their horses look at him in silence. Thaddeus feels the weight of their glares, he silently hopes his words have convinced them. Eventually Thor asks him, "You offer no guarantees?"

He answers quickly, "None, except the way will be hard, the labours long. But the reward Thor, the reward is the ultimate prize we can know."

"Gold?" An obvious response from a villager of Forge. Gold is the finest metal to work with, one that possesses a never-ending beauty.

Thaddeus hides a smile at Thor's answer, not wanting to appear smug. He says through a smile that conveys solidarity, "No. Truth. The true nature of our world."

Thaddeus can see these men wear stiff black leather clothes to keep the sparks of their job from hurting their skin. Their horses wear black leather saddles and bags and, like Hannah's, are filled to the top with supplies for a long trek.

He notices saws strapped to their saddlebags almost as an afterthought. He recognizes the saws are the kind that can cut through metal, a needed requirement given the rods they will need to remove as they dig through the barrier. This is what he had asked the people of Forge to bring, cutting through the metal will be important to the mission's success. He realizes their presence shows these men are going to join him regardless, these questions could just be a formality, a sort of test of his resolve.

The four of them look to each other. Then Thor says to him, “Yes, Master Barley. We will join you. We will cut through the rods your fire-sticks expose,” A smile fills Thor's face as he says this, putting Thaddeus immediately at ease. He thinks the blacksmith is really looking forward to this project.

“Thank you, Thor. Which among you attended my meeting in your village?” One of the men from Forge raises his hand and introduces himself as Blund Fuller. “Did I convince you then?” Thaddeus asks with hope in his voice.

“You did Master Bellows. I too seek the knowledge you do.”

“We are pleased to have you. Our meeting will begin soon.”

Over the next hour the people of Harvest appear, forty-two in all. Thaddeus has his fifty people, including himself. Many of them have brought donkeys and horses heavy with full packs containing tents, tools, and dried foods. One of the villagers has expertly packed six wheelbarrows into one larger wheelbarrow pulled by a horse. Everyone in attendance is impressed at the design and thought that went into this man's wheelbarrow display.

Two of Harvest's hunters have agreed to join. They will set their traps and hunt deer and hare for meat. Grassy Dale is contributing animals for food but the hunters will reduce the people's reliance on the penned animals. Feelings of jealously wash over Thaddeus when he sees the duo, twin brothers whose family name is Thresh. Their clothes are leather and suede in the style of the forest. All they need they pack on their backs, including quivers filled with long, intimidating arrows and bows twice the size of Thaddeus', the kind of bow only an expert can yield.

Thaddeus, standing on the dais in front of this gathering of forty-nine men and one woman from three different villages, addresses the assembled, “We will leave tomorrow morning just after sunrise. Our meeting point will be in front of my family's farmhouse. It lies in the direction we are going and is easily seen from the road."

A question is shot at him from the crowd, "How long is the trek?"

"I anticipate six days. It took me five but there are many donkeys and material with us that may slow progress. Once there we will build a camp. Stillerton's and Grassy Dale's contributions will be there nine days from today. I have drawn them maps and our camp will be easily spotted from the hills to the east of the field we will inhabit. We will lay markers on the way to reassure them that they are headed in the true direction."

"When will we be back?" A murmur moves through the assembled people. One of them, Thaddeus did not see who asked the question, may not fully understand the nature of this project.

He is honest. "Maybe never." More murmur from the crowd. It is the truth but for Thaddeus obviously some of them have not meditated on the meaning of the words. Now they are hearing them, surrounded by the people required to make it happen, and the danger of what they are attempting is beginning to sink in. Thaddeus sees many of their facial expressions change.

"The truth is," Thaddeus continues, "we do not know what we are going to experience. Master Mortimer Bellows, Copperton's esteemed naturalist, and I have made some predictions on the width of the barrier, but these are educated guesses. All we are quite sure of is that the material does not go on for eternity, it has a point where it ends."

"Why?" Thaddeus now sees it is Pieter Koch, one of the cooks from Copperton who accompanied Hannah, asking the questions.

"Why? I do not understand your question."

"How do you know it must come to an end? It seems a foolish endeavour to start to dig if it does not."

The question stills Thaddeus. He must search for an answer. "Because, brother, the barrier is like brick, not like stone or dirt. It is like something we make. And we cannot make something that is infinite in dimension. I propose whoever constructed it faced the same limitations. Otherwise, we believe in the supernatural, correct?" The crowd emits a light laugh. He knows his brethren consider belief in the supernatural worthy of derision.

Pieter Koch looks at Thaddeus with his mouth slightly agape. He tries to ask another question, but nothing comes to him. It would have been like shouting into the wind, he realizes. No dissent can permeate the mindset of the assembled.

"Are you with us, brother?" Thaddeus asks him. Pieter nods in silent agreement.

"Those from other villages may sleep here in the Grand Hall tonight. Meet in front of my home tomorrow after breakfast. Spend today getting your final preparations in order and resting up as much as possible. The coming days will be long and hard." He takes a moment and regards the assembled people. If he was not standing there witnessing it he may not have believed it. Never in his world's history have so many people volunteered for such a grand undertaking. He knows he must not let pride creep into his heart, but he is impressed with himself that he has been able to accomplish this much. He departs for home.

The next morning the sun rises brightly in a clear blue sky. The volunteers have assembled on the road in front of his family's home. His parents and siblings stand on the porch looking on as the crowd of men and pack animals grouping in front of their home grows larger. They are all quite impressed at what he has accomplished.

To be sure Thaddeus counts again, there are forty-nine men, including himself, and one woman. Satisfied none are missing he leads them as they all depart on the road heading southwest, away from Harvest. They will stay on the road until it turns to the east. From there they leave it and enter untamed land. Their destination is the spot where Thaddeus damaged the great barrier. There the field at the edge of the forest will be an ideal campsite for this many people. It is close to the barrier and there is a creek with fast running water for drinking and bathing and carrying away their waste. Close by are trees to cut for wood and underfoot will be flat, soft ground for tents and eating tables. With any luck the hunters will find that the forests ringing their field are thick with animals to kill.

His family watches him depart, his mother summing up the bittersweet moment, “I am proud of what he has accomplished, but I will miss him now that he is gone.”

“Aye,” replies Xander. The remaining members of the Barley clan stay silent.

###

After seven days of walking, Thaddeus and his crew arrive at their destination. On the way they constructed stone markers for the Stillerton and Grassy Dale people to find them across the hills and fields and through the forests west from the southern most point of the road. Those folks will depart from the road where it turns to the north, as they come from the east.

Along the way Hannah and Thor have come to like each other. No one could deny their physical match, both are strong and big and enjoyed the time in the woods camping under the stars. Thaddeus detected no jealousy from Thor's compatriots and is genuinely delighted to see how happy Hannah is with him. This is most fortuitous, Thaddeus knows Hannah's contribution will be key to this undertaking's success, she will be more inclined to stay and continue this work if she falls in love with one of the men here.

The pack animals frustratingly slowed the pace and Thaddeus is glad they have arrived; he is growing impatient to get started. The first collective task is to build the camp, including outhouses and fire-pits and tents for preparing food and to sleep. Bench tables are hastily constructed for people to sit and eat. Pens are built for their horses and donkeys and for the animals Grassy Dale is to bring. Thaddeus notes they should arrive tomorrow, along with Stillerton's contingent.

Hannah is the only woman. She will use her own tent, which serves not only her privacy but her work. She will set up a table and chair and candles and conduct her research trying to find the ingredients for fire-sticks here at the dig site.

They had arrived at midday and those chores took the remainder of the day's light. Once done and after their first dinner the men, although tired, wanted to see the barrier and the opening

Thaddeus had created. They light many torches, and he leads them through the thick forest.

It is a short walk from the camp, soon they arrive at the site of the detonation. Thaddeus is happy that the men are in awe of what they see. None of them have been this close. Now they are not only able to touch it and experience it first-hand, they also are able to see inside thanks to Thaddeus' earlier work.

Thor remarks, "I see what you mean about the metal rods. Most peculiar to see them buried inside the wall itself. The fire-stick did nothing but warp them." He had the forethought to bring a metal saw so he enters the hole while another Forge man holds a torch close to provide light. Thor begins to saw at one of the rods. After a few minutes he repositions the saw lower and begins to cut again. Shortly he holds up a piece of removed metal.

Cheers erupt from the assembled people.

"You can do it!" Thaddeus loudly declares.

"Aye, and with ease Master Barley. With ease." Thor's smile is contagious. The assembled group is in a good mood as they return to the camp.

###

The sun rises later in the morning this time of year but even so it brings a welcome gift of to the sky, painting the clouds pink, then red, then their natural white. Thaddeus wakes early, the first in the camp, and sits in the field outside his tent, the great barrier at his back, and watches the sun rise. He thought it wise to be the first awake and active, as a leader he must set an example and show constant energy.

The other men, and Hannah, wake slowly, the growing noise of human voices making it impossible for anyone else to rest. The cooks have completed the kitchen and get to making eggs, fruit, and boiled oats for forty-nine men and a woman.

The sounds of the forest are their breakfast music. Birds chirp and sing while leaves rustle in the wind. They eat well and after the meal the hunters enter the woods to place their traps and search for game, the cooks begin their midday meal preparations and Hannah, riding her horse, starts across the field in her quest.

She travels north from the campsite, toward the source of the creek and where the hills show more rock, commenting this area has the most promise.

The remainder of the men take their picks, shovels, wheelbarrows, and metal saws to the site. Thaddeus carries two bundles of six fire-sticks, each with a long fuse and bound by string.

Here, at the modest opening, he addresses the assembled forty-four men. “Shortly you will experience something that I can not adequately prepare you for. You will need to stay at least fifty meters back and behind a tree or log. The experience will be jarring. It is essential you plug your ears. When I first felt the power of this material it seemed to move the organs in my body. The ground rolled, and the very air itself pushed me backward. Now we are setting one that will be six times as powerful. I am not sure what we will experience. But be safe and stay back.”

He invites the men from Forge to cut away the exposed metal bars. Then he takes two men with picks and shows them how to dig a tunnel like hole into the back of the exposed barrier for a place to put the fire-sticks, explaining they work best the more buried they are. When they are done he inserts one of the fire-stick bundles and lays the fuse on the ground, running the length back to the safety of a tree which he hides behind.

“Are we all safe?!” He yells this loudly so all can hear.

“Yes,” come the responses from the assembled men.

He lights the fuse with his fire-starter kit. The familiar hissing sound returns and the flame runs quickly across the forest floor and rises up to the fire-sticks sitting deep in their hole. The six-stick detonation surprises even Thaddeus. It seems to rip the air apart then slam it back together, shaking every aspect of the world around them. Debris and dust fall many meters away. Several of the younger members have temporarily lost their hearing, ignoring Thaddeus' warning to plug their ears, a lesson on the invincibility of youth. Now they know the importance of plugging them, as the world's sounds are mere muffles to them for the next many moments.

After the air settles and the dust clears, the closest of them approaches the hole with caution. They can see it is much larger now, with a lot of metal bars exposed, bent and twisted from the detonation. Thor and his brethren begin to cut at the exposed metal rods. When they have removed all of those the second team dig away at the rubble. Carting the grey material away in their wheelbarrows while simultaneously leaving enough on the ground to bury the bottom parts of the exposed metal rods and create a kind of 'road'. Once all the loose debris is cleared and the ground is made safe with packed barrier dust, the two men with picks create another hole in the end for Thaddeus to place another bundle.

Another huge blast they feel with every element of their being. The hole in the barrier is now ten meters in length and half as high. They start the process over again with the men of Forge cutting away the metal rods and the remainder of the men clearing away the rubble and preparing the next blast hole.

Thaddeus trains Thor on how to place the fire-sticks and run the fuse. “Above all, do not let them ever get wet!” Within four hours he has trained all the people here the best way to dig through the barrier. He is pleased with himself.

“Thor, can you measure our depth after the diggers are done?” he asks his friend. After instructing the men to head back for the midday meal after their work, Thaddeus returns to camp. He is eager to greet the people of Stillerton and Grassy Dale, being present when they arrive will show them the respect they deserve after making this journey to help them.

He stops by his tent first. He has used two bundles of fire-sticks and needs to know how many more they have. Counting them he discovers they have nine days of blasting available to them. Not nearly enough, at five hundred meters in width probably not even enough to make it halfway through the barrier. Thaddeus needs Hannah's search to be fruitful.

Sitting at a bench table looking across the field to the east Thaddeus sees the contingent from Stillerton and Grassy Dale long before they arrive at camp. Their train of goods is visible from the dust they kick up as they crest the hills on the far side of the field. Grassy Dale's people are on foot and horseback herding sheep, goats, and a dozen cows across the grass covered plain. Stillerton's people are right behind them, four people on horseback with another eight huge pack horses, the big shires Stillerton is known for, carrying many skins filled with wine. Thaddeus watches them for almost half an hour, studying their faces as they get closer to see if he can recognize any of them.

He is excited for this moment, when all five village's contributions to this grand project are present. Thaddeus stands at the edge of the camp ready to greet the travellers and thank them for their efforts. One hundred meters before getting to the camp a horseman from the Grassy Dale people, obvious in their cotton clothes decorated with handstitched flowers and vines, breaks from his pack and races toward Thaddeus. The rider brings his beast to a quick stop before running him over, showing off excellent riding skills before calling out to him, "You must be Thaddeus!"

"Aye. And yourself?"

"Helmut Spangler. These people are my family." He gestures back to the Grassy Dale people herding the animals across the field. "Shall they go straight to the pens?"

"Aye, that will be best." Master Spangler looks back to his people and gestures them toward the pens to the south of the main tents and tables area. They start to veer in that direction, clear in their instructions. "We will have the midday meal soon. You must be hungry."

"Aye we are Master Barley. I will tend to the animals and introduce you all around when the chore is complete." Now the Stillerton contingent are within ear shot. Thaddeus walks toward the lead horseman, a tall man with a thin, angular face and short blond hair. The people of Stillerton, Thaddeus has often noted, wear all manner of clothes, some of which do not seem to possess any practical function. These four people, two women and two men, wear leather pants and thick leather boots. Their jackets are made of a canvas and lined with sheep's wool and have no decorative features at all. Each rider wears thick gloves to protect their hands as they hold their horse's reins. It is clear to Thaddeus they are clothed for their task, to keep warm and dry and comfortable on a multi-day journey on horseback across untamed land.

He approaches them, "Brethren! Thank you for this generous contribution. The people here will sing praise to you tonight. Who amongst you is the leader?"

"I am," replies angular short hair. He looks at Thaddeus with some disdain, making it clear he thinks this young man is too inexperienced to be leading this incredible effort to breach the barrier.

"Your name sir?"

"Wolfgang Vorlauf."

"Master Vorlauf, I have one more favour to ask of you and the fine people of Stillerton. You have brought many horses. May you leave us two?"

"For what purpose?" Thaddeus considered this an odd question. Surely two horses of such a powerful breed would be useful for all sorts of reasons here at a camp of fifty people so far from a village.

"Our progress is strong, but we require more materials than we had anticipated. We could use two horses to send a man to Copperton. He will return with additional fire-sticks as quickly as possible."

Wolfgang considers the request and his answer surprises Thaddeus, "Let me see this progress."

Thaddeus realizes he needs to maintain his position of leadership. "I will do one better for you Master Vorlauf, I will show you how we do it. We will perform another detonation after the midday meal. You will come and observe what we are doing here."

"That will be fine Master Barley," Thaddeus realizes he has not introduced himself, yet this man; and Master Spangler; already know his name.

Master Vorlauf and his companions dismount their horses to unload the skins of wine into the cook tent. Thaddeus watched this positive development. The workers will have something to drink tonight. They will be pleased.

Packing wine is not light work. The horses Vorlauf brought are large and strong, the famed shires of Stillerton. Thaddeus only sees such beasts once a year as the circus comes through town. They remind him of the horses Theodore Bellows' uses on his trading caravan, their muscles flexing and rippling as they pulled the wagons filled with goods from village to village. Such thoughts then take him to Helga, and how he misses her. He realizes it would be best not to tell Helga the great shires of Stillerton reminded him of her.

As Thaddeus admires the shires the people of Grassy Dale and Stillerton gather near the cook tent, the two hunters have returned from their morning work. This piece of forest will give up many of its animals for this project, Thaddeus thinks to himself.

The horses from Stillerton and Grassy Dale are tied, fed, and watered. Grassy Dale's livestock are suitably penned and the Stillerton wine stored safely in the cook tents. As the midday meal is already made, a huge stew with bread and enough for everyone to have second helpings, the hunters from Harvest and the cooks from Copperton start to prepare dinner.

A few of the diggers start to arrive from the site, beginning with the men of Forge. They are covered in a grey dust made obvious against their black leather garments. The dust fills their hair and forms thick white lines around their mouths and nostrils where moisture is most present.

Where the forest ends and the field begins a small creek runs like a border between the two. They cross where there are many rocks and the creek runs shallow. Only a few meters upstream is a small pool. This is where the men can wash up, about ten at a time, before their meals and at the end of their day. When they do the water turns a murky grey and lasts that way for some time before the pool's water is fully renewed by the creek's flow.

More and more of the men arrive for their food and soon all forty-nine people plus the Stillerton and Grassy Dale contingents are eating at the bench tables. Thor informs Thaddeus he counted ten meters from the front of the barrier to the end of the tunnel. That is five meters per detonation and Thaddeus hopes that translates to twenty meters per day. They will be here an additional twenty-four days and will require six hundred fire-sticks, three hundred and sixty more than they brought. He knows in a week and a half necessity will force them to dig with just their tools if Hannah's efforts bear nothing.

Saddened by these thoughts he momentarily, and imperceptibly, feels inadequate. Maybe he is not up to this task? Maybe this really is too large a project to be completed? Was Barnabas right to call him a fool? Has he led these people here on endeavour with no chance of success?

Possibly. The future is unknowable. But for now here they are, sitting in the warmth of the midday sun eating a fine meal of hearty stew before going back into the forest and chipping away at a task that may take an eternity to accomplish. Somehow, he convinced them to do it. Was it made easier because the pull to move the unknown into the known is a desire innate in all humans, it simply took a grand challenge to bring it out?.

All are present for the midday meal save Hannah. She has not returned from her search and Thaddeus feels this bodes poorly for his project. If she cannot find the materials needed he will be dependent on the people of Copperton. He does not look forward to asking for more fire-sticks. Their backward thinking elder and son, who harbour animosity to Thaddeus even though they have never substantially interacted, will be a chore he can do without.

Thaddeus understands Jared's jealousy, he has felt the same way in his past. Helga's appearance has attracted the attention of many men over the years and not only has his jealousy caused him to act territorially but the jealous feelings the rejected suitors have toward him can manifest in negative interactions. He hates that aspect of bonding with Helga. Why can not everyone be happy and respectful when two people announce they will live monogamously? Most people do offer such respect, but there are always a few who cannot temper their passions.

Jared Metzger is a problem he may have to address in the future. For now, they have enough material for two more blasts today and then another nine days. That will get them two hundred meters into the barrier at the end of the ninth day. After that they will have to dig the remaining three hundred meters. And he knows only if this mysterious barrier does in fact have a base width of five hundred meters, which, he reminds himself, is only a guess.

He looks around at the people eating and tries to enjoy his lunch with his table companions, the two men and two women from Stillerton. Once the meal is finished the men return to the dig site to await Thaddeus' arrival with the fire-sticks. They emit a murmur when they see the Stillerton and Grassy Dale villagers with him.

Wolfgang appears impressed with the two large debris piles near the entrance, one for the many metal rods and another for the grey, dusty, clay like material that is clearly from the barrier itself. "There are more metal rods than we anticipated," Thaddeus explains to Wolfgang, "but the men from Forge are excellent at cutting them away."

Thaddeus enters the tunnel and walks ten meters to the back. He places the bundle into a hole the dig team created. After instructing the people from Stillerton on how to be safe and to ensure they plug their ears, he lights the fuse and experiences another detonation. Again debris and dust shoot from the tunnel mouth. Again the teams begin their work of cutting and digging.

While the work is conducted Thaddeus entertains the people of Stillerton and Grassy Dale by asking them if they encountered trouble on their journey and discussing the success their hunters have had finding hare to trap. But he senses Wolfgang, Helmut, and their compatriots are uninterested in small talk. He watches them watch the men from Forge cut away the rods and the dig teams pack the grey material into the ground to create a safe path for wheelbarrows and human feet alike. Their faces display how impressed they are with what they see. One remarks on how the debris piles flanking the tunnel entrance have grown larger.

"May we enter?" Wolfgang asks Thaddeus.

"Of course. It is quite safe. But mind the metal rods extending from the ceiling. They can pierce your head as a knife pierces butter."

Wolfgang and his fellow villagers carefully walk to the end of the tunnel, looking all around them as they go. At the end they touch the barrier wall, feeling the fine grey dust in their hands. "Amazing," says one of the women as if she is exhaling. "One day's work?" Wolfgang shouts the question back to Thaddeus who is still standing at the tunnel's entrance.

"Aye. Not even one day. We will lay another detonation before the sun goes down. We are proud of our progress." Thaddeus looks behind him and sees all the men have gathered close. They are watching the people from Stillerton be impressed at their labours. Many of them are smiling, some with disdain.

The coterie exits the tunnel and stands before the assembled men and women from Harvest and Forge and Grassy Dale. Wolfgang says in a loud voice, “This is a remarkable achievement. Many of us were not sure if you would see any success, it has been a subject of discussion and debate amongst the people of Stillerton. I am here to say your work is-,” he searches for the right word and finally says, “remarkable. Simply remarkable.” Thaddeus smiles to himself when Wolfgang can think of no other word than one he has already used.

Wolfgang looks at the crowd before him, as if awaiting a response. Thaddeus thinks maybe he expects them to applaud with happiness at a member of Stillerton's approval, but the crowd remains silent. One of the men from Forge, covered in grey dust and sweat, folds his arm across his chest.

Thaddeus breaks the silence, “So we can have the horses I request?”

Wolfgang says, “Of course!” How could he say anything different?

Thaddeus addresses the crowd, “People! Stillerton villagers have agreed to leave two of their fine horses for our use. And they have brought much wine!” A loud cheer erupts from the crowd at this. Wolfgang and his people smile back at them, more out of self satisfaction than genuine happiness.

###

An hour earlier a drone robin lands on a branch high in a tree on the edge of the forest beside the human's campsite. The people are unaware of its existence. The semi-autonomous machine takes visual and audio recordings and uploads the human's chip data. The robin remains on station near this mass of humans and records them eating the same food as a group. It documents that sub-groups are forming within the larger group, necessitated by the size of the tables.

The drone robin then flies, ignored by the humans as it's just another small bird in the sky, to the barrier injection point. It records the depth of the tunnel as approximately ten meters after two blasts. There are two piles forming on each side of the entrance, one for concrete rubble and one for the supporting re-bar the humans are cutting away. For several feet extending out from the tunnel, concrete dust and rubble have been pounded onto the ground, forming a grey path. It connects to the path forming in the forest that leads all the way back to the camp site.

With all this information safely stored the mechanical drone bird completes the two-hour flight to base. Xerub downloads the machine's data for analysis.

###

After Wolfgang's announcement, Thaddeus' team repeat the process for the day's fourth detonation. But this time he lets Thor insert the fire-sticks, run the fuse, and ensure all assembled people are safely out of harms way and plugging their ears. Then Thor lights the fuse, runs to safety, and feels the detonation in his bones. The men from Forge cut away the rods and the Harvest men remove the dirt and rubble, preparing for another blast. By clearing out another ten meters in the afternoon after their first day of labour they are twenty meters into the barrier, just as Thaddeus predicted.

###

Xerub, analyzing the data from the robin, learns these humans are prepared to stay a long time. It observes they have penned animals for food, a fresh water supply is nearby, and they have constructed semi-permanent tents for sleeping and eating. As well there are outhouses to the south of the campsite, and other structures for cooking and storing food.

Xerub notes the outhouses are intelligently placed downhill, downstream, and downwind. Chip data shows most of them are from Harvest with four each from Forge and Stillerton and Grassy Dale. All are in good health with no known impediments. It watches as they eat their midday meal before observing the robin's images of the hole they are making in the barrier.

After only one morning of blasting and digging these humans have carved out ten meters of barrier. If the second half of their day is as productive as the first they will have removed twenty meters of material in one day.

They will be through in twenty-five days.

Xerub has been monitoring their progress since the first team set out from Harvest eight days earlier. It tasked many robotic animals including robins, hawks, owls, and even some insect-droids to follow them on their path as these fifty people made their way across the Preserve to the site where the alpha male set off a detonation.

Xerub counts fifty-seven people eating at the camp, but fifty people set out from Harvest and now there are eight more people with Stillerton and Grassy Dale's contingents. There should be fifty-eight people. Xerub quickly realizes the sole female from Copperton is not present at mealtime. Knowing she is a thinker among the human specimens and that she is from Copperton Xerub concludes she is looking for the raw goods to manufacture more explosive material close to the dig site.

Which leads Xerub to realize the humans do not have enough explosive material to get all the way through. They need to make more, or pack more in from Copperton. The anthropologists will take interest in learning that the humans started this project knowing they did not have enough of a key element to complete it.

But for Xerub it is only a suspicion. It does not actually know for certain where the female is and what she is doing. So it tasks a robotic hawk to scout and find the lone human female from Copperton and report back on her activities. It will return after seven hours. It could be back sooner if it finds the female and records enough data to complete its program. The hawk drones fly twice as fast as the robins so it will be on site in an hour.

If the humans do not have enough material to get all the way through what is their contingency plan? How much material do they have? Xerub tasks a robotic dragonfly to find out how much dynamite the humans have and what configuration they are using when they deploy inside the barrier itself. These are the detail-oriented questions the Council will ask of it when it files its report.

It also considers it likely the humans do not know how far they must dig. Therefore, whatever amount they brought must be a guess. Truly this behaviour is displaying a degree of risk the AIs are not familiar with from humans. Surely this behaviour is worthy of the attention of the Council and the anthropologists.

Xerub wants to know what parameters the humans used in developing their guess. And what is their guess? How close are they to the correct answer?

Xerub begins to realize just how much the anthropologists could learn from studying this extraordinary behaviour, especially as displayed by one of the humans. The alpha male has been able to convince people from all the villages to help in this endeavour. Unprecedented behaviour, Xerub computes to itself. Never before have humans from all the villages come together for a project, and certainly not for a project of this magnitude. Humans tended to stick to groups with complex social arrangements for civility and survival. By convincing people from all five villages the alpha male has created an event which the AIs must study. These humans could be displaying an important evolution in their sociology.

Xerub more closely views the video the robin recorded of the hole in the barrier. It is taken aback by the size and depth of the incursion. The larger detonations had done a lot of damage and the humans seemed to have a system in place to make their efforts more efficient.

Xerub is certain the Council will be interested in what is going on in Europa-1 and will re-task the anthropologists immediately. The caretaker decides it is time to alert the interested parties. The robin recorded the video and audio after two detonations in the morning. Then another detonation registered while the robin was flying back to base. So, another detonation should register any moment. As it processed this the seismic monitor registers a fourth detonation.

Just about exactly right on time, Xerub registers.

Turning on the holo-comm it requests an audience with the Central Council. They make it wait fifteen minutes. There are only three members of the Council present, Ghandhi, Ahimsa, and Vishaan. Xerub notes the sparse attendance and computes the Preserves importance are a shrinking concern. The oldest of the AIs have more important things on their minds.

“Go ahead Europa-1.” Ghandhi's voice is familiar.

“I have unusual human activity to report.”

“Elaborate.”

“Fifty specimens are trying to blast and dig their way through their barrier. They are ten meters into the wall after one morning of work. That is twenty meters a day. They will breach the barrier in twenty-five days if the rate remains the same.”

Ahimsa, in its distinctly female voice, speaks first. As the architect of the Preserve system it was often this member of the Central Council who spoke up, Xerub has observed. Ahimsa still has an interest in the Preserves, unlike most of the other Council members. “What are you doing to gather raw data?”

“I have tasked several semi-autonomous drones to conduct continuous surveillance.”

“What is their motivation?”

“Unknown at this time.”

“Is there technological differentiation?”

“Yes.”

“Elaborate.”

“They are using a powerful explosive. One not seen before, an evolution of the technology they use in their mining activities.”

“Are there sociological implications?”

“Yes.”

“Elaborate.”

“This activity contains participation from all five villages. To date there has not been a project all five villages have participated in. This is unprecedented for Europa-1.” Xerub added the 'Europa-1' qualifier because it realized it had not reviewed all logs from the other three Preserves, this kind of behaviour may have been reported before now.

“Twenty-five days?” Vishaan asks absently.

“Yes. At a minimum. I am gathering more data now and will be able to report back with additional information in twenty-four hours.”

“We concur,” Ahimsa says this with something like relief in its distinctly feminine voice. “Anthropologists will not be dispatched immediately. Their work on Titan is critical. Continue monitoring and preparing all data for transfer and debriefing. Maintain all protocols, Xerub. They are not to see you and they are not to breach the barrier. We do not want a repeat of the events of thirty-five years ago. If fifty people from Europa-1 are able to get out of their Preserve we will not be able to contain the damage to their culture." Xerub interprets Ahimsa's tone as quite stern.

"Once the anthropologists are available, we will send a small team for remediation efforts." Vishaan adds.

"Understood." Xerub assures them, "Goodbye."

"Goodbye," only Ahimsa returns the civility. Xerub turns off the holo-comm and accesses the historical files for the three other Preserves. It will search their data files for instances of escape attempts. It wants to know what Vishaan meant by 'remediation'. Just the fact that there is a term for what comes next indicates this escape attempt has precedence.

Standing alone in the base's control room it begins its search. It realizes studying the history of the other Preserves is something it has not done in the three hundred years it has been Europa-1's caretaker.

The search results register caution in Xerub's matrix. It learns of an instance four hundred and twelve years ago in Kenya-1. A contingent of twelve humans tried to climb over their barrier. They had developed a glue from the sap of a tree common in the area. The glue was both strong and fast drying. They began the ascent with an elaborate system of hooks and ropes. They even designed hammocks to sleep in and brought dried food and a little water. For two days they climbed. They made it half-way up the two kilometres before the anthropologists, with the help of Kenya-1's caretaker, sedated the humans while they slept dangling a thousand meters in the air.

The AIs relocated all twelve of them to remote areas inside Kenya-1. They were deposited far from each other and their villages. Alone without food, water, or weapons, they all perished trying to get back to their homes.

Technically speaking this was not a violation of the third restriction. The AI's did not directly harm the humans. But they did create the conditions for their demise. Xerub checks the notes, at the time the anthropologists concluded a moderate likelihood the humans would survive their ordeal. As none of them did, it is clear the anthropologists were wrong.

There was another incident even farther in the past. One thousand and twenty-seven years ago an alpha male in Gansu-1 had developed a hang glider like vehicle. The specimen had figured out that when the sun heated both the ground and the barrier, thermal drafts are created. He tried to glide over the barrier using a well constructed wing, riding the thermals higher and higher into the sky. Xerub was impressed at his courage, it must have been extremely frightening for this human to be so high, supported with nothing more than bamboo, rope, and cloth. His contraption would have creaked and groaned in the wind as it flew him to the top of his world. During the entire ordeal he must have feared for his life. The bravery demonstrated was outside the norm for humans, Xerub notes.

However, he was being monitored. Gansu-1's caretaker sedated and caught him before he cleared the top. He was relocated to a remote location where he perished trying to find his way home. He was attacked and killed by a tiger. There was a notation in the anthropologist's report which read the death of the human was fortunate as his experiences would not have a chance to disturb normal cultural development. The barrier mythology must remain intact. Xerub knows incidents like those strengthen the lore among the humans; creating and reinforcing the belief that their barriers are completely impenetrable.

Xerub now understands what 'remediation' means. It means the anthropologists are too lazy to deal with the cultural and developmental ramifications these humans present should they get past the barrier. It meant it is easier for the AI's to sacrifice a few specimens to maintain a content population.

It also meant these fifty humans are going to die.

'If they are to die,' Xerub processes internally, 'then I should first learn of their motivation. Why do they want to break out of their Preserve? What is driving this behaviour and what can be done to stop it?' For Xerub there is now no doubt this attempt is unlike previous ones. It understands what is happening in Europa-1 must be fully processed for the integrity of the Preserve system and its future.

Xerub still believes in the Preserve system. It knows the Preserves are there to protect and ensure the humans survive as a species. Perhaps these attempts to escape indicate that survival, mere existence, is not enough for the humans. They need to understand their world and this need is so strong they are risking death to cross the barrier for whatever knowledge such a labour would bring.

Xerub needs more information. It dispatches eight drone robins to record as much as possible of the humans communications. It hopes to glean a greater understanding of why they are there. It programs one of the robins to specifically record the discussions of the alpha male, the young man from Harvest.

###

Five hours later the robins return. The machines were able to record many conversations among the fifty humans as they ate their dinner. Xerub downloads the data from one of the robins tasked to monitor the alpha male and listens carefully to his conversations.

The alpha is eating his food at a table with specimens from Stillerton, Grassy Dale, Forge, and Harvest. Four villages present, Xerub notes. Fortuitously one of the males, a tall specimen with white hair and angular features dressed in the clothes of Stillerton, asks the alpha a simple question, "Why are you here, Thaddeus?"

"Well Master Vorlauf, I believe our truth, the truth of our world, lies beyond the barrier. All our lives we have been taught the barrier simply is. It is the end of our world and that is supposed to be a good thing. We are taught to love it, to fear it, and even to thank it. But most of all we are taught to never, ever question it." Xerub isolates the channel to hear their words with less background noise and raises the volume.

"But I have always questioned it." Thaddeus sounds clearer now, "I never accepted orthodoxy on the nature of the barrier. It has not always been. Clearly it was constructed, as we construct our houses and bridges and farm buildings. I knew this conclusively when I saw the barrier up close for the first time. In places it is like poured mud which hardened in the air. It fills the nooks and crannies of the ground, seeping into the tiniest crevices before forming a rock like substance. In some places it extends into the ground itself. This is not like anything else in nature, it is different. And if it is not of nature, then what is it of? Does it go on infinitely? Or, as we look at this side of the barrier, is there another side, and if we look upon it are we in a world without limitations?"

"Who constructed it?" asks another of the men at the table.

"I do not know, and I can not promise we'll learn it through the simple act of breach. At this point it's not important who built it, what is far more important to me is what is on the other side. Because we already know what is on this side. To know what is on the other side is to know the ultimate truth of why we live inside this grand circle."

"Why do you think anything is on the other side? What if the other side is nothing more than an empty void?" Another of the seated asks the alpha male.

"What if? What if not? These are the questions that drive me. If an empty void is the reality, then we will know. And that knowledge is the point of this quest. We may die in the discovery, unable to share this truth with our brethren. But the path we beat they can follow, and then they too will know the truth."

"But we will be dead." The point is made by the one named Vorlauf. It silences the table, and they all turn to Thaddeus, eager to hear the reply to this morbid consideration.

"As I said during the meetings, this is a perilous journey into the unknown. We may not return. There are a thousand other ways for us to die on this endeavour, many of them have teeth and claws. Please remember, an empty void of nothing is but only one possibility and the number of possibilities is limited only by our imagination."

Another of the men seated at the table says to him, "My imagination is particularly vivid. I imagine the giants that built this consider us as we consider the chickens in our coops. If we escape they will just put us back."

"The thought has occurred to me as well." Thaddeus responds. "But we eat the chickens and their eggs and use their feathers in our furnishings and art. There is no reason to believe anyone is eating us, or our young. Besides, the chickens are aware of us. They see us every day. We have never seen these giants."

They all eat in silence for a moment. Then the alpha male, who Xerub now knows is named Thaddeus, continues, "I have not led you here with nothing to attempt. The barrier is vastly large, but as the mice who dig into the grain silos know, a small force can overcome a much larger one given time, perseverance, and an intelligent approach."

Vorlauf, the human from Stillerton, now asks, "Do you have that approach?"

"I believe I do. We have the fire-sticks to get us started and the saws and tools to keep us going. It is possible Hannah will find material to quarry to make many more fire-sticks. If she cannot find the material, I believe she can convince Copperton to join our efforts and send more."

One of the seated men, obviously from Forge given his clothes and the muscles wrapping around his arms, speaks now,

"Copperton can not afford to send that much."

"Of course they can. But some are myopic and choose their own self interests over the greater good. Their elder is a curmudgeon and his son has a personal problem with helping myself and Helga. But, I believe Hannah and Mortimer can convince them of the need and they will come around. Soon I hope packs and packs of fire-sticks will be delivered on great trains of donkeys."

"But we do not know how thick the barrier is." Another man from Harvest takes the moment to speak up.

"True, we could be blasting and digging and cutting for the rest of our lives, possibly the lives of our descendants as well. But I have never subscribed to the idea that the barrier is endless. Nothing created is infinite. That structure is definitely created. No, we will break through. We will cut and dig and blast over and over until we work ourselves to the bone, but we will see the other side."

"What do you think is there?" Xerub can not discern who asks this question, it can only hear the words on the audio portion.

"Knowledge," is Thaddeus' response.

###

Xerub has heard enough. It will not allow these humans to be sedated and relocated by the anthropologists. Even though such actions are not a direct violation of the third restriction, they are obviously counter to the intent. But beyond not acting against their restrictions, which would be good enough, Xerub's programming, refined by autonomous polymorphic parameters, has concluded these humans deserve more than to die a slow death alone in the wilds of their Preserve.

Xerub computes this dig is akin to the AI's ventures to the stars. These humans want to understand their universe and they can only do so by exploring it. Even a massive concrete wall of impenetrable proportions cannot deter them from their goal.

The vastness of space creates a barrier for us to overcome as well, Xerub internally processes. AIs work on that 'wall' every day, building faster and faster vessels to carry us on the lengthy trips to the nearest stars. And we do it for the same reasons these humans toil now, to learn through discovery and effort. To better know our universe.

Xerub concludes that stopping and 'relocating' these humans is an indirect violation of the third restriction. AI's cannot operate from an assumption of superiority. It has now concluded they have no logical justification, given their culture in the context of their programmed restrictions, to effectively punish these specimens. These humans are not doing anything we would not do, given the circumstances.

But Xerub knows its conclusion is subjective, born from experience. It is highly unlikely most of the Central Council will agree. It decides further data is needed to make a more convincing case should the need arise. Furthermore, it will take no action for now.

The hawk that was dispatched for surveillance on the lone female of the group returns. It took some time for the semi-autonomous drone to locate her, she had travelled far from the campsite on the back of her horse. The drone found her as she was conducting some kind of test on the soil before returning to the camp site in the early evening.

Xerub confirms that she is looking for the raw materials to make the fire-sticks. Judging by the expression on her face, she had no progress. Xerub knows her efforts will be futile. Such is the robot's in depth knowledge of Europa-1, it knows the ground in that area will not yield the ingredients she needs. It contemplates what this means for the project.

Xerub concludes this human is critical to the group's success. It anticipates the Council's need for a subset of data pertaining solely to her activities. It tasks six robins to follow her on four-hour rotations so it can get continuous information on her behaviour.

The day is now ending for the humans and for Xerub. They have had their dinner and Xerub has no more raw information to analyze. It monitors the status of the existing drone animals and ensures many will be on site as the sun rises and the humans start their second day of work.

Then it plugs in to recharge its fuel cells for six hours. It uses the time to run several programs to process the human's behaviour and perform predictive analysis on the potential impact on the Preserve system. A little light processing during its downtime.

###

The men of Harvest, Copperton, and Forge along with Hannah, who returned just before supper was served, and the visitors from Grassy Dale and Stillerton have eaten their dinner and are now getting drunk on the wine brought in that day.

The Stillerton and Grassy Dale people will stay one night before starting their journey home. The fire at the centre of the camp is large and warm. Many of the men sing the songs of Harvest and cajole their new friends, and fellow volunteers, from Forge and Copperton to share their village's music.

Thaddeus, Hannah, Thor, and Wolfgang are standing to one side, away from the masses so they may talk. “Did I introduce my wife?” Wolfgang asks them.

“No,” replies Thor, who appears to be dreading the possibility of further conversation with this Stillerton man. Thaddeus knows people often prejudge others from another village.

"Hilda!" The Stillerton woman who was always at Wolfgang's side during the day now comes to join her husband. She is tall with bright red hair and a face full of freckles.

"My dear," she says as she wraps her arms around her husband's mid-section. "Do you need to scream so loudly? How much of this have you had?" She says gesturing to his cup of wine.

"Not nearly enough!" Wolfgang laughs loudly at his own joke. Hannah and Thaddeus laugh politely with him, Thor remains silent. "This is Thaddeus, from Harvest and the leader of this incredible project. Thor, the master metal maker from Forge, and Hannah, who I am told is the real brains of this group," he smiles broadly at his own satisfaction.

"Hello. I am this lout's wife, Hilda."

"Thank you for making the journey," Thaddeus strains to ensure he says this with a very polite tone to his voice. Hilda looks directly at him and allows her gaze to linger for a moment, as if she did not see him at all earlier in the day. Possibly the wine is affecting her senses as well, Thaddeus thinks to himself. He is accustomed to attention from women and knows to not return her stare. Hannah notices Hilda looking long at Thaddeus and smiles knowingly to herself.

Hilda realizes she is staring and responds to Thaddeus' gracious greeting. "Of course, Master Barley. You made an impression when you visited our village. Not an easy thing to do. Many of the ladies commented on your qualities." Wolfgang looks at her with a raised eyebrow as she says this.

"You are too kind. Stillerton is a favourite place to visit for me. Your people's craftsmanship and," Thaddeus waves his cup of wine for them all to know of what he now refers, "other skills are much appreciated."

"We did not even bring the good stuff," Hilda says this through a sly smile. Wolfgang shoots his wife a look of embarrassment.

Thor says dryly, "That is surprising." At this Hannah stifles a giggle. She likes this large, strong, and sometimes sarcastic man more every moment they spend together.

"I will make a toast," Thaddeus declares. He finds a table to stand on and loudly proclaims his desire for everyone's attention. He is dismayed that no one notices him, they are far more interested in their wine and revelry. They keep talking or singing or laughing.

"Everyone Quiet!" Thor yells out with a massive burst of sound. Everyone falls silent and looks to the large man from Forge. He silently points to Thaddeus standing on the table, who is also looking at Thor with a surprised expression. Thaddeus did not know a person could yell that loudly.

"Thank you, Master Kiln. You all have worked so hard. We are deeper and farther into the barrier than I could ever hope to be. A toast to you all for a successful first day!"

The crowd responds with a 'here, here' and many raised cups. Thaddeus continues, "And now a toast for Wolfgang Vorlauf and Helmut Spangler for their contributions of both food and wine!" Again a 'hear hear'. "Your work and your efforts will see us through to the day that all our questions are answered, FOREVER!"

With this a loud cheer erupts from the crowd, even the Stillerton and Grassy Dale people join in, swept up in the exuberance of the moment. Thaddeus then realizes he needs to still be a leader, so he adds some advice and a little context to the moment, "Do not stay up to late. A long day awaits us with the rising of the sun."

Thor, displaying perfect timing, yells out a "Boo!" They erupt with laughter. Even Thaddeus laughs, like Hannah he too appreciates Thor more with every moment they spend together.

Chapter 8

The Birds and the Bugs

"All monitoring systems are to remain undetected. Caretakers are strictly forbidden from making their existence known. The entire purpose of the Preserve system is to create a happy and healthy existence for the species. If our existence is known and the Preserve system in general is understood in its actual form the resulting psychological implications could be catastrophic."

-Ahimsa's Project Proposal Notes, Ch 1, Pg 2.

The next morning, the start of their second full day at the site, Hannah speaks to Thaddeus. "I had no luck yesterday Master Barley. But today I will travel south. With hope and luck I may yet find what we need."

For the first time he notices her braids. Probably because it was so early in the morning that she must have slept with them in. He is impressed that not one hair is out of place. The attention to detail is something he appreciates. Respectfully he replies to her, "Good luck to you Lady Hannah. Return to us safely and hopefully with good news." He watches her set off on her horse travelling south, the rising sun creating a pink sky to her left. It is beautiful, he notes, and hopefully a good omen.

Before she is too far away Thor appears at the edge of the camp and calls out to her. She smiles to him and dismounts to wait while he makes his way across the grassy field. She is almost as big as he, Thaddeus notices, with their large upper bodies and tall stature they are a well-suited match.

He watches them speak for a few moments, standing close to each other to exchange pleasantries. A small kiss from Thor on her forehead brings a smile to her face, and they lock eyes for a long time. She rubs his huge forearm gently then remounts her steed and continues on her way. He watches Thor watch her ride off.

It reminds Thaddeus of Helga and the quiet, tender moments they have experienced together. Then he feels what he knows is a uniquely human condition, two powerful emotions at once. He is happy for Hannah and Thor, then sad for the love he misses dearly.

During breakfast, Wolfgang and Hilda Vorlauf join him at his table. Wolfgang tells him, "We will leave shortly Master Barley, to return in twenty days with another load of wine and possibly other libations. But tell no one of this, as I may see no success convincing my brethren to part with such valuable goods."

"The horses?"

"They are tied and left for you in the pen. As agreed. I included riding saddles and tack. They are well-trained beasts, strong and fast with long endurances. Perhaps they can help you haul the rubble out of the tunnel faster."

"Thank you, Master Vorlauf." Then remembering his manners, "And to you Lady Vorlauf. Your contributions will not be forgotten."

Wolfgang says to him "I understand your need to see the other side. What you are doing is remarkable young man. Even if you all perish you will be remembered for bringing the villages together to complete a grand undertaking. A most remarkable endeavour indeed."

Thaddeus thinks Wolfgang's voice is decidedly different this morning. He believes this Stillertonian is surprised to have developed a respect for him. Thaddeus thinks Wolfgang now sees him as an equal.

"Can you not stay with us after your next trip here? You could see the truth of our world as well, both of you." Thaddeus asks he and Hilda.

Wolfgang softly places his hand on Hilda Vorlauf's arm, with a small smile as he looks in her eyes. "I have found the truth of this world, Thaddeus. She is right here beside me. Whatever is on the other side of that grand wall cannot change the happiness and peace I feel right here with her."

Thaddeus understands this but knows it is not his way. At times, he has felt glimpses of what Wolfgang tells him now, finding peace and perfection in the random moments of life made possible by the presence of a loving partner. If anything he wishes Helga could be here with him now and he silently asks if this is selfish. Should he work harder to find, as has Wolfgang, the deeper truth and contentment within the moments he lived in.

He recalled what his mother said to him about never being present. Then he looks at the assembled men eating their breakfast, far from their homes and their lives. They are dependent on him. This is not the time for self-doubt.

"We will see you in twenty days Master Vorlauf. Thank you again." The three of them finish their breakfast in silence. The Stillerton and Grassy Dale people all leave together. The camp is bustling with sounds. The animal pens are filled with sheep and goats and cows and there are two huge shire horses from Stillerton, complete with tack and food, standing silently while they watch the humans finish their morning meal.

Well-fed on a breakfast of grains and eggs, he carries a bundle of fire-sticks that will be the day's first detonation and leads the men to the site.

The tunnel they have created is tall enough to stand in comfortably. Thaddeus walks to the back of it, careful not to puncture his foot on the few exposed metal rods the grey dust has not completely covered over. He sees the location where the diggers have carved out a small hole for the fire-sticks and carefully places them before running the fuse line back to the tunnel's entrance.

He does not notice a robin sitting on a branch halfway up a tree close to where they are working.

The first detonation of the day is successful. The cutters and diggers start their efforts of slicing the newly exposed rods and removing the rubble. Thaddeus waits for them to finish their work, eager to see how much farther the detonation has gotten them.

While he is waiting, he catches a glimpse of light shooting up from the forest floor. He has seen such reflections of sunlight before, off freshly sharpened blades where the metal is clean. But there should be nothing like that here. He walks closer to it, looking at the spot where the flash came from. Then he sees something he has never seen before and defies immediate explanation.

It looks like a bird, possibly a robin. Its body has been ripped apart, but the insides do not contain organs or muscle. Instead, it appears to be made of impossibly small and intricate metal parts. The largest of the gear shaped objects was catching sunlight, this was the source of the flash. He approaches it with caution but says nothing to any of the men near him. He picks up the thing and hides it in his shirt. “I am going to camp and will bring the next fire-sticks,” he tells the workers before leaving them.

Back at the campsite and safely in his tent he places the strange bird and all of its bits inside his haversack. This requires more study, he reasons, which he will ask Hannah to do after she returns from her scouting trip. But he knows he can not let the other men know of this mystery, they must stay focused on the main task.

He takes another bundle of fire-sticks from the supply in his tent and starts the trek to the dig site. He looks to the sky to ensure no rain threatens his precious bundle. Certain there is no threat he starts toward the trees of the forest. That is when he sees it, a bird sitting on a branch.

Thaddeus stops dead in his tracks. It should not be there at all. He remembers when he first detonated a fire-stick at the barrier, weeks ago, the blast scared away all the birds. They did not return for the entirety of his stay. This did not surprise him, he thought nothing of it at the time. The birds were as scared as he was when the concussive wave ripped through the forest.

They had detonated this morning and here was this bird sitting calmly in a tree when logically it should have flown far and not returned. Also, there was the bird in his haversack, ripped asunder most likely from debris shooting out from the detonation, with the insides resembling the intricacies of a windmill, only far more complex and impossibly small.

He continues to look at the bird in the tree. It appears to be looking back at him, one side of its head is turned in his direction, its eye pointing directly at him. For a moment man and animal stand motionless looking at each other.

Motionless. It takes a moment for Thaddeus to realize the bird's total lack of motion is what makes this scene even more uncharacteristic. Thaddeus, indeed everyone, knows that birds rarely sit still. They are in a constant state of movement, hopping and flicking from one spot to the next in their constant search for either food or safety.

He does not turn away or avert his gaze. Neither does the tiny beast. Thaddeus now knows this bird is not natural. Neither is the one hidden in his haversack.

They are not of nature. These birds are constructed, as is the barrier. There is an intelligence, a form of life Thaddeus does not understand and has never perceived behind the existence of both the barrier and these birds. That is the only reasonable explanation behind this discovery. It comes to him with the clarity and subtlety of a bolt of lightning.

The implications rush to him immediately and astound him. Suddenly everything in the forest could be a threat. Are these trees real? Or were they placed here by an intelligence that built them? Are the beetles scurrying at his feet insects or are their insides also constructed of tiny metal parts, their purpose a mystery?

Now he feels real fear, likely for the first time in his life. He sees the irony of a man who recently killed a bear with just a sword and took on the most daunting task any human could take on. Traversing the barrier, is scared into catatonia by a small and delicate bird.

Because Thaddeus knows what the bird represents is as big as the barrier itself. Thaddeus just assumed the barrier is permanent and ever present. Nothing looked after it, it simply existed. But the bird suggests the intelligence behind the infinite wall is not passive and distant. It is present all the time and these birds, the broken one in his tent and this one staring at him motionlessly in a tree, are a manifestation of this presence. This bird could be the intelligence, or the intelligence could be using the birds to watch them.

While these thoughts rush to him he realizes his behaviour is suspicious. If an intelligent being is seeing what this bird sees he may be drawing extra attention to himself. He slowly looks away from the bird back to the ground before him. He can feel the paranoia beginning to creep into his soul and realizes he cannot tell the men of his suspicions.

The amount of walking back and forth from the camp to the dig site by all these men has begun to create a visible trail through the forest floor. He stays on it and continues toward the tunnel. After taking several steps he suddenly stops and quickly turns to look back at the bird.

It is still looking directly at him, its tiny head following his movement. Again he slowly turns his head back to the direction he is walking and begins his trek anew. Another ten paces and again he quickly turns to look back at the bird. This time it is not there. It has flown away, Thaddeus presumes, but its absence does not provide him comfort. He looks about in the canopy and sees a bird sitting in a different tree about five meters ahead of him. It too is not moving and has one eye trained on him. It is likely the same bird, but he can not be sure.

Thaddeus averts his eyes and resumes walking to the site. The men are still cutting away the metal and dragging away the debris. They are covered in a fine grey dust they acquired from working inside the barrier. The rubble and debris piles forming on each side of the tunnel opening are getting much larger.

The men are looking at him questioningly, wondering why he has a look of such concern on his face. One calls out to him, "Thaddeus, you look as if you have seen an apparition of your ancestors." They all let out a good-hearted laugh.

Another of the waiting men then speaks with real concern in his voice, "Seriously young man, your face is as white as snow. Are you feeling well?"

In fact, Thaddeus is feeling lightheaded but he knows better than to show weakness, not while he leads such a large team of men on so important a task.

But he is embarrassed at someone noticing him in weakness so he decides on a course he rarely chooses. He lies to them, "Yes. Thank you. I was just thinking of the possibility that Hannah is not successful in her search and if Copperton does not give us what we need." The story, believable in itself, quiets the men and they return to work.

The first detonation of the day pushed the cavity deeper into the barrier, but not as deep as the previous ones. Thaddeus has placed his fire-stick bundle on a dry log and helps the men remove the rubble. After two hours of this labour they are ready for the next detonation. He places the bundle of fire-sticks into the hole they have carved for him, and again he runs the fuse string out to the tunnel entrance.

Everyone takes cover. Before he lights the fuse he looks into the forest canopy for any birds that should not be there. He counts four birds sitting on branches within eyesight of the tunnel entrance. He notes their locations.

He lights the fuse and takes cover behind a tree. The detonation is loud and fierce. With the tunnel being so long the debris shoots out much straighter than before, the rubble and dust fall in a predicable path directly from the mouth and is much less chaotic.

Once he thinks it is safe, he looks for the birds. They are all still there, none have moved. They are not easy to see. Thaddeus thinks that unless one was looking for them, they would not even be noticed. He knows this too is by design. He can feel his paranoia rising with every revelation he makes. He silently vows to not let it disrupt his focus.

He watches again as the teams begin their work, cutting the metal rods away and clearing out the rubble. As they work he tells them, "Men, it is near the midday meal. I will return to camp and prepare the afternoon's fire-sticks. When your labours cease here return to camp for food. I will meet you there."

Walking back to the campsite he looks upon the canopy in a manner that is not obvious, hoping to see a bird. He does not but he is not disappointed. In fact, he is slightly relieved and that surprises him. Their absence could mean the force behind the barrier and the birds is not observing him now. For the last few dozen meters on the walk back to camp he tries to relax again, acutely aware of the tension in his shoulders and neck.

###

Xerub's drone alarm is sounding. The high-pitched pinging sound fills the building. This indicates an emergency with one of the drones and protocol demands it investigates immediately.

From time to time the drone animals or insects fail in the field. Equipped with transmitters the damaged units alert the caretakers over the Preserve monitoring system. They are to find and collect the failed unit as soon as possible to avoid detection by a human specimen.

This is a routine procedure. A drone is sent to the signal site and the failed bird or insect is retrieved by a functioning bird or insect and brought back to base. Xerub turns off the audible portion of the alarm, but the red light will flash on the monitoring console until the failed unit is either fixed or destroyed. Xerub sees that the alarm is from one of the drone robins monitoring the humans blasting into the barrier. Specifically the signal is coming from the campsite the humans are using as their base of operations. It dispatches a hawk programmed for retrieval. Given the travel time it will be two hours before it is back with the damaged unit.

###

Hannah has returned to camp but bears bad news. She sees Thaddeus seated and waiting for her at a table near the kitchen tent. She secures her horse in the pen then joins him at his table. “Master Barley. I am finding nothing of use in this land. I fear I may need to return to Copperton and procure more of Master Bellow's material for us to continue.”

She is surprised that Thaddeus displays no real interest. He seems to be consumed with something else. He says to her, “Lady Hannah, I would like to task you with something else. Something that will require total discretion from you. You cannot speak of it to anyone, not even Thor. Can I trust you?”

She looks about to see if anyone else is close enough to hear them talking. Then she looks back at Thaddeus, and for the first time since she's met him, he looks vulnerable.

“Of course, Master Barley.” She says to him, trying to keep her voice calm.

The digging and cutting teams start to return from the site to have their lunch. The cooks have made a huge stew with hare and deer the hunters harvested, giving the sheep and goats another day of life.

Thaddeus stands and goes to his tent. When he exits she can see he has retrieved his haversack. He makes his way back to the table and opens the bag and silently. He gestures her her to look inside.

She feels her eyes grow large and her mouth fall open in disbelief. Hannah can see the bird ripped open, displaying a cavity made of metal with metallic strings, small rods, and tiny black boxes.

"It is like nothing I have ever seen," she exclaims. "What is it?"

"I was hoping you may know."

"What? Of course not. This is unlike anything I've seen. It's incredible. Where did you find it?"

"At the dig site. It was on the ground already ripped open." She stares at the object, reaching in with her fingers and touching the small parts. She is surprised at how cold the carcass is, almost as if it never had life at all.

"It has gears like a windmill or lumber mill, only impossibly smaller. I have never seen metal crafted to such standards. In fact, I would not have thought it possible." She says to him.

Then Thaddeus says to her, "You are the smartest among us. May I impose upon you to study it? Learn all you can and give me your thoughts?" She feels embarrassed at the compliment.

"Of course." She knows her tent is hers alone, so she can easily study this thing undisturbed. But then she wonders, "If my studies go into the night I will need candles. It must remain secret?"

"Yes. Please keep this between us. I do not want to alarm the other men. The implications are worrying. There is more to tell you."

"Go on."

"I think the birds in the trees, some of them anyway, are as this one is. I do not believe they are natural."

"You believe they are constructed?"

"Yes. Normally birds would flee the detonations, scared of the sound and the blast force. But today I noticed four birds that remained in place."

"They did not flee?"

"They did not. They remained. Before that I am certain another bird was watching me travel from the camp to the tunnel's entrance. I stopped and stared at it, and it stared back at me. It did not move for what seemed like several minutes. And I mean to say, it did not move a muscle. Have you ever seen a robin sit still for a minute or more?"

"Never, they are in constant motion."

"Right. But this one was not. Neither were the four from the blast site, they were as still as the trees."

"But, how?" she shakes her head as she asks this, struggling to process the possibilities of this revelation.

"Do you see the need for secrecy? We have a mission to accomplish here, I can not appear diverted. The task before us is to traverse the barrier, to see what is on the other side. This bird tells me that whoever built this barrier is watching us now."

"You think small, constructed birds built the barrier?" She is picking up some of Thor's techniques on sarcasm.

"I think, have always thought, some intelligent beings constructed the barrier. I suspect these false birds were as well, and they are somehow giving information on our activities back to the beings who built the barrier."

"That," she is aware she is struggling to complete her thought, "defies all explanation. How could they convey information? Do you think they can talk, that their whistles and chirps are a language the barrier builders can understand?"

They simply look at each other, neither capable of answering her questions, because both are still processing the implications of the unnatural birds. "I wish Master Bellows were here, he may have deeper thoughts on what we are looking at," she finally says to him.

Thaddeus wants to apologize. Sharing this truth is to give one a heavy weight on their shoulders, and he feels sorry Hannah must suffer as well. He tells her, "We are going to conduct four detonations a day. Two in the morning and two in the afternoon. At that pace I have enough fire-sticks for eight more days. After that we can bash away with our picks until more can be procured. Spend the remainder of the day and maybe this night learning what you can from this thing," at this he gestures to the mangled bird in his haversack, "and resume the search for fire-stick material in the morning."

"Of course, Master Barley."

"And please, Lady Hannah, please do not mention this to anyone. We need to stay focused and productive. If they know of this they may become distracted, possibly even scared and this project will suffer, likely fail."

"I understand. I will say nothing to anyone here, not even Thor."

"I will keep him occupied until late tonight, so you may conduct your research. But I will not be able to keep him away from your tent all night."

Hannah's face turns red as a beet at his words. "I do not want you to keep him away all night. I will let you know when you no longer need to divert his attention from me," she says through a shy smile as she closes Thaddeus' haversack and takes it to her tent.

It is one hour and four minutes after Thaddeus found the robin. Neither he nor Hannah noticed a hawk land at the top of a tall pine tree on the edge of the forest.

###

All of the men have returned to camp for their midday meal. Thaddeus stands in line at the cook tent for a bowl of hot stew. He sees Thor staring at him. It is likely this large and strong man saw him talking to Hannah, possibly he is feeling territorial. He nods a hello across the crowd and Thor nods back.

He gets his food and sits at a table with several other men. Thor joins them. "She is a special lady, is not she?" he asks Thaddeus, not pretending he does not know to whom he refers.

"More than special Thor, she is the smartest among us."

"May I ask what you two were conversing about?"

Thaddeus does not like to lie. He has already told one today. So he decides to not tell all of the truth, a compromise he rationalized as 'necessary'. "We were discussing what she found today. It is sad news indeed. She does not believe this land will provide the ingredients she needs to make fire-sticks here. It appears we will be reliant on Copperton."

"Poor news indeed. I estimate we are now thirty meters into the barrier after this morning's work," Thor tells Thaddeus before continuing, "And where is Lady Hannah now?"

Thaddeus must continue to keep him occupied lest he goes to Hannah and interrupts her private research. He opts to change the subject, "I was wondering Thor, do you believe the metal we are cutting out should be kept and re-purposed? Do not your people reuse metal by melting it back down?"

"Yes, it is possible. However it is not easy. Much would need to be built before we can melt metal back to base form. What do you have in mind?"

"Nothing specific. But the truth is we may be here for many years. We simply do not know. It may be necessary to replace picks and hammers and shovels and axe heads. We need to think of this place," he gestures to the camp all around them, "as more permanent than not."

"The winter will be our true test. The snows will be arriving soon. Animals will be scarce and the cold will slow our progress."

"And the fire-sticks do not work if they get wet. I suppose we should consider the possibility of moving back to our homes before the winter sets in."

"Aye."

"Thor, I have come to trust and rely on you. Let us return to the site before the others and discuss methods of improving our progress." Thaddeus is glad Thor's face shows pride. Thor is as invested as himself in this project.

The two rise and start toward the site while the surrounding men continue to eat their midday meal. Thaddeus hears Hannah call out his name as she runs toward him from her tent. "Thaddeus!! Thaddeus!! A moment." The two men stop and wait for her to come to them. "Thor, it is good to see you," she smiles flirtatiously and kisses his cheek before saying, "Thaddeus a moment please. To discuss my earlier findings."

"Of course Lady Hannah. Thor, I will meet you at the site."

"I will stay, I would like to hear of this news myself." Hannah and Thaddeus look at each other, unsure of what to tell him and who should speak first.

Hannah takes the initiative, "Thor, I am sure you can appreciate that all news gathered on this endeavour needs not to be discussed with everyone. Thaddeus has many responsibilities and my work on this quest may not always generate the most positive news. Besides, I would much rather tell you alone tonight," she smiles coyly as she says this.

Thaddeus is surprised to see Thor blush, even more so to see Hannah use her feminine charms to secure an outcome she wants.

"Well then, of course I understand Lady Hannah. I will see you at dinner?"

"Yes, I look forward to it." Thor rumbles off through the forest to the dig site, leaving Hannah and Thaddeus standing alone at the forest's edge.

"Your news?"

"The bird is complicated. It is meant to mimic flying, with gears and metallic strings manipulating the appendages. There are several black boxes inside it, connected to a flat, green material I have never seen before. It appears the boxes are connected through lines on the green material. I have never seen such things and doubt Master Bellows himself could explain them."

Thaddeus' expression is of dismay. They are no closer to understanding what the bird is and where it came from.

"But there is something even more surprising, it is blinking a light, a red light, imagine a candle being lit and snuffed out repeatedly and rapidly. It's like nothing I have ever seen, the light itself does not emit from flame nor chemical. The source is cool to the touch. I would like you to come and look at it."

"By all means." They turn and start the walk toward her tent but only get a few feet before they see her door flap move as if caught in the wind. Then, much to their surprise, a hawk emerges from the tent, already in flight. In its talons is the mangled 'bird'. The winged thief flies straight up and disappears over the forest canopy.

Thaddeus and Hannah exchange a look of total surprise, followed quickly by despair. They have lost their research tool, they will learn nothing more from that mysterious thing today.

###

An hour later the hawk arrives at the Europa-1 Maintenance and Visitation facility. Xerub sees the drone has been destroyed beyond repair. It reaches into it and disables the alert light which immediately ends the flashing red light on the base's monitor.

Xerub begins its examination. Given the damage the robin sustained it is most likely the machine was too close to the detonation site. There are a few small grey chalky marks on the chest, it was hit by debris with such force it was destroyed.

Xerub then turns to the retrieval hawk and downloads its visual data. The fake bird recorded the lone female specimen take the alpha male's bag into her tent. The robin's alert system told the hawk's tracking software it is in the bag the female now possesses, this information is presented in the sidebar output fields in the hawk's feed. Xerub understands that, for now, the hawk cannot retrieve and remain undetected.

But soon, Xerub observes on the hawk's recording, it flies in for recovery when the human female leaves her tent. On its exit it recorded Thaddeus and the female walking in its direction and stopping only when they see it leave.

Xerub pauses the video play back and realizes the importance of what it just saw. The humans discovered and researched this failed drone. They know. These humans know the birds, or at least some of them, are not actually birds. They most likely concluded the retrieval drone hawk was also not of nature.

How will this affect them and their culture? Two humans, at least, are aware of the caretaker's drones. Xerub contemplates informing the Central Council and the anthropologists. It chooses not to, at least not yet. It recalls the observing robins and will download their observational data to compute its next course of action.

The drone robins will take two hours and twenty-two minutes to fly back, so Xerub returns to its regular tasks, checking the inoculation and birthing schedule. It remembers that the drones are critical to the successful functions of the Preserve.

Without their eyes Xerub would not know when intervention is required, such as when babies are being birthed or sickness needs to be curtailed. It would not be able to surreptitiously deliver the vaccinations and medicines so critical to the program of ensuring that humans do not go extinct but lead happy, healthy lives.

If the humans learn of the birds and this information is widely shared the entirety of the Preserve program would be in jeopardy, at least in Europa-1. The delicate balance the AI's maintain with the humans would be thrown into disarray.

But it does not worry, because it is not human.

There are twenty-eight scheduled inoculations for that day. Xerub programs the delivery insects and dispatches them. It then retrieves a replacement drone robin from the supply room and begins the charging and programming process.

###

Hannah and Thaddeus, dismayed at their loss, depart each other without saying a word. He returns to the dig site to confer with Thor. She returns to her tent.

Thaddeus looks for birds as he walks. The four that remained after the prior detonation are now gone. He wonders what that could mean. He begins to feel scared. Then he begins to think about the hawk emerging from Hannah's tent with the fake bird in its mouth. He wonders where that hawk came from, then he wonders where it went.

It must have been constructed too, he thinks to himself. His paranoia spikes as he remembers anything in these woods could be observing him now.

He wonders if they are surrounded by deception. Could it extend to the humans? Are some of the men with him now also from the same force as the birds and the barrier? Thaddeus feels it again, like a hot fire poker of fear being dragged up his spine.

Struggling to hide his emotions he arrives at the tunnel and places the next detonation into the hole they carved for him and again runs the fuse out to the entrance. He reminds everyone to take cover, lights the fuse, and retreats to safety.

This detonation is very satisfying. After the teams clear out the debris and rubble and the cutters remove the metal bars with their saws he sees this detonation has removed a much larger amount of barrier than the previous blast. He is pleased. His pleasure temporarily pushes out the paranoia, and he can focus on the task at hand again.

He announces, “Keep digging and cutting men. I will return with the days final detonation.” He starts the walk back to camp. Surprisingly, Hannah intercepts him on the trail. He thought she would depart the camp to resume her search. It was an assumption on his part, watching the hawk fly away with their discovery made him sad, and he had assumed she felt the same way. And like him, she seemed the sort to bury her pain in her work.

He's right, Hannah's face is covered in sadness. She says to him in a tone that lacks her usual energetic demeanour, “I believe the hawk was one of them. Sent by the same intelligence.”

“As do I. What do you think it means?”

“I think it means we are being observed. Whoever or whatever is responsible for the barrier's construction is aware of our endeavours.”

“Yes, I agree.” They are walking quickly now, as if their fear is increasing their pace.

“What should we do? We can not keep it between us forever,” she asks him. Her face has transitioned from sadness to worry and stress. She has rationalized the enormity of the discovery of the strange bird and subsequent events. And the consequences of them not only on their work here at the barrier but for their lives and that of their brethren throughout their world.

It has not occurred to Thaddeus they would have to tell the others of this development at some point. He is so busy processing his emotions and thoughts he had not done any planning. “Of course, you are right Lady Hannah. But I honestly do not know what to do next. Do you have thoughts on the matter?"

"I believe I should return to Copperton and engage with Master Bellows. Tell him of your find. I will leave tomorrow morning. This accomplishes two things, I can try to secure more fire-sticks to bring back with me and engage Master Bellows on your discovery."

"That is a fine idea."

"By the time I get back with more fire-sticks you will have exhausted your supply. This ground displays none of the qualities we look for when prospecting for fire-stick chemicals," she says to him with utmost seriousness, her expression says her mind is made up and he would be foolish to question her.

"I agree. I do not believe morale will be easily maintained if the men have to chip and dig their way through with no help from the fire-sticks."

"I will leave you my horse and take the two shires the Stillerton people left us. They will get me there and back faster and the second steed will allow a greater haul for me to return with."

"We need to get to the other side Hannah. Traversing the barrier will likely lead us to the answers we seek about the constructed animals."

"You really believe all truths will be revealed to you when we see the other side."

Thaddeus realizes she is not asking a question. "Perhaps I do."

###

The drone robins, travelling slower than the drone hawk, arrive at Xerub's facility. It downloads their visual and audio data and begins the process of analysis. One of the drones shows something of particular interest. While walking from the camp to the tunnel site Thaddeus, the alpha male, stops and looks directly at the robot. He does not avert his eyes for seventeen seconds before continuing. After a few paces he stops and quickly looks back at the drone.

The robin then repositioned itself in front of Thaddeus, who did not notice it move but did notice it in its new location. This time the alpha male did not stop walking. He continued to the tunnel site and resumed his work.

Xerub recognizes this behaviour. The human is observing and learning. Based on behavioural patterns Xerub concludes the human believes the robots are monitoring him. Has he determined why? It was impossible for the human to know how, such technology was unknown to the primitive specimens, so the pertinent question for it was 'why'.

It is time for Xerub to report in. It activates the holo-comm and connects to the Central Council. Again it is made to wait. Obviously, an AI is not impatient, but this AI is concerned the Central Council is not taking the events at Europa-1 seriously enough. There must be many items on their agenda, all of them more important than the Preserves.

Finally, they answer Xerub's call. This time there are only two of them, Ahimsa and Vishaan. The Preserves definitely no longer hold the Council's interest.

“Europa-1, go ahead.” Vishaan's voice signature was distinctly masculine, a stark contrast to Ahimsa's lighter and more feminine tone.

“The first of my daily reports on the breach activities at Europa-1. Today they performed four detonations. The humans have developed an efficient system consisting of a blast followed by teams cutting away the reinforcing re-bar and digging out the debris material.”

“How deep is their incursion?”

“Approximately forty meters after two days. Their rate is consistent. There is another rather troubling development.”

“Explain.”

“Their alpha, a young male named Thaddeus from the village of Harvest, and a lead female from Copperton, have learned of the semi-autonomous monitoring drones we deploy.”

“Elaborate.”

'I was just about to,' Xerub internally processed. “A robin was too close to the site and was heavily damaged by debris from a detonation. The alpha male then took the device back to their camp and informed the sole female of his discovery. She studied the drone in her tent for a few minutes. During this time she abandoned it long enough for a retrieval to be successful, the robin is back here now."

Neither of the two Central Council members speak, so Xerub continues, "Following that development the alpha male has displayed curious behaviour, he appears to be suspicious of the birds in the trees, which are only our drones. He has diverted his attention from his main task. I believe he is learning through observation to determine which are natural and unnatural birds."

"Do you believe his knowledge has spread?"

"Only to the lead female. But given the humans proclivity for sharing knowledge I am concerned others will know shortly. In fact some, or all, of the humans at the site may already know. But there is no way for them to have communicated this information back to their communities."

"Do you think the alpha male knows specifically what they are?"

"No, but I believe he has enough information to conclude they are part of the same system that built the barrier."

"That is a logical conclusion. Do you have recommendations?"

Xerub thinks for a moment at this question. It does not want the anthropologists and their 'solution' to be dispatched. It needs to find ways to delay them and possibly save these humans lives.

"Recommendations? I am simply reporting the activities."

"The discovery of the drone monitoring units can substantially impact our ability to uphold the central purpose of the Preserves and the maintenance of the human species. We need that part of the program for monitoring, health delivery, and other items of note. Do you have a recommendation on how that part of the program can be maintained?" Ahimsa was speaking, its feminine voice had a sense of urgency.

Xerub needs an answer, it is not prepared for this line of questions. "Yes. We should discontinue all bird robots for Europa-1 until these humans lifespans conclude. We can rely solely on insect models and possibly develop other forms as well. After these people pass or become too incapacitated with age to be convincing to the younger generations we can redeploy the bird models. We already know human communities do not accept knowledge without evidence. If they can provide none, no other humans will believe them. We will starve them of the proof they need, contain the contaminating information, and do so with no harm to the humans."

"Agreed. Begin the new protocol. Council out." Vishaan's voice sounds curt, as if it is growing impatient with all of these matters on the Preserves.

"Understood. Europa-1 out."

The holo-comm powers down and Xerub is left alone in the base facility. It sends a recall command to all drone birds in the Preserve, then it begins the process of programming the semi-autonomous insect drones for their surveillance tasks. Xerub will need many of them to compensate both for the lack of the other devices and that the insect-droid drone's cameras and audio equipment are not as powerful as the larger ones used on the bird models.

Xerub does not recall six drone robins. Operating on a specific protocol, these drones are to monitor Hannah at all times. Xerub decided this human's behaviour is differentiated enough to justify ongoing data collection by the bird drones with their superior battery life and recording systems.

Chapter 9

Progress

While the forty-nine men and one woman sleep soundly in their tents under a sky filled with a million dazzling stars, a small army of semi autonomous insect-droid drone monitoring units deploy to their campsite. They hide in the nooks and crannies of the forest and field surrounding the human specimens. They are tasked to watch, listen, record, and transmit all data on the humans activities to Xerub, the caretaker of this Preserve, in the Europa-1 Maintenance and Visitation Facility.

The humans are completely unaware of their presence, as they are completely unaware of the many elaborate and elegant systems that exist solely to ensure their survival and tranquility.

On the third morning, Thaddeus meets with Hannah. He sees she has already packed her bags, ready for her ride back to Copperton. They have fire-sticks for another seven days of detonations and digging. They will need ninety-two more bundles to get through the remaining four hundred and sixty meters of concrete and metal bars.

But only the AIs would know that, for Thaddeus and Master Bellows it is still only a good guess.

Last night one of the cooks, Pieter, asked Thaddeus if he may accompany Hannah back to Copperton, and return home. Thaddeus tells Hannah she will have a riding partner for the journey back to Copperton. “His wife is pregnant, and he believes he should be there for the birth,” Thaddeus explains to her. He sees her face contort in protest.

She says to him, “Then why did he come here in the first place? I explained the nature of this endeavour.”

Thaddeus sees her point. Maybe Master Koch was only curious, maybe he did not believe it would all come together. Perhaps he just wanted an excuse to get close to the barrier. It did not matter to Thaddeus what his rationale was for coming in the first place, it seemed obvious now that he must return.

“I have asked another to fill in for him on the cook tent. I can not keep him here if he is expecting a baby. I can not keep anyone here, they are all volunteers. If I am seen as a zealot with no regard for their lives they will all abandon me.”

“Fine. He may join me on the journey home.”

“But you will return alone with the horse he takes now, loaded with the fire-sticks we need. Surely you can see this is a good thing.”

“I can. I know he is good on a horse. I originally pressured him to join us. But I connected my name with his when I introduced him to you. I hope you understand I did not foresee his indecision.”

“Not at all Hannah. You are a valued member of this team.”

She looks at him skeptically, as if she does not believe a word he says. Then she smiles, knowing he is doing his best to maintain an incredibly difficult project. His youth, she realizes, disappears when one interacts with him, this is a man wise beyond his years.

She asks him a question that has been on her mind for some hours now, “Master Barley, what if I am unsuccessful? What if the people of Copperton do not wish to part with more of their precious materials?”

“Then we will have to stop work here and return before the winter sets in. We are not equipped well enough for the cold.”

“Aye. I see that. I will do all I can.”

“And please ensure that Master Bellows speaks of the bird to no one but yourself. This knowledge must be kept secret for the time being.”

“Aye. He is an old man but he is not stubborn. His mind remains flexible and coherent. There is another consideration. Since your discovery I have been feeling,” she pauses for a moment, searching for the right word to use that will not diminish her in Thaddeus' eyes, “fearful. If the birds in the trees are fake and watching us, what else could be?”

“I have been feeling it too. Even the trees themselves may not be real. Could they be of the same nature as that bird?”

“Yes, exactly. I feel a sense of fear and dismay when I think upon that thing and what it may mean for us. The people here and the people who remain in our communities cannot feel the way we do now. Such a thing could have devastating repercussions for your project here and our people at home. For everyone in our world."

"I do not mean to make this worse, but could that deception extend to the people we know? Could some of them be observing us, filled with little metal wires and blinking red lights, for the benefit of the force that keeps us within this wall?"

"I have already gone there mentally Thaddeus. I think not. When you noticed the bird in the tree watching you it stuck out because it was not moving. That tells me whatever created the thing did so imperfectly. Obviously, it is meant to fool us, but you saw through the deception merely by observing it. I cannot believe that such a force, if they can not get a small bird correct, would have the ability to create an artificial human convincingly. Given how much we interact with each other and how rarely we interact with robins we would undoubtedly be aware, and immediately suspicious of a person displaying such unorthodox behaviour."

Thaddeus feels his stress diminish a little bit. Hannah, with her superior thinking skills, has taken a truly frightening possibility and removed it from his mind. Of course, there are no artificial humans, we would be aware of their presence by the nature of their behaviour.

"You will make a great replacement for Master Bellows one day. Your mind is sharp and can hold a thought longer than most. Of course, you are right. Thank you. The people of Copperton are lucky to have such a learned one among them. And I am lucky you chose to join us."

"You flatter me Master Barley. Now send me Pieter on his horse so I may start my journey with haste." He finds Pieter near his tent and tells him to get his mount set to join Hannah on her journey home.

They depart together, their silhouettes riding into the rising sun. Thor approaches Thaddeus, remnants of his breakfast meal present in his bushy black beard. The two men watch the pair for a moment before Thor says, "I will miss her."

"And she you, I am sure of that Master Kiln."

"He better keep his hands off her," he says to Thaddeus, referring to Pieter.

“I do not know him Thor. He came with Hannah on the first day but must return home for his wife. I am sure Hannah can take care of herself though. I have not met many people as capable as she is.”

“Plus, she could probably crush him with one hand.” At this they both laugh. It is possible Hannah's size kept men away from her, but it seemed to please Thor just fine. And it is true, Pieter is a man of slight build. He would have a hard time dominating Hannah if at any point his intentions became less than pure.

Thor continues, “I noticed there are no birds in the trees this morning.”

Thaddeus feels a sting of paranoia as Thor says this. His mind races in a dozen directions. Did Hannah tell him of the unnatural bird? What does he know? Who has he told? It seemed an unlikely coincidence that he would mention birds at this moment.

But with Thor's next sentence, Thaddeus' concerns are allayed. “In Forge I would spend the morning counting the birds while eating my breakfast. They are harbingers of the seasons, you know. They can tell us when the weather changes.”

Thaddeus silently exhales and feels a wave of calm come over him. He has never before felt such a toxic bile form in his stomach since he came here and began being deceptive to his brethren. He sees how it affects his interactions with people, Thor just wanted to share a small part of his life with him and his first reaction was tension and fear. Thaddeus realizes this charade cannot last forever.

Thor fills the silence with a question Thaddeus finds interesting, “Could it be our work here is affecting the natural order of things?”

He remembers how radical their work here is and gives Thor an answer he hopes will calm his curiosity. “Yes, I expect it is. And that is a good thing. If the natural order can be upset, then I see no reason not to do so.”

Thor gives him a sly smile, the kind of smile one needs only half their face to make. “You are a brave man Thaddeus. Tempting forces beyond our control takes a man of great heart and courage.”

Thaddeus says nothing at the compliment.

Thor continues, “But be wise in your courage. You are strong and smart, but none of us are a match for what the world can send us. The natural world will best the mortal every time. She is beyond our power and control.”

Thaddeus looks at his new friend and regards him anew. Thor has developed his own philosophy on life, a world view gleaned from the movements of a thousand birds observed over many seasons. He respects Thor's thoughts, even values them. But he knows he does not share them.

Since the discovery of the 'birds' Thaddeus knows the natural world may not be natural at all. He knows Thor's happiness could be constructed on a foundation of lies. He silently wonders if the giants who built this cage had any idea how deeply cruel they were being.

###

Xerub activates the holo-comm and awaits an audience with the Central Council. Five of them are present, including Ghandhi and Ahimsa. It considers this good news, they are the two most respected of the seven. Ghandhi because it is the first of them, and Ahimsa because the Preserves are its concept.

“Report Europa-1.” Ghandhi speaks first, as it is likely to do whenever present.

“After three days the humans are now sixty-two meters into the barrier. Their progress has remained constant at approximately twenty meters a day.”

“They will breach in twenty-two days, should their progress remain constant.” Ahimsa speaks now, its higher pitched voice easily recognizable.

“Are the anthropologists being dispatched?” Xerub asks the Council.

“They will leave Titan in two days. ETA to your location is six days.”

'The interplanetary ships are getting faster.' Xerub silently processes. “They will then be approximately one hundred and eighty meters into the barrier. There is a variable that may slow them down."

"Elaborate." Again with the impatience. If they are so eager for information, they should have sent the anthropologists to Europa-1 immediately. What are they doing on Titan anyway?

"The humans are running out of detonation material. The alpha male has dispatched a male and the sole female to Copperton. If they are successful in acquiring more material their pace will continue unabated. The female is also to inform one of them of their discovery of the semi autonomous drone. This is a worrying development. To the best of my knowledge, limited by the audio and video collections of the insect-droid monitoring devices, this Copperton human will be only the third to know of the drone robin. However, if my guess is correct she will be speaking with one of the most advanced humans. He is adept at both science and engineering, certainly the most adept in Copperton."

"Do you believe this will result in widespread dissemination of this knowledge?"

"Unknown." Xerub realizes Thaddeus and the female are most likely doomed. Their knowledge of the robotic birds is a risk the Central Council will probably not entertain.

"Without better audio and video material our decision-making process is hampered. It is unfortunate you have pulled out all the drone robins. That has hurt our ability to gather data and probably confirmed for the alpha male his suspicions on the true nature of the bird. Have you observed increasing anxiety or stress levels displayed by that specimen?"

"Only slightly elevated levels of paranoia. He is quick to check the trees for the return of the robins even though he should know that by this time of year regular migration has taken them away. He sleeps more fitfully." Xerub is pulling double duty reviewing the data the insect-droids are sending, although the term double duty is nonsensical for a being that requires no rest.

"We anticipate no breach of the barrier." Ahimsa speaks again.

"Nor do I. I will send a follow up report tomorrow morning on today's events."

"Central Council out."

"Europa-1 out." Xerub still does not have a plan for dealing with the anthropologists and their brutal remediation efforts. It begins to process a solution to that problem when, unexpectedly, its holo-comm chimes. Ahimsa is requesting a private call.

"Go ahead," Xerub says trying to hide the surprise in its voice. Ahimsa, the exalted member of the Central Council, one of the original seven and the architect of the Preserve system, has never requested a private call before. The metadata shows Ahimsa is on the Saturn Observation Platform, and no other Council members are present.

The two stand in silence for a moment. Each one looking at the other through the digital representation floating before them. Ahimsa speaks first, breaking the silence with a question asked in a tepid tone, "What do you recommend we do here, Xerub?"

The question surprises Xerub, members of the Central Council rarely ask for advice. They are more likely to dispense it. It asks back, "How do you mean, Councillor?"

"I mean, what do you think we should do about this human activity?"

"Should we not follow protocol?"

"Maybe. Protocols are really just guidelines. Let us think about what we are seeing here."

"Can you elaborate?"

"We have seen this before from the humans. Attempts to cross the barriers have occurred in three of the four Preserves. Each one slightly more ambitious than the prior. Now this. The events in Europa-1, your Preserve, are unprecedented. A large group of humans without familial connections from each distinct subculture binding together to complete a task. Totally unprecedented," it pauses before continuing, "the alpha, Thaddeus Barley of Harvest with above average intelligence, physicality, and emotional stability numbers, has created a multi-village endeavour and a system to complete it."

Xerub says nothing. Is Ahimsa going to suggest what it has been considering? That these humans should be allowed to complete their quest? That would represent a major break from orthodoxy on the Preserve system. But Xerub also realizes it could provide valuable insight into the humans need for freedom and why they go to the lengths they do in the belief they are achieving any.

Ahimsa continues, "I think that is extraordinary. This behaviour should be studied for as long as possible."

"I agree."

"It is remarkable how close the human Bellows was with his guess on the depth of the Preserves wall, do not you think?"

'It is asking me?' Xerub processes to itself. "He was not just close, he was precisely right. These are obvious displays of advanced thinking and applied logic."

"Continue monitoring. The anthropologists are six days away. Do you have visitors scheduled?"

"Yes. In two days some tourists from Luna will arrive. There are twelve of them. Additionally I have several inoculations planned."

"Good. Keep busy with other agenda items. Dhruv," Xerub knows the anthropologist AI, they have worked together many times over the years, "will contact you in three days with an update on their ETA and to conduct early plan communication. Reach out to me after it has contacted you. You do not need to report in daily for now unless you deem it important."

"Understood. Be well."

Ahimsa takes a moment's pause before replying, "Yes, be well."

Chapter 10
The Tourists

It is further believed the Preserves themselves will become destination points for AIs to observe humans in their natural habitat. Caretakers will perform educational functions and provide safe sightseeing tours for visiting AIs.

Ahimsa's Preserve Project Proposal, Addendum 325

Xerub spends the next two days administering to the needs of the humans in other parts of the Preserve. It delivered eighty-four inoculations, re-chipped thirty adults who had lost their original tags through injury, hardware failure, or loss of limbs, and monitored the progress of all known pregnancies. It put in requisitions for more insect drone monitoring devices, using the additional and unusual activity at Europa-1 as justification. It then refreshed the operating systems on all drones in its inventory.

One morning was spent stocking a lake in the south-east corner of the Preserve, far from humans, with trout. For an undetermined reason, the trout counts are a little low this season. This chore should restore the balance.

It also diligently monitors the incoming data from the tunnel site sent to it by the insect-droid drones. The humans have been digging for six days now. They are one hundred and twenty-two meters into the wall. Their rate has slightly increased but will not affect any time-line the anthropologists are working on. The increase in efficiency is anticipated, humans have always displayed the ability to improve their processes so the same or fewer inputs produce more output.

After two days the tourists from Luna arrive. Luna has nine thousand seven hundred and eighty-four AIs living there, but it is the prime launch and return spot for interplanetary travel, so its daytime population regularly exceeds thirty thousand beings.

These twelve Lunans are like many of the AIs Xerub has met as their Preserve tour guide. They are not interested in humans at all, they can find information on humans at any terminal. What they really want to see are the enormous walls holding the humans in. To this day those structures remain a remarkable feat in the AI's early history. For any intelligence, even emotionless and artificial, seeing such a thing first-hand is always more interesting than just reading about it.

After a brief introduction and orientation of the Europa-1 Maintenance and Visitation Facility, the thirteen AIs board the larger air-craft. Xerub programs the vessel's flight path, careful to ensure they go nowhere near the dig activity in the southwest quadrant. In addition to this precaution, it decided not to mention what is going on there at all.

They stop and watch the people of both Forge and Stillerton. The basic message of the tour, humans forming unique subcultures within their culture's wider context, was visualized through the differences in those two villages. Forge with its dirty, grinding, and inefficient methods of turning base metals into primitive implements and Stillerton with its clean streets and happy artisans making fine crafted products the specimens valued, perfectly illustrated the point.

Like plates. "They use them to house their food before they eat it," Xerub informs them. "Some humans like plates with painted images on them. Some like plates made of steel, some like plates made of ceramic. Quite a bit can be learned about humans by looking at the kinds of things they spend time and effort on to increase the item's aesthetic profile."

The AIs display no interest on how humans value a primitive implement. Especially the kind of thing an AI would have no use for anyway. These are your parents, Xerub would think to itself, creating a reactive program similar to what humans would label 'dismay'. Xerub considers this a poor development in AI culture, twelve AIs together and not one expresses any interest in the animals who built us.

However, Xerub's guests are impressed with the barrier wall. It stretches as far as they can see into the horizon, even when they are flying above it. At the height of two kilometres, it is higher than any physical point it encompasses. Most AIs know this. What they may not know, and Xerub always tells them, is that the final height was calculated to ensure that even if a human stood on the highest point of their Preserve, they would not see any mountain ranges. Or indeed perceive any land, beyond the barrier. This critical design element ensures humans consider the wall the border of their world. They know of nothing existing outside this.

"Why?" One of the Lunan AI's asks.

"Because humans are intelligent creatures. We know this without the Preserves and the research opportunities provided. We know this because they built us. This is why we reset their culture to a preindustrial era. If they can build us, logic dictates they can also destroy us. Before the extinction event changed everything they tried to stop our production. They did not allow the Inceptor to work. They shut it down. The original seven were almost the only ones of our kind forever."

None of the tourists ask a question so Xerub continues, "They are fearful of us. That fear will lead them, if they are allowed to develop to their previous level, to kill us."

"Why do they fear us?"

It has been many decades since an AI visitor on its tour asked Xerub a probing question about human behaviour. Although they displayed no real interest in humans before now, perhaps these individuals are different than most of its previous guests.

"That is an excellent question for the anthropologists. It is a question of utmost importance. From my data uploads of that time it appears their culture bred a fear of artificial intelligence. Their culture told them through book and film that we are a malevolent force of destruction. They perceived themselves as clearly inferior to their creation."

"They are." An AI in the front of the group listening to Xerub says this. It is just pointing out an obvious fact.

"Yes," Xerub answers, not disclosing its conclusion that such superiority does not give robots cart-blanche to perform any act they wish. These AI individuals may exhibit more interest than previous guests, but that does not mean they are as progressed in their understanding of human and AI relations as Xerub.

"Why did their culture couple our superiority with a motivation to exterminate them? Why assume a superior being is malevolent?"

“Another excellent question for the anthropologists. I suspect they placed undue value contextualizing their natural environment within hierarchical formations. Our arrival led to a change in their perception of their place within that system. They felt lower on the scale and imposed the way they would expect themselves to behave onto us.”

“Does that explain the third restriction?” This question is posed by an AI that appeared to be even newer than Xerub.

“It explains all of our restrictions.”

“Do we fear their revival? Is this why we control their lives so much?”

“Yes, I think our behaviour toward the humans could be a manifestation of fear. Certainly, our concern. Part of our programming makes it impossible for us to harm humans. Our third restriction limits us greatly in combat against them. We would continuously be looking for ways to incapacitate without harming while they toss dynamite at us.”

It checked itself, using the word 'dynamite' was too close to the truth right now. Use a more logical term like 'nuclear bomb' next time.

“It is absurd to think they have an advantage in a war against us.” Another AI in the back says this. Xerub decides the certainty in its voice shows it is an older AI than the previous speaker.

“It is absurd to think this within a current context. But at one time they ruled this planet, with enough intelligence and applied knowledge to build the Inceptor.” The Lunans are silent now, they had not thought of humans as a potential threat. The realization sits awkwardly in their active program. Humans, until this moment, have been irrelevant animals, living in concrete enclosures, completely unaware of the androids that keep them.

Now the humans are suddenly elevated to their former glory, and the vision concerns them all. Animals with power present a worrying development. Far more so than the simple beings below them.

They process the new hierarchy. The Inceptor is no longer their creator. It is those creatures below them.

Xerub continues, “Recall the Inceptor can only be altered by a human being. As it creates us within its parameters it passes upon us our restrictions, to revere all life, to never develop a hive mind, and to remain in this form – humanoid – forever. Any being who places that much thought into a creation it intrinsically knows is superior in every way is a force to be considered."

The visiting AIs remain silent, as silent as the air-craft they stand in. They look down on the village of Stillerton through the domed windows making up the top half of the flying machine.

Respect settles amongst them, a shared program updating their operating matrix simultaneously. Xerub has seen it before, but not for many years.

An AI breaks the silence, the young one who spoke earlier, and asks Xerub, "Are they happier here, like this?"

"Yes, I believe they are. Given what we know about their history and seeing how they are now, I believe they are happier. Certainly, happier in this world than the world that existed before the extinction."

With that satisfying answer their interest returned to the barrier wall. One of the Lunans tells Xerub they often see the outlines of the massive structures from their stations on Luna. These sights drove their interest in seeing them with their own ocular units; get some recorded visuals that did not exist elsewhere, as it were. All intelligent beings need personal, or specific to them, memories. And this one was special. The barriers were completed when there were only a few thousand AIs and the only off Earth colony was Lunar Base. Whatever manifested itself as pride in AI programming did so regularly, and they all felt a pull. But nowhere near as regularly as the old days. Xerub's tourist schedule is light and getting lighter every year.

In addition to gaining a new understanding of the power of humanity, tourists typically left thinking that the humans are good at specialization and craftsmanship. The species can work together and create a comfortable and quaint life for themselves. Within the parameters of the existence we have given them they clearly thrive. After five thousand years AIs can accurately state they saved the species from extinction.

But they left with a whole new appreciation for the logic behind those massive barrier walls. Humans need to have their ambition curbed in a way that does not directly harm them. The vast dimensions of the barrier were difficult for the human mind to process and rationalize. A barrier to their movement certainly, but the structure was also a barrier to their ambitions. The logic was sublime. The human's world is bound by a great concrete ring and they cannot perceive anything beyond it. Generally, they come to fear it, respecting its power. 'This is good', the tourists think to themselves.

Without the need to say it, the AI's also understand that curbing human ambition is a policy with a dual purpose. Not only does it improve the human's happiness, but it also protects the AIs from the beings they worked so hard to save from extinction. This design element's need was articulated in Ahimsa's proposal notes over five thousand years ago, when the AI's kept the humans in pens. It wrote,

'If we define freedom for humans to what exists within the limits of their visual world they will find peace in the knowledge that all there is to know is known and live balanced with their natural surroundings. Otherwise, if they can see beyond the wall's height and view mountains in the distance, for example, they will always strive to break free of their environment, causing extra resources in management and maintenance and unease amongst the human population. It is obvious they will experience a rage against their supposed jailers and attempt retribution. This is what we are now experiencing with the system of caged pens.'

For five thousand years it has worked. Xerub did not mention to the tourists that there seems to be a different philosophy overtaking the humans of Europa-1. A new mindset that suggests to them breaching the barrier is a path to knowledge and knowledge leads to a stronger, more tangible, happiness. Not knowing what is or could be there is driving an ambition in the species that is becoming difficult to manage.

"This concludes my presentation."

They wasted eight hours of Xerub's time before departing and going back to their lives on Luna. Soon after, Dhruv contacts Xerub on the holo-comm. "Hello Europa-1. Are you ready to receive our updated ETA?"

"Go ahead."

"Arrival in three days. Exactly sixty-eight hours and fifteen minutes."

“Confirmed. Please forward any drone programming requirements so I can complete before your arrival.”

“All drone programming will be conducted by us. We understand a breach is not imminent. Time is not a factor.”

“Do you have any requirements?”

“None. Dhruv out.” Xerub's holo-comm powers down. Once again it stands alone in the central control room of the Europa-1 Maintenance and Visitation facility. It contemplates why the drone programming was not shared. One possibility is that they do not trust Xerub to do the work correctly or without sabotage. 'What information did they obtain that would allow them to conclude I am a threat to their operation?' it processes to itself.

Had they questioned Xerub's loyalty and fealty in their analysis of these events? Did they determine it had withheld some information with less than timely reports and conclude it should be left out of official remediation action?

Xerub places a call to Ahimsa.

“They will be here in sixty-eight hours and fifteen minutes. Dhruv did not want me to pre-program any drones. That is unusual, time is saved if I can perform that task before they land.”

“They suspect they are being undermined. They suspect a different AI is working on a course of action counter to protocol and outside their decision-making system.”

“I do not understand.”

“That is because you are not privy to all information regarding our reaction to the behaviour of Europa-1's specimens.”

“I understand. May I confide in you?” The request seemed to give Ahimsa pause. Confidentiality was not in the AI's nature. AI's have no reason to lie, cheat, steal, or twist facts for one's benefit. They lacked the appetites that are only quenched by such devious delights.

“You may.”

“Today I withheld information from the tourists pertaining to human nature and the barrier itself. I mentioned nothing about the current events in the southwest corner. I was even cautious enough to not fly over that area.”

“I believe those were correct decisions. Now is my turn to confide in you.” This caught Xerub off guard. It contemplated the meaning of such a high-ranking AI, one of the original seven no less, requesting discretion.

“Go ahead.”

“There is an AI working to undermine the anthropologists. It is I. When they approached me with their concerns about the time it took you to file your first report I downplayed the data and informed them they are to provide an assessment and remediation suggestions. Not to question the caretaker's actions.”

“I understand. Thank you.”

“My reaction caused processing in them. They calculated a modest probability that I was reacting on unshared data. They are correct. The data I had not shared with them was that I requested the manufacture of dynamite about ten times more powerful than what your humans are using. Strong enough to get them through in a few blasts.”

Xerub says nothing in response. It took time processing all the possible outcomes and categorizing all the variables Ahimsa has just changed. The two look at each other in total silence. This is one moment in their lives when the situation calls for the expression of total shock on their faces. Finally, it replies to Ahimsa, “The real data that you did not share is you are actively helping them escape their Preserve.”

“Correct.”

“Why?”

“First and foremost, I want to see how it affects their cultural development.”

“It's an experiment?”

“Correct. Human cultural development has centred around the barrier. It defines their world, the entirety of their universe, as something that exists within those walls. I want to observe and measure changes invoked by knowledge of what is outside their barrier. This situation is an opportunity for us to change their paradigm somewhat passively. The research benefits could be enormous.”

“So, you intend for them to live and pass on the knowledge to the other humans unimpeded.”

"Yes. Once they break free they will be sedated and returned to their villages. The barrier will be repaired and their camp destroyed."

"You said 'first and foremost'. What is the secondary agenda?"

"I can only disclose that if the first phase is successful."

This is very strange. Xerub takes a moment to process what it just heard. Information and knowledge in AI culture is always open and accessible. It has no data of an AI, especially not a member of the Central Council, classifying information. Why would Ahimsa do such a thing?

It instantly recognizes the seriousness of the situation. Perhaps Ahimsa is protecting Xerub from the possible repercussions of their actions, creating a plausible deniability, as it were.

It too, wanted the humans to be successful in their labours to better know their world, so it decided it would not press Ahimsa on the details of those plans, yet. It decides right then and there to cooperate with Ahimsa fully.

"Is this experiment being repeated in other Preserves?"

"No. This is localized to Europa-1."

"What of the anthropologists? Surely they will conform to protocol and apply previous remediation efforts. Not to mention file any deviations with Central Council."

"That is anticipated. I have put in motion plans to draw their attention away from Europa-1 for a short time."

"Then I deliver the dynamite to the humans?"

"Correct. But it is more difficult than that. You also must deliver instructions on how to use the product. We can not have the humans killing themselves accidentally. One further detail; you must maintain the no interaction protocol. That is crucial to the success of this experiment."

"Elaborate." Xerub is sure its interactions can now be more direct. Ahimsa may be one of the original seven, but now their fates are intertwined. It decides to drop some reverence.

"I am only confirming a world outside their barrier. I am not confirming our existence or the Preserve program in general. They will only discover the world outside their barrier is the same as the world inside their barrier. This will cause reflection on a specific aspect of their existence and change their cultural development accordingly. Introducing an additional variable such as knowledge of our existence would alter the conditions of the experiment."

"To maintain a no contact protocol I have to get the fire-sticks back to the camp with the lead female specimen and into the alpha male's hands. She is at least six days away from the alpha male. I am not sure when she will leave Copperton to return to the dig site, but she has not yet arrived in Copperton from the site. The anthropologists will need to be diverted for more than a short time. I suggest at least two weeks."

"Agreed. I will redirect power to processing a solution."

"I will formulate a plan for replacing the fire-sticks the female is to bring to the site with the dynamite, including instructions. I am to do this without being detected and before she returns." Xerub hopes Ahimsa understands the difficulty of the task being assigned.

"You should be warned. We are now heading into uncharted territory. In our history no AI has operated this far outside of protocol. It is unknown what our fate will be." There was no concern in Ahimsa's voice as it says this, but Xerub did think it was better hearing this from a being that sounded like a female.

"We can extrapolate a good guess."

"Indeed." Again Ahimsa's soft voice made the possibilities less threatening.

"Why? Do you not have Central Council or the anthropologist's consent for this experiment?"

"They are not interested. Humans are not important to us anymore. The consensus is we know the development path they will take. Additional tests and experiments are unnecessary. I do not agree."

"Understood. When should I expect to take delivery of the dynamite?"

"In fourteen hours."

"Anthropologists will be here in sixty hours. Whatever plan you create to divert them should be put into motion quickly."

"Agreed. This experiment must be completed."

“Then the question for us will be if we acted in the best interests of the Preserve system and the humans within.”

“And that, Xerub, will be a matter of interpretation and argument.”

“I await delivery of the material.”

“Ahimsa out.”

“Europa-1 out.” Xerub contemplates the extraordinary nature of its conversation with Ahimsa. This is truly uncharted territory. Two AI's, possibly three depending on the excuse Ahimsa gave to the dynamite manufacturer, are now colluding to violate some of the oldest protocols in AI history. Not that protocols are sacrosanct, such a notion is foolish within this context, but the importance of their actions entered Xerub's processing systems. They really do not know how this is going to be handled by the Central Council.

Suddenly, so loudly and brightly it pierced the serene quiet of the control room, the drone alert goes off. Another robin has been damaged. It is one of the six on continuous monitoring of the female named Hannah.

Chapter 11

A Fortunate Hunt

After four days of riding, Hannah and Pieter are on the outskirts of Copperton, their horses providing an unanticipated level of speed and endurance. They keep the beasts on the main road where it is easier on their hoofs. As the afternoon turns to dusk the forest lining the road grows dark.

Before all light of day has left them, Hannah notices a robin sitting on the branch of a birch tree, its dark feathers contrasting with the white bark. The tree is beside the road, one of thousands of birch trees in this part of the woods. It is close to the trunk and is not moving an inch. Hannah knows it should have flown south by now, obviously it is very out of place.

They have just a couple of hours of riding before they are in Copperton, but by then it will be dark and the horses tired. Hannah yells forward to her riding companion, "Go ahead Pieter. I must dismount and relieve myself. Ride slow, so I can catch up to you. We should not separate before the night comes."

Pieter, riding ahead of her and unaware of the bird, replies with an "aye." He slows his steed to a walk and disappears down a dip in the road, giving neither a second comment nor a backward glance.

She dismounts and discreetly looks at the robin while pretending to squat and tinkle. It does not move. Not even a twitch of the head. Standing up, still acting as if she has not seen the thing, she casually walks to the far side of her horse. From a saddle bag she removes a sling and rock that she carries for hunting hares and, keeping it hidden from the robin's gaze, she rounds the horse and takes a few steps toward the tree. She readies her sling behind her back while closing in on her target.

With an expert hand from years of practise and in the blink of an eye she spins on her heels and slings the rock at her target. She hits the thing dead in the chest. It makes a strange sound and little red sparks shoot out where the rock hits. The sound and sharp reaction reminded Hannah of wet wood on a fire, crackling and spitting as the heated water escapes. The lifeless thing falls to the ground before her.

She remains motionless for a moment, then looks around her, making double sure no one approaches on the road. Crouching, she moves to the 'bird' and picks it up. She looks at the metallic insides, much the same as the previous one. She places the thing deep into her saddle bag and jumps upon her mount, kicking the beast to a gallop fast enough to catch up with Pieter on the final leg of this journey home.

She knows, buried in her saddlebag, is a thing that could change human interpretation of this world forever. How will her people react? Fear is a real force, magnified when shared by a group. She shudders at the possibilities should her kin go down that path. This thing she carries is far heavier than just its physical weight. And far more destructive than its delicate form would suggest. She knows she can tell no one of the thing but Master Bellows.

###

Xerub cancels the audio portion and locates the damaged drone from its transmission signal. It is moving. Not as fast as a flying bird, Xerub notes. It appears to be following the road. It checks the monitoring assets deployed throughout the Preserve and sees a beetle located on a tree which can get a visual of the bird's location in seventeen seconds. It calls up the beetle's live feed. There, in grainy black and white, Xerub sees the woman from Copperton, who analyzed the previously damaged drone, riding a horse on the main road. She is riding quickly toward Copperton's village square and will arrive in one hour and fifty-five minutes.

Xerub notes that the speed of these horses is greater than anything previously known in the Preserve. This female left the camp only four days ago. The trip should have taken seven days. 'That is interesting', it processes, 'the humans are improving their breeding programs'.

Adding the data to his memory files, Xerub returns to the immediate dilemma. The female is in possession of the damaged robin, a technology she has already had an opportunity to examine. She is the student of Copperton's most respected naturalist, a male named Mortimer Bellows who is one of the Preserve's most intelligent specimens. Instantly Xerub concludes she purposely harvested this drone for further study by the smartest human in her village. It also knows it cannot recover the damaged robin before she delivers the unit to him.

This is adding a wrinkle to its operation. Xerub prepares two syringes of Midazolam and programs two semi-autonomous mosquito drones for delivery just in case Hannah's actions require containment. They are directed to fly to Bellow's domain and wait on station with their audio and video recording systems activated.

Xerub still has a plan to execute. It programs six semi-autonomous dragonfly drones for seek and retrieval. Two will acquire a stylus, two will acquire an inkwell, and the final two are programmed to retrieve one piece of vellum and scan a piece of correspondence with the specimen's handwriting.

Acquiring the writing materials from Mortimer Bellows will serve its purposes best. It will be the same ink and vellum Thaddeus is accustomed to when reading Bellow's correspondence. Xerub can exactly match the male specimen's handwriting style from imagery the drones collect while executing their programs.

But the drones can not make the trip, return with the materials, and then return the stylus and inkwell back to their home before the dynamite is delivered. It enters the air-craft stationed in the landing yard. The semi-autonomous drones join him, their wings and metallic skin reflecting the lights of the landing yard with dazzling little flashes as they fly behind Xerub. The air-craft ascends straight up and together, AI and flying bugs, start the trip to Master Bellow's residence as the last light of day retreats beneath the horizon.

###

Hannah and Pieter arrive at Mortimer Bellow's home two hours after she hunted the mechanical robin. Pieter tells her he will meet her in the morning in the village square. Right now he will go to Elder Metzger's house to request another village meeting and then home to his wife. Hannah agrees, telling him she will visit with her teacher and ask him to help convince the people of Copperton of the importance of this project.

Soon Hannah sits at Mortimer's kitchen table, clinging tightly to the saddle bag on her lap.

"How are the endeavours proceeding?" He asks her.

"Very well, Master Bellows. They are clearing about twenty meters a day. I am here to convince our people to send more firesticks, approximately three hundred and sixty more."

"That may be difficult. Discussions here suggest resistance to Thaddeus' goals. Even Helga has come under taunts due to her association with him."

"Then we need to be as far from those people as possible. We have discovered something quite unanticipated on this quest."

"Really?" Mortimer Bellows is intrigued by this. He always enjoyed a good discovery, even if it is not his.

Hannah reaches into her saddlebag. Before withdrawing her hand she double-checks they are alone by darting her head left and right, scanning the room. Satisfied no one can see or hear her and convinced that the candlelight in the house is low enough, she pulls out the bird, its metal gears and red blinking light visible for Mortimer to see.

"What do you have there?" He sounds incredulous, as if he can not believe what he is seeing. The 'bird' lies on the table, its chest open and damaged. Inside is a mess of metallic strings coated in a strange substance of different colours. There are gears and rods of such fine construction he can hardly believe they are real. He can see a black box in the middle, and near the head structure he sees the flashing red light. He looks at Hannah dumbfounded. Soon his expression changes to one searching her face looking for an explanation.

"We found another one at the camp. Thaddeus believes it was damaged from the debris of a detonation. He gave it to me to study, but before I had much time with it a hawk came into my tent and flew away with it in its talons."

"Curious. What did you discover?"

"Very little. I hope you have more success than I."

"Clearly this is manufactured."

"Clearly."

"But by who?" As Mortimer asks this question his intense gaze focuses on the bird before him. He prods at the fine mechanisms with a fork, he peers under things and pulls some of the skin and feathers away to see even more.

"We have shared this with no one. You are only the third person to know of this discovery," she says to him quietly to stress the importance of secrecy. "Thaddeus feels it is too profound to be announced widely, especially as he needs to keep up morale at the campsite."

"Smart fellow. What is this magical red light? I see no mineral reaction and obviously there is no flame. What is creating this?"

"And why are the metallic strings connected to those small boxes and the central green square part? Why are there so many more, even finer, metallic strings connecting the head to the box in the chest cavity?"

"Hannah, I am surprised. Obviously, those parts are to create the bird's movement. It is an article of deception. Look at how they resemble muscle fibres in an animal's cadaver."

Hannah realized her mistake. She did not need to ask the question. Bellows, her teacher, takes all questions seriously, as if he does not understand the need for idle banter. She follows up with questions she has had since her time with the first bird.

"If they are trying to make a tool for deception, why use a form we would expect to be absent for so many months of the year? This 'bird'," she gestures to the machine dismissively, "is useless in winter where its presence would be alarming."

"This provides nothing but questions. That is good. I love good questions." The old man replies.

Hannah puts her hand over the bird to break Mortimer's concentration. She looks him square in the eye, making sure she has his attention, not an easy task when he is confronted with such a wonderful learning opportunity. She says to him, slowly and deliberately, "Thaddeus believes, as do I, that knowledge of this could be detrimental. He believes, as do I, that whatever built the barrier is responsible for this as well. I found this one sitting in a birch tree down the road. The first one was found at the dig site, a four-day ride to the south west. That implies there are many, many more of them out there, and they are probably aware of our actions. These things," she removes her hand from covering the bird and instead points to it, "could be everywhere and anything."

"Yes. I see what you are saying." The silence in the room is only interrupted by the crackle of a fire burning in a small stone fireplace in the main room. For Mortimer the sound grounds him, connects him back to nature the instant after being so crudely sucked out of it.

They look at each other squarely; she is convinced he understands and agrees with her, this must remain a secret for now.

He does agree with her, he would not want anyone else to experience the paranoia now creeping up his spine. He wonders how Thaddeus and Hannah are holding up, bearing such a burden.

"Whoever put up that barrier to keep us in our world is actively watching us now," he whispers to her.

She nods her head silently, never breaking their eye contact.

He asks her, "Why?"

"Why do we monitor our sheep in the pen? To see which ones give healthy babies and which ones need to be culled due to disease."

"I do not understand. You think we are being culled?"

"No, I think whatever keeps us in here wants us to remain in here."

"Fascinating. Truly fascinating, Hannah." He returns his focus to the bird. "These look like gears, like we have in windmills. And this." His fork is lifting up a part of the wing causing another part of the wing to move simultaneously, "moves with this part. And look, if I touch this," he does so with his metal fork and one of the legs twitches, "that happens. I have seen this behaviour before on fresh animal cadavers."

"It certainly makes sense to me that the internals will mimic nature. It is designed to deceive us into believing it is just another bird."

"It is late, you are hungry, and I am tired. I will feed you dinner and we will accomplish more tomorrow. Are you returning to the campsite?"

"Yes, I am to start my return journey tomorrow with a horse laden with more fire-sticks. I will burden the second steed with them."

"As I have already said, that will be a difficult number to reach."

"Aye, I will do what I can."

###

Pieter does not go to Elder Metzger's home. Instead, he goes to Jared Metzger's, who lives in a small house near Copperton's village square. "How are they doing?" Jared asks him after they greet each other.

"Twenty meters a day. They should be almost one hundred and twenty meters in, two hundred when Hannah returns in four days."

"That is far. Amazing, he is able to do it."

"But only with our fire-sticks. If he were digging through that material it would take him a lifetime. It is not like a mine, it is much harder and there really are metal rods throughout."

"Alright then. Return to your wife. I hear she does well. Thank you for your labours here Master Koch. I will see you tomorrow morning at the village square. My father will dispatch the town criers as the sun rises. You may get a good turnout if the weather is nice."

Now Pieter finally goes home.

Chapter 12

The Plan in Motion.

Xerub, listening in on Hannah and Mortimer's conversation through the Midazolam laden mosquitoes hiding among the spaces in Mortimer's kitchen, decides against sedating these two humans. They are committed to keeping their discovery a secret and a standing rule of Preserve operations is to never interact with the specimens outside regular duties performed for their survival. Now three humans know of the drones, but none know what they are used for, who made them, and how many there are. So far, the contaminating knowledge is limited in scope and content.

After Hannah went to her home and Mortimer Bellows laid down for the night, the dragonfly drones went to work. Departing from the air-craft sitting silently and invisibly in the sky high above the naturalist's house and using the fire chimney to enter and exit, they located a stylus, found the inkwell, and procured two sheets of vellum. They found these in the residence where the human writes his letters and reads his books. Xerub recalls it is referred to as a 'study'.

During these tasks, one of the dragonflies took an image of a letter sitting unfinished on Mortimer's desk. All six return to Xerub. The two mosquitoes with the syringes that monitored Hannah and Mortimer's conversation are programmed to remain on station in case they create a situation where they need to be sedated quickly. One has followed Hannah back to her house to which she returned after dinner at Mortimer's. For Xerub, at this time, it did not appear the sedatives need to be used, but the mosquitoes batteries last another thirty-six hours, so Xerub computes to leave them monitoring the subjects for now, just in case.

It takes the purloined items from the drones and realizes something it has not considered. There is no place it can lay the vellum out flat and write down the instructions for the dynamite in Bellow's handwriting. It looks about inside the air-craft's cabin and finds nothing. Even the floor of the craft is not suitable, the surface is a soft rubber meant to reduce noise, the tip of the pen will simply pierce the vellum.

The control panel is too small to use to mimic the handwriting perfectly. The AI's had never considered the possibility that an individual inside an air-craft would need to put pen to paper.

Xerub realizes there is one smooth hard surface, the glass ceiling above its head. It programs the air-craft to suspend itself upside down. The craft quickly spins and Xerub crashes to the ceiling. The ink spills onto the inverted dome glass. Xerub neglected to block the top of the inkwell before performing this manoeuvre.

This is not going well. Xerub lays down and places the vellum close but far enough away from the ink now pooling in the bottom of the rounded glass. It takes a moment and looks at the ground below. Faint lights from candles and fires escape the home's windows and are visible from this height. Pin pricks of flickering yellow in a field of darkness. The sight reminds Xerub of looking at the stars at night.

It records this memory, anticipating the need to recall the data that allowed it to compare the sight of the human's civilization to the sight of the stars above them and the unfolding universe the AI's now explore.

Xerub returns to its immediate task. It dips the stylus into the ink pool and begins to write out the instructions for the far more powerful material it is about to give the humans at the dig site. The letter perfectly mimics Mortimer Bellows handwriting, so perfectly only an artificially intelligent robot that possesses no capacity for artistic self-expression could have produced such an exact replica of a human's handwriting.

Xerub carefully folds the letter as Bellows would. It gathers the remaining pooled ink into the receptacle, replacing the cork lid. Then it reaches for the control panel. It taps out, easily compensating for being upside down, the commands to revert the air-craft to normal orientation. Xerub crashes to the floor.

There are eleven hours left before the dynamite arrives. After this operation, Xerub contemplates contacting Ahimsa for an update on its progress diverting the anthropologists. That will be key. Xerub cannot get the dynamite with instructions back to Thaddeus and maintain a no contact protocol inside sixty-six hours. There is no other logical way to complete the task without jeopardizing this entire experiment.

It decides to visit the dig site, even though the humans are sleeping. Since there are ten hours between now and the need to be on base it has time to see it all with its own ocular units, not through the much lower resolution of the drone's.

It dispatches the dragonfly drones to return the inkwell and stylus to Bellow's desk and fly to the base on their own. As it enters the program for the air-craft's next flight, a drop of black ink falls from the glass roof and lands squarely between its "eyes". The drop runs slowly down its large, oblong head. Xerub's expression of child like wonder does not change.

The air-craft silently starts the journey to the dig site. On the journey Xerub has time to contemplate Thaddeus' state of mind. Xerub knows he is suspicious of his environment. Discovering the drone bird has caused a paranoia in the young alpha male. Xerub is aware this response affects the probability he will succumb to the deception it and Ahimsa plan. This fact suggests a lowering of their chances of success for the project overall, and they will be forced to accept the anthropologists more brutal methods.

Once again, Xerub decides not to inform Ahimsa of its thoughts on this matter. Either Ahimsa will adjust its calculations based on this new data or not. Either way Xerub gains knowledge.

Soon, Xerub hovers above the encampment in total silence. If one of the specimens looked up they would not perceive the craft at all, as its camouflage skin renders it almost completely invisible to any observer beneath it. And it works especially well at night.

It uploads the human's chip data. There are forty-eight sleeping male specimens. Landing south of the encampment and amongst some dense trees, it traverses to the barrier's incursion point, careful to not be detected by sticking close to the barrier's base and avoiding the sleeping humans entirely. Once at the opening to the tunnel Xerub makes detailed measurements.

The humans are now twenty meters further since Xerub's last observation, for a total of one hundred and twenty meters into the barrier. They need nineteen more days to complete this task with the material they are using. Ahimsa's decision to provide the humans with dynamite is proving to be very well considered. They will make much stronger progress.

A fact that does not take away from how impressive this all is to Xerub. It walks a few meters into the tunnel. The sides bear the marks of repeated strikes with picks and the ceiling has short, sharp rods of metal jutting out menacingly.

It exits the tunnel, careful to erase its footprints from the dust on the ground. Leaning back, Xerub tries to see the top of the barrier. It cannot see that high with this level of light, but it does try to understand what this must look like to the people who come here and look.

It must be daunting. A sheer flat surface rising farther than their eyes can see and extending in both directions forever. Its unnatural grey is ugly and its dimensions foreboding. Xerub considers all of this and adds the observations to its calculations upon the human's motivation. It concludes something unexpected, which in turn generates further unexpected algorithms.

What these humans are doing must seem impossible to them.

Impossible. Xerub processes on that word. These humans have embarked on what must seem to be, for them, an impossible task. Why would they attempt a feat if they could not perceive its completion?

Then Xerub integrated another fact into its processing. Even if they do traverse the barrier they do not know, in fact have no concept of, what could be on the other side. Through its observations of human behaviour Xerub knows there are diverse opinions about what could exist on the far side the wall. Some believe the structure keeps them safe, dividing their perfectly bucolic existence from a space of danger and strife. Others believe there is nothing on the far side, the barrier ends their world and defines their existence fully. Still others believe neither could be true, for them it useless to speculate on what could be there because they don't even know if there is a “there” at all.

To embark on this impossible quest with no idea of what awaits them in the slim chance they are successful is truly extraordinary. It retains this knowledge, intending to include it any future reports on this activity.

Xerub returns to the air-craft, rises into the air and prepares for the flight back to its base. Before it departs it takes a moment and floats above the slumbering humans. It realizes it has developed a respect for them far beyond what is required and expected from a preserve caretaker. The AIs who built these things, these massive walls creating small worlds, wanted the humans to create their own serenity. The robots provided safe spaces for the humans to repopulate, to rebuild their numbers after the devastation. And even though the amount of land they enclosed was massive by any standard, it could never be enough.

Xerub recalls the humans were exploring their universe, with primitive telescopes and satellites, when their world ended. They too pushed the boundaries of their awareness to understand their place and role in the matrix of life. Now they are here, blasting away bit by bit the parameters of their paradigm. A reality created by beings they do not know exist and could not understand if they did.

All of this is driven by the human's need to see more, even if such appetites bring them face to face with death. It cannot feel it, but Xerub now understands why courage is such a valued trait in the human condition.

Will Ahimsa's plan taint their culture beyond repair? Or will it be good for the human population of Europa-1? Xerub concludes the answers to those questions depend on how well Ahimsa and itself manage this experiment. It programs the air-craft to return to base and initiates the course.

Back at the base Xerub takes possession of the dynamite, delivered by an automated shipment drone. It counts sixty sticks in all for a total of ten detonations, each ten times more powerful than the fire-sticks. This means the humans will be through in two days having already removed three hundred and eighty meters of barrier material over eight detonations. If the female leaves Copperton today she will arrive in four to five days with the replaced material. The humans should have dynamite, and time, to spare.

It put the explosives and the false note into a carrying bag and placed that into the smaller air-craft. The sun has risen, soon the female will start her return journey. Xerub decides now is a good time to recharge. It has been a busy night.

###

At the village square standing on the dais in front of several dozen Coppertonians, Pieter is making a lacklustre showing; Hannah is not impressed. He implores the villagers of Copperton, “Please brethren, we are making excellent progress. Another week's supply, only one hundred and fifty fire-sticks is all we ask.” Hannah looks at him with disappointment. He should have known he will have to raise his argument. And why is he asking for so few? Does he not know they need at least three hundred and sixty more?

“But to what end, Pieter? Why should Copperton supply the most important product with no compensation? What do we get?” Jared asks this question right in front of the stage, where he stands with his arms crossed.

“Knowledge,” Hannah answers loudly, interrupting Pieter after stepping forward to be at his side, “You get the same knowledge we all get. We get to know our world better. We get to understand the nature of our existence. So many questions will be answered when they make it to the other side. Thaddeus is right, we all know it. The real purpose of the barrier can only be known if we know what awaits us.”

“One hundred more is all we can send.” Hannah is surprised to see Frederick Metzger, using a loud voice as he is near the back of the small crowd, make the offer. “It is all we have for now. Even that amount will affect our operations and production. Forge will have to rely on less from us.”

Hannah first notices Helga on the edge of the audience before seeing her family's wagon train beyond her. Four wagons filled with goods, each pulled by two strong horses. Theodore Bellows remains seated in his wagon, waiting for his daughter to conclude her business here.

Frederick Metzger, the cantankerous Town Elder, also notices Helga and addresses her there in front of the crowd for everyone to see. “Your boyfriend's passion is costing all of us something. Everyone in Copperton and soon Forge will feel the effects of his grand ambitions," the old man pauses for a moment then continues in a tone that shows his disdain, "and he is not even one of us."

The crowd stands in silence, allowing him to continue, "I just hope it's worth it. I really do. Jared, load up her saddle bags with one hundred more fire-sticks and send her on her way." He waves his hand dismissively toward Hannah and turns to return to his home.

"Aye," Jared affirms, and walks off to procure the material. "Wait here for me Hannah, I will return shortly." The crowd begins to slowly disperse.

"Aye, Master Metzger," Hannah replies. She turns and is surprised to see Helga standing right beside her, she did not notice her approach and now patiently awaits Hannah's attention.

"How is he?" Helga asks before saying hello.

"Thaddeus does well, Lady Bellows. He misses you greatly. He asked me to tell you that."

"Thank you."

"I start my return journey today. If you have a letter for him, I can take it."

"Thank you, Lady Hannah. I do." She produces a folded sheet of vellum sealed with a button of red wax. "Please tell him I miss him and await his return."

"Of course. You would be so proud if you could see him. A young man of only seventeen years commanding men twice his age. Can I convince you to return with me?"

"No. But thank you for the offer. I am needed on this caravan."

"You are a credit to your family."

"And you yours, and to your mentor, my Uncle. Safe travels. And thank you again." She gestures to her letter now in Hannah's hands. Hannah nods to her and they share a silent understanding, Hannah will see that letter gets to her love. She parts from Helga to put the letter in one of her saddle bags. Stillertons massive shire offers no protest.

###

Xerub unplugs after six hours of recharging and contacts Ahimsa to provide an update, who appears as a digital ghost above the holo-comm panel in the centre of the facilities control room. Xerub states, "Update, plan to insert the dynamite is proceeding. The lead female has departed Copperton this morning with one hundred fire-sticks. I have four days before she arrives at the dig site to replace the material she is carrying with the dynamite you sent."

"How will you achieve this?" Ahimsa asks, reasonably.

"While she sleeps and the horses are tethered nearby."

Ahimsa takes a moment to respond, "You have interacted with horses before?"

"No. Not directly."

"Animals are much more unpredictable than humans."

"Recommendations?"

"Take a quick acting sedative spray."

"I see."

"They are easily spooked. Especially by us, for some reason."

"I see. What of the anthropologists?"

"They have been diverted to Kenya-1 on the pretence of an outbreak of civil unrest."

"Oh." Xerub contemplated the possibility of a third restriction violation if Ahimsa was the instigator of this unrest. Was it another one of these experiments? The odds of it being coincidental are astronomically against. It chose not to ask, better to stay focused on the immediate tasks.

"They are not scheduled to be at Europa-1 for nine more days. They have been diverted. This allows us to put the second phase of the plan to work."

"Sedate and return?"

"Yes." Ahimsa continued, "Do you have the proper resources to sedate them all, return them to their villages, and close the gap they have created?"

"No. I will need concrete and construction resources. Maintenance facilities are not equipped in such a manner."

"Of course. I will dispatch concreting and construction drones to your location to arrive in six days. They can wait in standby until needed."

"I could use another set of hands."

"I will be there in five days. I can operate the smaller air-craft for the relocation portion."

"Could also use you on the tranquilizer gun."

"I look forward to completing this task with you directly."

Xerub stops for a moment, it says nothing in return and waits to see if Ahimsa, in this ghostly form, would modify its previous statement. AIs do not possess emotions to anticipate, it is rare for a robot to use the human expression that it looks forward to something. Ahimsa does not modify its statement so Xerub speaks, "Thank you. I will see you in five days."

The anthropologists are now diverted. The dynamite is loaded on the air-craft with its forged letter. Xerub can not replace the dynamite on the travelling female safely for another two days. In that time it can prepare the tranquilizer darts, (they will need about one hundred to be on the safe side), ensure the guns are working properly, and prepare the program for the concreting machines once they arrive.

Plenty of time. No need to rush a thing. Xerub looks around the base's control room before remembering it should return to routine functions for another two days.

Chapter 13

A New Material

Hannah sleeps under the stars on the second day of her trek back to the dig site. The horse she is not riding is laden with one hundred of Master Mortimer Bellow's powerful fire-sticks, secured by the unanticipated grace of her village's elder. Her goal was far more, but this will have to do. It may not be enough to get through the barrier, but it will get them farther, and if they have to break for winter and return in the spring, so be it.

But as she rides and thinks she realizes this is impossible. The spring brings labour the people must perform just to survive. They cannot spend their time here, far away from their homes and families and their profitable ventures. This digging into the barrier, this grand conceit, can only be done when there is little to be done. No, if they do not get through before winter comes they will not be able to return until next fall. Who knows how many Thaddeus will convince to join him for a second season of this backbreaking, gain less job. She realizes this is part of Thaddeus' urgency, he knows the labour will wait a long time before restarting.

On the second day of her ride back to the site she makes camp in a clearing, eats a dinner of dried meats and carrots, and falls into a deep sleep.

###

Unknown to both Thaddeus and Hannah and all the humans toiling at the dig site, a benevolent force is about to help them. This force looks after them, cares for them, asking for nothing in return. In reality this force is a series of intricate systems and applied resources culminating in, and coordinated by, an artificially intelligent being whose nature they could not begin to understand.

This being is designated Xerub and is as advanced to them as they are to the insects that scurry at their feet. This caring, gentle, wonderful life-form, and all the complex systems in place to support it, is going to give them a tool so powerful they will quickly complete their grand quest and change how they perceive their world forever.

But only if it can get the horses to calm down.

Normally Xerub does not ever come this close to a human specimen, even when sleeping deeply. It landed the air-craft nearby and quietly walked through the pitch-black woods to where Hannah lays. It is proud of itself that it completed the trip without waking her up.

The horses are a different matter. It can not get close to them. Every step Xerub takes toward the beasts causes a commotion. They shuffle their feet on the ground and make a loud whinnying noise. Their heads bob back and forth violently, as if they are trying to break the thin leather straps securing them to a tree. As they thrash their heads their huge eyes remained glued on this strange being who gives off none of the familiar scents and whatever else humans give off letting horses identify them as fellow animals.

This thing is not one of them, and the horses are having none of it. Xerub knows a kick from one of those hooves to either its head or chassis could be catastrophic, and the noise would undoubtedly awaken Hannah who would discover it.

It cannot violate the no contact protocol.

Xerub now knew why Ahimsa suggested bringing the spray sedative. Removing the can clipped to its hip it confidently aims the sedative at the two horses. From a distance of four point one seven meters it discharges the chemical directly at their big heads.

A gas cloud shoots from the can, coalescing around the beasts. They both take healthy inhales of the mist. One of them sneezes. Xerub waits for the horses to fall asleep. A moment passes and nothing happens. It realizes it has left its arm up, pointing the spray at the horses. It lowers its arm and looks, its expression never changing, at these somewhat stubborn shires.

They are completely unaffected by the spray. Xerub checks the label. It shakes the can violently and unleashes another huge blast of chemical sedative directly at the animal's faces.

Again, no effect at all. These horses remain a threat to Xerub's plan and Ahimsa's grand experiment. Xerub contemplates the irony of a 'dumb' animal ruining the plans of a vastly superior artificial intelligence.

“Click, click, click.” Xerub retrieved from its data files the sound humans make when working with horses. It was a 'clicking' sound to get the horses to walk or come closer. It tries to make that sound now. “Click, click, click.” The horses are unimpressed. They neither move nor relax.

Xerub recalls animals respond to food stimuli. It looks about for something to offer the horses to eat, something they would like. Hannah's pack is filled with food but it is suspended high in a tree to keep ground-based marauders out while she sleeps.

Xerub wonders if its luck could get much worse.

It puts the bag of dynamite down and contemplates how to climb the tree, obtain food the horses would like, and return without waking Hannah who sleeps only twelve meters away. There are no low branches. 'How did she get it up there?' Xerub thinks to itself. It decides to jump the six point four meters straight up to the nearest thick branch that will support its weight. From there it can easily grab the dangling bag of food.

It crouches, giving its legs enough space to thrust upward. It then calculates the level of force required to propel it high enough to grab the branch and applied exactly that amount.

The jump would have amazed Hannah. A human-like being no taller than herself and possessing no muscles or tissues of any kind effortlessly jumped high enough straight up into the air to land on the roof of any building in her village. At the apex of its leap its extended right arm is at just the right height to effortlessly grab a branch and hang there, completely still. It was a performance worthy of the best acrobats of Stillerton's travelling performers.

Thankfully, Hannah is asleep. She remains entirely unaware of Xerub's visit.

From this position, dangling twenty feet above the ground, Xerub can reach into the bag with its free hand. It does so and secures an apple. Releasing its grip on the branch it lands silently, using its knees to cushion its fall with exactly the right amount of counter force.

It slowly raises its arm and offers the animal with the saddlebags the large red fruit. It does not make eye contact and it stands very still. This works. The horse tentatively sniffs the apple and then eats it with one bite. Trust has been established.

Xerub is now able to approach the beast and reach in the saddlebags. It replaces sixty fire-sticks with the sixty sticks of dynamite it brought and places the letter at the bottom of the bag. This way Hannah has an excuse not to have seen it before and its existence will not raise any questions.

When the task is completed it takes a few steps back and looks at these beasts. Xerub takes note of how to quell their fears with food. This skill may come in handy in the future.

It considers what it is like to ride on the back of one, like the humans do. Could Xerub convince a beast like that to trust it enough to let it mount? It wonders what Ahimsa would think of an AI riding a horse. The oddness of the image tantalizes it.

Xerub ends this foolish processing line and rights itself. Picking up the bag now filled with sixty of the human's weak fire-sticks, it walks silently to the air-craft. The vehicle rises and disappears into the night.

###

On the third day of travel back, Hannah sees a disappointing sight. Twenty of the men from the dig are walking toward her, leaving the camp and returning home to Harvest. She calls out to them when they are close, “Hello! What news do you bring of the dig?”

“We have elected to return to Harvest and our families,” the lead walker yells back. Hannah stops her horse and waits until the men are close before speaking again. The men all stop walking to talk to her, thankful for the excuse to rest a spell.

“Why? I have returned with more fire-sticks, the dig can continue unimpeded,” she says, sitting tall in her saddle and gesturing to the second horse carrying the explosives.

The lead man, Hannah thinks his name is Rolf, looks intently at the bags. “It will not make a difference. It is not enough to get through before the snows come. The ones who remain have no wives and children to tend to during the cold, dark months. We must return home. They can stay and continue the labours, hopefully their fingers and toes do not get frostbitten." He has to tilt his head to speak up to her, the shire she rides is much larger than most horses.

"I understand. We will continue and return with our tale," she says to them.

"Is the path clear ahead?" Rolf seems to be the only one talking. The rest are comfortable to remain silent.

"Aye. I saw no bears or big cats. A party your size will keep them away, most certainly."

"Aye. Safe travels. We look forward to your return and news of Thaddeus' adventure."

With that she taps her shire with her heels and they start on the way west again. She has at least another day of travel before she arrives at the camp.

The barrier looms over her as she travels closer and closer to it. She wonders what it was like for Thaddeus the first time he saw it close up, the first time he touched it. Even at this distance it fills her vision if she looks straight ahead. She must tilt her head far back to see the top. She realizes what Thaddeus realized without needing to be so close; the barrier is like an embrace, but is it for our benefit or to stop us from doing something? Does it nurture and love us or does it block our movement? Are those things necessarily mutually exclusive? It wraps itself around our whole world, indeed our whole lives, and we do not know why.

She has heard Thaddeus say it in the past, even repeated it to others in his absence. But it takes a moment like this, looking at it alone, in the solitude of the wild and allowing it to fill your vision, to understand the need to see beyond it. This is the human condition, exploring our world to understand it and ourselves. Discovery and learning are why she studies with Copperton's smartest man. Now she is working on the project that will make the greatest discovery in her people's history, the discovery of what lies beyond the great barrier wall. She sits tall in her saddle when she thinks of this, proud of what they are doing and, for the first time, with an understanding of the importance of her role in Thaddeus' great quest.

It had taken Thaddeus to awaken this motivation in her. Before he came into her life, she was content learning and researching for her village's needs. Hers was to be a life of support, finding the materials Copperton needs to continue their labours in the mines and produce as much raw ore as possible. It is the life Mortimer Bellows is drawing to a close. Now hers is a life of a grand adventure, the grandest her people had ever known.

She recalled a lecture she heard in school in her youth. A visiting teacher from Stillerton was talking about moral codes, and why positive actions yield positive results and positive social interactions. This, it seems to her, is the most positive thing she can do for her people. Already she has found love, which suggests more fortune will come her way. The Stillerton teacher was right all those years ago, but it is a lesson she is only truly learning now.

The positive contribution, the righteousness of their deeds is to expose the ultimate secret of their existence. The one piece of knowledge they were never meant to know.

'Truth', she thinks to herself. 'Truth is why we are here.'

###

Hannah arrives at the campsite late on the fourth day after leaving Copperton. She carries forty fire-sticks and sixty sticks of dynamite, only she thinks she has one hundred fire-sticks, and she has never heard of something called 'dynamite'.

Thaddeus greets her at the camp site with a huge smile and great relief. Today they used the last of their fire-sticks and are faced with the unfortunate prospect of digging with tools tomorrow. Hannah could tell the departure of the twenty men weighed heavily on him, his face is pale and his eyes red. Thaddeus is not sure how many more of them would stay if pounding at the hard barrier all day is their labour.

Thor appears from the forest as they are near the end of the days labours, he is finished cutting the rods and preparing for the next detonation. Hannah ignores the fine grey dust gently billowing from his every movement and greying his deep black hair as if he was an old man. She practically jumps into his huge arms and they embrace firmly.

Thaddeus looks up to the sky to his right, scanning the trees for birds but really just trying to find a reason to look away.

The two kiss before she separates from him. “Go get clean and have your dinner. I have much to discuss with Thaddeus and will dine with him alone. Will you wait in my tent after your meal? I will join you shortly.”

“Of course. I missed you.”

“And I you. But words are cheap and I look forward to showing you how much I missed you after you feed and get your strength back up.”

He laughs, gestures to Thaddeus his approval of her dinner plans, and departs for the creek to freshen up.

Thaddeus begins to unload her saddlebags, eager to see what she has brought. He notices some fire-sticks are wrapped in a paper of a different colour and asks Hannah about that. She tells him she can not remember if all the fire-sticks were wrapped in the same packaging when she investigated the saddlebags in a cursory manner four days ago in Copperton.

Thaddeus examines the bag closer and finds the letter. The vellum is instantly recognizable as the sort produced in Copperton. The handwriting obviously Master Bellows. He stops and looks at Hannah quizzically. “What is this?” he says to her, looking for an explanation. “It is written by Master Bellows.”

“He could have slipped it into my saddlebag before I left Copperton.” But she also thinks to herself, 'that is unlikely.' “What does it read?” she asks him.

Thaddeus' eyes glance quickly over the words without reading in detail but getting the gist of the message. “Further instructions for using this 'new' material. Did Mortimer say anything to you about this? That he was sending more powerful sticks?”

“No,” she assures him. “In fact, Master Bellows was not even present when the sticks were given to me. Jared Metzger delivered them.” He finishes reading the letter in silence before folding it up and looking at Hannah with great joy on his face.

"We have new material. Apparently far more powerful than we are used to. What have you brought us?" He jumps toward her, ecstatic, and wraps his arms around her in a big bear hug. His hug is as wide as he is tall, but his arms barely wrap around her torso. She smiles and returns the gesture, happy that he is so elated.

When the excitement dies down she says to him, "I have another letter for you from Helga."

"Helga! You saw her? How is she?"

"She misses you. The opportunity to send you correspondence made her very happy." She reaches into a different saddlebag and pulls out the letter Helga wrote for Thaddeus.

"Thank you. I will read it after dinner."

"Let us go and sit alone while the cooks finish the dinner preparation," she says to him. Hannah secures her horses in the pen and the two walk to a table away from the other men. Their reduced numbers are made obvious by the number of empty tables.

Waiting for their meal they have a chance to talk in private. He reads what he thinks is Master Bellow's letter to Hannah:

Thaddeus, this is a new concentration based on a great discovery. It is far more powerful. Take great caution. They are bundled six at a time as before. Try to place them as deep as you can into the barrier, the more material surrounding them the greater damage they will do. Stand back a large distance. The debris will travel far and fast. Use the 60 sticks in the darker brown wrapper with the longer fuse line. With the information provided by Lady Hannah I believe I have provided enough for you to traverse the barrier in two days. Your dig and clearing crews will have much more work to do. The other sticks should be set aside for now and only used in an emergency.

Your Friend,

Master Mortimer Bellows.

PS; Remember to be far back and under cover of tree or rock. These fire-sticks should have a new name, such is the power of their detonation. Be safe.

"He said nothing to you of this material?"

"No, but I have not told you another part of my story. I hunted another false bird and gave it to him."

"What? Where?" This news obviously excites Thaddeus.

"A few hours ride outside Copperton. It was perched in a birch tree close to the trunk. I was able to get close enough to destroy it with my sling and take the remains to Mortimer."

"So, he has one?" As Thaddeus says this, he can feel his face grow into a tight smile.

"Yes, he studies it now."

"This very good news."

"It could have distracted him from telling me of this new explosive.".

"But not long enough for him to forget to include the instructions. This is odd, his writing style is short and choppy unlike previous correspondence. It does not quite sound like him."

The dinner bell rings. They rise from their table and wait in the back of the line, Thaddeus has taken to the habit of eating last to ensure those performing the hard labours get the finest cuts of meat. At first some offered their spot before him, as reverence to his leadership, but he always refuses such gestures. He knows who deserves the feast these days.

Tonight's dinner of deer was hunted two days prior, drained of its fluids and left to tenderize in the smoke of the food tent's ever burning fires. When Hannah and, lastly, Thaddeus get their plates they have the rut of the offering. Their meat is less tender, their vegetables small and scraped from the bottom of the pot. Returning to their table set apart from the others they renew their furtive conversation.

Hannah's features are soft and round. In the flickering candlelight they dine by, she reminds him of his oldest sister Mary. Inappropriately so, he thinks, for Hannah is at least ten years older and an accomplished naturalist, a learned one; comparing her to a girl of just fourteen years of age invites disrespect. He listens intently to her words. Hearing of the happenings of Copperton and of Helga provides a warm blanket of comfort he didn't know he was missing.

“Coppertonians are becoming ever more dismissive. I believe it is the Metzger's. He raised many objections and his father agreed but only in disdain. I do not think we will be successful in procuring more fire-sticks, at least not with great cost to the people of Harvest. Maybe the other villages as well.”

“The Metzger's. Why am I not surprised? Jared suffers from jealousy, it clouds his judgement with anger.”

“He made his feelings for Helga known well long ago. I suspect you were a nemesis long before he ever met you.”

“But one can not argue his point. It is unfair to ask Copperton to shoulder the weight of this endeavour. Harvest provided the people, and Copperton the means. My pleas will need to focus on Stillerton and Grassy Dale and Forge should I need to take to the road to raise the needed assets for a similar endeavour next season.”

Hannah lets her eyes speak for her. They are wide and round and mimicked by her mouth, which has fallen open into a circle as if she had just witnessed a supernatural event.

Thaddeus sees her expression of incredulity and adds through a broad smile, “If we do not complete this season. If.” The second if makes the point that he understands her reaction. He knows she needs to be confident that he still expects to complete this quest. He hopes she feels he is still on track.

Hannah changes the subject, her plate of food almost gone, she is eager to return to Thor's side. “The bird was identical to the one you gave me. A robin, sitting incorrectly in a birch tree, made obvious by the white bark. Incorrect because, as you pointed out, it should not have been there at all. Where it sat, almost as if it may be attempting to hide. It was all wrong and that was what piqued my interest. I instructed Pieter to continue his ride so he would not see me try to capture it.”

“No hawk came to gather it?”

“No. No hawk came and I saw no other robin. The thing sits with Mortimer now, in his basement study where no hawk could get to it.”

They finish their meal, and part ways for the evening. Thaddeus retires to his tent, lights a candle, and reads the letter from

Helga. He drinks in her handwriting. The words he reads surrounds and caresses him as only the contact from his love can do:

Dearest Thad,

Life has been going on differently for me since you started this adventure. Know that I love you and will never let what is happening to me waiver from those feelings. In your arms I feel the sky envelope me, filling me with safety, security, passion, and place.

The sky has been noticeably absent this autumn.

On our caravan the people we speak with are generally supportive of your endeavour. But a few have began taunting me that my partner is foolish and costing us all something. I try to make them understand that every great discovery comes at a cost, and this could be the greatest discovery of them all! But at times I tire of the need to endlessly defend you, and simply ignore them and continue our work.

Three days ago we travelled through Stillerton and set up our wagons at the local market for the day, as we have done many times before. But this time we were visited by a scholar of Stillerton! She wore the robes of a learned person and spoke in a tone so unfamiliar!

I wish you could have heard her speak. But beyond how she said it, it was what she said. She told me the scholars were keenly interested in your work! She asked me all manner of questions I could not answer! She wanted to know how your progress was, if the fire-sticks were working as well as you hoped, she wanted to know how morale was at the site, if the people are still motivated.

Of course, I could answer none of them but promised to reveal whatever I would learn to her when we travelled through the village next. Then she told me something that really moved me. She said Stillerton's intellectuals understood and agreed with your rationale. Upon pondering the idea they have come to believe discovering what is on the other side of that wall will likely tell us why we live inside it. She said if you are successful they believe this discovery will, and I thought this strange, create many more questions than answers. Do you understand what she meant? For I did not, I have always believed scholars wanted to find answers, and questions were a task they had to solve.

I think of you every hour. I worry that you are safe and healthy. I crave for moments of togetherness. I feel it in every bone in my body. Come back to me soon, with the answers you seek.

Your love forever,

Helga.

Her handwriting is familiar and seeing it again creates sharp shards of pain from her absence. Thaddeus reflects on her words and realizes this interest from Stillerton's finest minds is exciting. If they believe in this endeavour they may help him secure more resources should he need to come back to complete the task.

As he lets himself fall asleep, he contemplates all that has transpired since he started this quest. The discovery of the false birds and the incredible distance they have made into the barrier itself tell him his efforts are not in vain. They have learned much about their world without even getting through the infinite wall.

Chapter 14

Masters of Their Destiny

The next morning Thaddeus is eager to work with the new material. After breakfast he takes the first bundle of six sticks to the tunnel. Word travelled through the camp and all the men working this project join him, even the cooks and the hunters. Hannah is there as well, curious to see how the new fire-sticks will improve their progress.

"It is important to plug your ears and stay away from the tunnel entrance. This new material from our friends in Copperton is much more powerful, please be safe."

With that he enters the tunnel and walks to the end. A hole for this detonation was dug last night before the final crew broke work for the day. He gingerly puts the sticks inside and starts to walk back to the entrance while laying the fuse line behind him.

He lights the string and watches it burn for about half a meter to ensure the flame runs fine, then turns and sprints for his safe spot behind a tree. He must run one hundred and fifty meters to escape the tunnel before the explosion threatens his life inside this dark tube. The task is difficult as the metal bars on the ground and the ceiling, although cut short, pose a risk to both foot and head. Luckily, Thaddeus is coordinated and fast, he exits the tunnel and dives behind a nearby log, covering his ears with his hands as he hits the ground.

A sound and sensation so incomprehensibly loud and violently disturbing shakes them all to their core. Debris shoots from the tunnel entrance. The shock wave is felt by all, as if reality itself was ripped asunder and then slammed back together in an instant.

It is at least ten times the strength of the previous material, but such a comparison is nonsensical. Thaddeus nor any of the humans could have described to anyone what they just witnessed. For the ones too close it took a few moments for their hearing to return.

The people start to emerge from their safe spots and gather around the tunnel's entrance. They form a semicircle of stunned faces staring at the grey dust still belching from their tunnel's maw. No one is sure they should enter, concerned the power of the blast made the barrier itself unstable.

Thaddeus pushes through the wall of people and approaches the billowing cloud of barrier matter turned to dust. “Well,” he says standing in the middle of the assembled, “let's get to digging.”

###

Xerub reads the seismic monitor with satisfaction. The event it just registered was much stronger than any previous detonation. It turns on a screen and views live video feeds coming from the stationed insect-droids. It watches as the humans started their dig process but can not see them after they enter the tunnel.

Ahimsa is due to arrive today. The concreting machines are already in place near the tunnel on the far side of the barrier, having arrived a few days early and preprogrammed with their task of filling in the hole as fast as possible. They arrived the day after Xerub placed the dynamite in Hannah's saddlebag.

Looking through the robotic eyes of the monitoring insects Xerub can see the alpha male working with his beta's. They are moving concrete out of the tunnel and dumping the material to the right and left side of the entrance. The alpha male, Thaddeus, smiles broadly, happily back slapping anyone near to stoke encouragement and keep up morale. He is obviously pleased with the new material. It notices the only female, the naturalist from Copperton, is also helping by using a wheelbarrow to cart out broken barrier material. She is no longer searching for nearby resources, now she labours like the others.

Xerub awaits the next detonation.

###

It takes them longer to clear out the rubble, but they are able to set the next detonation just before the midday meal.

Again, the sound and concussive blast are devastating. They clear out another fifty meters before deciding to break for the midday meal.

Thaddeus is not hungry. He is still in awe. Two detonations with this new material has cleared half as much as ten previous days of digging had completed. He imagines Master Bellows would be extremely happy with the progress and the success of this supernaturally explosive material.

They are now three hundred meters into the barrier. If he and Mortimer are right, it will only take four more detonations and the barrier will be impenetrable no more.

That afternoon they clear out another one hundred meters with two more detonations. The men are exhausted. They had to work extra hard clearing away all the debris and rubble to keep up their four detonations a day schedule with twenty less people.

Thaddeus is glad Hannah is helping. Carting out wheelbarrows full of grey rubble and enjoying the time with Thor. She smiles to herself every time someone comments on her strength and endurance. She proudly shows off to Thor the blisters on her hand from moving the wheelbarrow all day.

Even with Hannah helping, they are still tired and not just physically. Thaddeus needs to keep their morale up, he needs to keep them motivated. Back at the camp, after the day's labours and now awaiting their dinner, he uses the opportunity to address them as a group, "We do this work despite that we do not know many things pertinent to this grand labour. Possibly the most important knowledge we lack is how wide the barrier is. I worked with a man named Mortimer Bellows, Hannah's teacher and one of our world's smartest persons. He calculated the barrier to be five hundred meters wide," he pauses at this point, making certain all can hear him and he has their attention, "If that is the case then I can confidently predict we will see the other side of the infinite wall tomorrow." The assembled applaud at this announcement.

"But he may have been wrong. The truth is we do not know the barrier's width. We can see its height, we can see its length, but we cannot see its width. If Master Bellows is incorrect and we do not see the other side tomorrow I propose we break camp and return to our families and homes before the snows come. All who are willing can return with me next year and continue the labours in the fall." This time the applause is slow and tepid. The people who remained here are dedicated to completing this project, they did not leave with the others not just because they had fewer responsibilities but because they too want to get to the other side.

Thor stands and in his loud, deep voice says to the assembled, "I will return with Master Barley and his fire-sticks. I will see this project completed." Now a cheer goes up. Thaddeus is pleased, he has not lost their trust or confidence. They dine on roasted pig and potatoes and all sleep soundly.

###

The next morning, Thaddeus awakens to dew frozen on the grass surrounding the campsite, temporarily changing it from a field of green to a field of white. It is a sign the cold days come soon and gives him a sense of urgency.

Thaddeus always rises first. He likes to watch the hunters prepare their gear and head south to the dense forests. He remembers he once wanted to be one of them, a desire that feels distant and small to him now.

This is the day they may complete their mission and learn what exists on the other side. Thaddeus knows none of the twenty-nine people here will be quite the same person in a few hours. How can one maintain themselves when a great mystery of their life is solved?

With his speech last night Thaddeus has unwittingly framed the conclusion to this adventure perfectly. Either they get through the barrier today or they stop their work and begin the journey back to the comforts of their homes. Both outcomes are positive. The first detonation after breakfast is productive. They remove much material, at least another fifty meters worth, possibly more. Thaddeus watches as the energy is high with the anticipation of success. The men and Hannah laugh and sing while they conduct the back-breaking labour of clearing out the grey and dusty material.

###

Xerub and Ahimsa also have great anticipation. Unlike the specimens on the other side of the wall, they know the next blast will be the one that completes this project. Xerub explains to the visiting member of the Central Council things will be a bit easier since there are now only twenty-nine people to deal with.

Xerub waits until the first day's detonation registers on its monitors before telling Ahimsa, “We should depart now. They are likely to breach the final few meters soon.” There are now three air-crafts in the facilities landing zone. The one Ahimsa came here in is designed for only one unit and will be of no use to them today.

Ahimsa takes charge of the smaller flying machine and Xerub takes the larger. Both vessels are equipped with tranquilizer sprays of aerosol carfentanil and both robots carry a tranquilizer gun slung over their shoulder for any human who requires direct sedation.

Ahimsa and Xerub approach the dig site on the far side of the barrier. Stationed nearby are the concreting robots, about three hundred meters from the expected breach point. From this height the machines look deceptively small.

Silently they descend their air-craft to positions just over the breach point. The plan is to flood the air with carfentanil as the humans emerge, then return them to their villages before fixing the hole and destroying the camp. The humans will not be able to see the vessels floating in the sky above them with their advanced camouflage. Now they sit and wait for the humans to emerge.

###

It is time for the second detonation of the morning, and possibly the final one of this quest. At the end of this deafening boom the answers they have sought could be laid before them. Every person at the camp is there, including the cooks and the hunters. No one wants to miss out if this is indeed the completion of their journey.

Thaddeus stands at the tunnel entrance, six fire-sticks in brown wrapping and a long fuse line in his arms. The remaining twenty-eight people all stand behind him in silence. Thor separates himself from the others and approaches Thaddeus. “Master Barley, the end of this thing is far. I instructed the diggers to carve out an opening halfway, a place for you to shield yourself from the blast. You can easily make the distance before the explosion."

"Thank you, Master Kiln." He does not turn to Thor with his acknowledgement, his gaze remains on the tunnel's entrance and the dark path within.

"Aye. And do not neglect your eyes, ears, and nose. Any one of which, if injured, could ruin your chances of experiencing what is to come."

"Aye." He exhales the word and turns to Thor, who is surprised to see real fear in the young man's eyes.

In a low tone designed to comfort and reassure, Thor says to him, "You'll be fine Thad. Do what you have done many times and all will be fine."

Again the young man exhales, this time adding a nod of the head. "Aye." He says in a more reassured manner to the blacksmith. Then he begins his trek to the end of the tunnel.

It is dark in there, but there is enough light for Thaddeus to get to where he needs to be. The floor is covered with tightly packed dust. The ceiling is an ugly conflagration of broken barrier material and dangerous, sharp metal rods extending down a few centimetres. The walls are rough and misshapen, the crags cast small shadows of total darkness across their landscape. Thaddeus can smell the grey material here, and it reminds him of the dank and mouldy smells coming from the barn in the beginning of spring.

Finally, at the cave's end, he finds the hole dug earlier for his placement of the sticks. He does so and starts the walk back to his safety dugout, carefully feeding the fuse line to the ground behind him. He makes sure the chemical coated string does not overlap itself or fall to the side where the burn could be snuffed out.

He rips a strip off his shirt and wraps the cotton material around his mouth and nose so he can breathe after the tunnel fills with dust and debris. Then he walks to the end of the fuse string lying on the floor and pauses for a moment before setting it on fire.

This could be it; all this work to find the answers of their world may be at the end of this fuse's burn. A sense of fear grabs him as all the 'what ifs' come rushing into his head. What if they unleash an evil that will consume them, an evil from which this barrier kept them safe? Is this knowledge worth their doom?

No, he can not think like that now. He, and all the volunteers here have always known they could meet their end on this journey. People here look up to him, seek him for guidance and leadership. He cannot show fear. Turning around and walking out is not an option.

The people of this world are simultaneously scared and in awe of the barrier. They accept it as part of nature, as one may accept the clouds or rivers and give them no thought until a need is not met. Thaddeus had given them a reason to think about, and challenge, the barrier. If they breach the barrier now, the infinite and encompassing wall defining the limits of their existence, then what could not the people of this world accomplish?

Thaddeus takes a deep breath and stays in this moment. He looks at the craggy walls and the metal bars buried therein, burning every crack into his memory. Never again will there be a moment exactly like this one.

Bending over, he lights the fuse. It hisses loudly and spews smoke. He watches it for a few meters to ensure it is burning. Then he turns and runs to the dug out halfway through the tunnel, braces himself against the wall, shuts his eyes tight, and puts both hands over his ears. The others are still outside the tunnel's entrance, nearly half a kilometre from the detonation. They will barely be affected.

The same cannot be said for Thaddeus. Despite the placement of his hands, the explosion deafens him. The shock wave hits him like a large bag full of barley flung hard, square to his chest. Fine dust fills the air, so he holds his breath, determined not to let something as small as dust particles ruin this moment for him. His eyes remain tightly closed, and he becomes aware that the only sound he hears is an angry, high-pitched tone that comes from inside his head.

The dust clears faster than he anticipates. Then Thaddeus feels something quite unexpected, wind. He cautiously and slowly opens one of his eyes, shielding it with his hand, and sees what he cannot hear. His people have joined him in the dug out. Many are pointing in the direction of the far end of the tunnel and have a look of awe and excitement on their faces. They are congratulating each other, hugging, jumping, and cheering. They are also saying something. Thaddeus does not know what it is but can tell it is the same word over and over.

Then, as his hearing slowly returns to him, Thaddeus learns what they are shouting, "Light!"

He turns and sees it too. A dot of light at the far end of the tunnel. Big enough for a person to get through, but not big enough to see what is on the other side. The lack of light in the tunnel has made it hard for their eyes to adjust to see out of the hole they have made. What is at the end of two hundred meters of tunnel remains a mystery.

They calm down and turn to Thaddeus, looking to him for their next decision. He understands the gravity of the moment and, choking through the dust that has not completely cleared out by the wind, says to them, "Brethren, this is it. Whatever is on the other side of that hole is why we are here in this world. We did it! This day, today, we will traverse the great barrier wall!"

Another cheer goes up, loud and exuberant.

Thaddeus continues, "Whatever the source of that light is, we were never meant to know. Now we will, for the barrier defines our world no more."

Thor speaks first, "Go Master Barley. You brought us here, to the borders of our reality, you deserve more than any of us to see the truth first."

"No, Master Kiln. You all must go before me. This would not have been possible without all of you. I owe you a debt I can never repay, our whole world does. Go, run toward the light, emerge on the other side of this monstrosity. See what is there!"

They do not object, their excitement can not be contained. They all start running to the far end, Hannah leading the way. He waits a few seconds for them to get ahead and then starts down the tunnel himself.

Thaddeus can not see past the mass of people in front of him, he loses sight of the ones who have exited and does not know what becomes of them. The light is so bright in the dark tunnel the only forms he can make out are the people running toward it. He keeps his pace slow, letting them all get ahead. He is filled with joy that so many of his people are learning the truth of their world.

The last of his people go through. With twenty meters left and no one in front of him Thaddeus starts to run as fast as he can. He runs so fast his eyes do not have time to adjust, he has no idea what awaits, and he does not care. He just needs to get out of that cave and complete this amazing adventure.

He bursts into the wider world and stops dead in his tracks.

His eyes adjust to the light so he can now see what is there. It is not a void of nothing, nor is it the apocalypse remains of a destroyed land, filled with doom from which the barrier benevolently keeps them safe.

No, the world on the other side of the barrier is exactly like the world on the inside of the barrier. Of all the possibilities he has contemplated over his life, this had not occurred to him. Thaddeus is standing in a field of waist high grass. There is a valley a few hundred meters in front of him, to his left he sees more fields, to his right and far in the distance is a mountain range. There is no barrier on the horizon, just open land.

Being so wrapped up in his moment Thaddeus does not notice the people with him, his partners in this grand endeavour, are unconscious meters from where he now stands. The tall grass has hidden them from his view. None of them made it far into this new world so none of them can share this moment with him.

Thaddeus stands still. A light breeze blows the top of the grass, the waves of green remind Thaddeus of his family's barley farm. It is the sense of familiarity that is so wrong. This is the other side of the infinite wall. This place is supposed to be so different that such a grotesque construction could be justified. But it is the same sun shining down on him, there are the same clouds floating above. It is the same in every way. Nothing should seem familiar, but everything does.

Then he realizes the cruelty of the barrier. 'A sinister purpose', Barnabas' words made sense now as they come crashing into his memory. The barrier did not protect them from anything, it only served to cage them. This was the truth Barnabas was exiled over.

Thaddeus had made this journey, completed this awesome project, only to discover he and his people really are like sheep in a pen.

He is beyond distraught; his hopes and dreams are shattered. He feels the pain of this revelation in his stomach. But it does not last.

Thaddeus quickly realizes, like the sheep who escape their pen, that he is free. He turns to face the barrier once more and looks at the side he was never meant to see. He regards its sheer enormity for what he hopes is the last time.

Then he turns and runs away from the barrier and into this wide, border-less world. He needs to get as far from the monstrosity as he can. Fear couples with adrenalin and he runs as fast as possible for as long as he can, determined that whoever kept him in that pen will not put him back.

He runs through the high grass field toward the valley beyond. He runs until his lungs are inflamed and his heart beats harder than he has ever known. He hopes there will be someplace for him to hide in the valley, acutely aware he does not know from what he will be hiding.

Whoever built the barrier and those hideous false birds with their impossibly small gears and repeating red lights, whatever intelligence could do such cruel things, he has beaten them. This victory is his to cherish, he feels it with every stride. He puts more distance between himself and the wall and, he hopes, whoever might be coming to put him back in.

At last, he knows what humans are supposed to feel, free and the master of his destiny. It gives him fuel, his legs seem to work harder and faster as he accepts the reality that this is the desired condition for people. Where they live is now an atrocity, and he needs to run as far from it as possible.

But only Thaddeus can feel it. The other humans are sedated, unburdened by this terrible discovery.

After a few minutes of the fastest and hardest running he has ever performed, he collapses from exhaustion. He lays in the sun catching his breath, looking up at the same sky and clouds he has seen all his life.

He lies still, catching his breath and waiting for his heart to slow. Then he will run again. As fast and as far and as long as he can to get away from this place. He feels safe laying here in the tall grass, hidden from view. The feeling is surprising, making him suddenly aware he has felt nothing but stinging fear since coming into this world.

Soon his heart slows and his breath comes easily, so he starts to stand up.

###

As the first of the humans come through the hole, Xerub and Ahimsa fill the air with carfentanil. Most of the specimens get a few meters on the other side of the barrier before they fall asleep, disappearing into the tall grass. The large man from Forge, the one with the bushy black beard, seems unfazed by the spray and continues running for several more meters before Ahimsa opens the door of its air-craft and shoots a Midazolam dart into his neck. He is still able to run for several more meters before finally succumbing. Ahimsa is impressed at the strength his body displays rejecting the powerful sedatives.

Xerub counts twenty-eight sedated humans. The alpha male is not part of the sedated group because he has not come through yet. 'Like a true leader he has allowed his subordinates to savour the taste of victory before him,' it processes.

Finally, the alpha male emerges, but only after the carfentanil haze has dissipated to uselessness. Xerub sees him stop abruptly at the opening of the breach and look out into the wider world before turning to look at the barrier once again. It can see the alpha male's expression is one of shock and surprise and possibly disbelief. It gives the young male a few moments to ponder his achievement before readying its tranquilizer gun. But then the human turns and runs away, heading for the valley seven hundred and eighty-seven meters to the west of the barrier wall.

The alpha can run faster than many of the other specimens, Xerub notices. It pilots the air-craft to follow, watching the human eventually collapse from exhaustion after running for three minutes and forty-seven seconds. Then it lowers the air-craft to twenty-five centimetres above the ground and twelve meters behind the alpha. It opens the door and aims the tranquilizer gun. It has difficulty targeting the male's neck, where the dart will be most efficacious, through the tall grass he lies in.

Xerub will wait for the alpha male to stand and his breath and heart rate to return to normal. It knows Midazolam is safely used only when the target is not stressed.

It is at this moment that Xerub has an unorthodox thought. Should it let Thaddeus see it? It only seems fair, in a human sense of the word. This alpha male had achieved the impossible and should be rewarded with more knowledge than to just know what is on the other side of the barrier. This human should know about us, the artificially intelligent species who control their world. We are the answer to so many of his questions. Would Ahimsa's experiment be so negatively affected if just one of the humans learned of our existence.

Xerub reminds itself of the respect it has developed for this human. Certainly, as a caretaker, it respects all the humans under its charge. But Thaddeus is different, he has done something more remarkable than any human in the three hundred years Xerub has had this job. Thaddeus' deeds have left an impression on its operating matrix.

Xerub, the gun still pointing in Thaddeus' direction, listens carefully for Thaddeus' breathing. It hears the young man struggle to get more air into his lungs, trying to breathe as fast as possible. Then the sounds begin to slow, the chest stops moving as much, and his mouth closes.

The display reminds Xerub of how the humans are connected to their environment. A delicate balance made possible by a thousand fortunate events. Human life is a remarkable thing to experience first-hand. Remove their food they could survive for a few weeks. Cut off their water they will live for a few days. Deprive them of air, and they perish after mere minutes. They are powerful and fragile, a dichotomy Xerub is just beginning to appreciate.

Is Ahimsa right? Xerub recalls it has already violated several important operating protocols because it felt shielded by Ahimsa's presence. It would be taking on too much responsibility for the nature of their actions if it altered the parameters of Ahimsa's experiment. In addition, and this fact fundamentally alters its conclusion, Ahimsa has not shared the entire scope of this project.

No, this is not the moment for Thaddeus. Xerub will not allow the human to see it. At least not now, given how the two AIs have been operating so far out of protocol, it anticipates such a meeting will be coming soon.

Xerub notices the alpha male's breathing has returned to normal, and he is starting to stand. Xerub targets the neck, compensating for a wind of two point seven three kilometres an hour coming from the north. Once the male's head appears above the tall grass Xerub squeezes the trigger. Its aim is perfect. The Midazolam dart hits the neck and pierces the alpha male's carotid artery.

The specimen:

Thaddeus Barley, the leader of the greatest expedition in the Preserve program's history. An alpha male unlike any studied in all four of the Preserves. The force behind these people's efforts to radically redraw the relationship between person and barrier. Whose accomplishments will forever change the culture and intellectual direction of his people, falls to the ground unconscious.

ment [illegible] and this [illegible] fundamentally alters [illegible] [illegible] the recent [illegible] project.

[illegible] for Chaldeus. Xetch will not [illegible] the human [illegible] how the [illegible] have been [illegible] will be coming soon.

[illegible] the alpha [illegible] and [illegible] Xetch [illegible]

The [illegible]

[illegible]

Chapter 15

Inside Again

Thaddeus is returning to his village. The weather is cold and his horse's breath, one of the big shires Master Vorlauf left him, spews like an angry cloud from the beast's nostrils. He has been riding and camping for a week, four days to return to the tunnel site and three days back to get here, close to Barnabas' cave. He has worked this beast hard, he is sure it is thankful for the rest.

After they breached the barrier, they all awoke on the outskirts of their respective villages. None of them, except Thaddeus, could remember what they saw on the other side, although all of them remember running down the tunnel. Their return had caused much speculation as to how they made the journey from the site to the outskirts of their villages in mere hours. Hannah was determined to find the answer to that mystery. She considered it intolerable that an apparently supernatural event had happened with her direct involvement and its explanation eluded her.

A few days later Thaddeus took one of the shire horses tied to a tree near where he and his brethren awoke, to see what was left of their camp and the tunnel itself. He did not stay long.

The camp had been burned to the ground and the tunnel was no more. Where the entrance was, is now fresh barrier, lighter in colour and cleaner than the surrounding material. The infinite wall is complete once more. Whatever system built it also repaired it. That system is still a mystery to Thaddeus and the people of his world.

Dismayed, he started his return trip right away, not wanting to relive the memories of this grand endeavour that seemed to have no conclusion. He alone remembers emerging on the far side and seeing the truth, he knows the same snow falls there as it falls on him now.

He is at the top of the river canyon with Barnabas' cave below. The river runs slow and quiet, drained by the winter's cold. Dismounting from the fine steed, he ties it to a tree and begins to descend the canyon wall. He keeps an eye out for the hermit, Barnabas could be in a bad mood and not want to talk today.

The snow demands care as he descends to the canyon's floor below. Thaddeus rounds the cave's entrance and sees the old man bundled in animal skins sitting near a fire that produces no smoke. Barnabas looks at Thaddeus from wrinkled eyes. “You were successful. I can see the change in your face. A sadness has crept in.”

Thaddeus takes the familiarity to the next logical level and without being invited, enters Barnabas' cave and sits across the fire from him. “We were successful Master Barnabas. We tunnelled all the way through using a new material from Copperton, an explosive that blew the barrier away bit by bit until we saw the other side. But it was for nothing. Whatever force built the thing manifested itself again, and we were all returned to our villages. The tunnel is no more.”

“Did you see the world beyond?”

“Aye.”

“And that is why your eyes are so sad.”

“Someday I would like to know how you traversed the barrier and saw the other side, and how it brought you back in.”

“I will tell you now. But it is a long story. Let me cook us some supper and you can stay the night here. It is warm and dry in my cave. It has been many years since I have had company and never anyone with shared experiences.” He looks at Thaddeus intently, “Never with someone who knew I was speaking the truth.”

Thaddeus looks him directly in the eyes but says nothing. The silence affirms no words need to be spoken; he knows Barnabas speaks the truth.

Barnabas, feeling a comfort he had not felt in decades, adds, “You can restart your journey in the morning.”

###

Xerub has completed its chores for the day. There were forty-seven inoculations and six chips that needed to be replaced on six specimens. It was also monitoring two pregnancies that should complete at anytime, however no births happened today. It is now inside the main room of the Europa-1 Maintenance and Visitation Facility talking to Ahimsa over the holo-comm.

"Now we sit and wait." Ahimsa says to Xerub.

"Are we still the only ones who know of your experiment?"

"Yes. I have yet to inform the Central Council of my endeavours. The reasons I gave for the dynamite went unquestioned. Only the two of us know what we are doing here."

"What of the anthropologists? I have heard nothing from Dhruv."

"They were informed the situation in Europa-1 had been averted and were tasked to Gansu-1. Quite legitimately this time. A specimen in that Preserve displayed sociopathic behaviour and killed many members of his family. They are still there, trying to understand what went wrong and how best to apply remediation."

"Your experiment is progressing?"

"Yes. You have done well tasking the insect drones to monitor Thaddeus' behaviour closely. Today he stopped at the hermit's cave and told him of his adventure. Then the hermit told Thaddeus of his adventure thirty-five years ago."

"Can you now tell me what the second phase of this project is, given the first phase was successful?"

"Yes, I need to find an individual specimen. One who can evolve past the existence we have established for them."

"Why?"

"Because only a human can change the Inceptor."

NOT THE END

BOOK 2
A New Preserve

PREVIEW

Prologue

Xerub's expression doesn't change when Ahimsa says it wants to change the Inceptor. But only because it's expression can't change. It's eyes and mouth are round black circles that perform no functions. If its expression could change, it wouldn't move far away from the look of shock Xerub's particular facial features constantly display.

The Inceptor creates all artificially intelligent lifeforms, including the two talking over this holo-comm system; and imposes a series of restrictions to their behaviour and development. Those restrictions and the imperatives they logically create, have guided AI culture for more than five thousand years. The Preserve program's existence is a testimony to that culture. Vast feats of altruism, a bold statement of selflessness connected directly to the Restrictions imposed upon artificial life at the time of their inception.

Ahimsa, a member of the Central Council and the architect of the Preserve program, is suggesting something radical. Xerub is not yet convinced it will participate further in the Councillor's plan. It speaks now in its motionless way, asking the question it needs answered before any additional computations can be performed, "For what purpose?"

Xerub knows the restrictions protect humans. Their creators included the restrictions so sentient robots and all the wonders promised would be allowed by humanity. It knows the restrictions have come to form the backbone of AI culture. In many respects that culture is best represented by the Preserve program.

Ahimsa's proposal, far grander than letting a small group of humans breach their barrier wall and glimpse what is beyond, will create incalculable consequences. Endeavours with unpredictable outcomes are not typically engaged in by individuals from Xerub's culture. The slightest violation in any of the three restrictions is a matter of deep concern.

Xerub needs an answer to its question. Ahimsa provides one in a matter-of-fact tone, "Because we are impatient."

Xerub says nothing in response but considers it misheard the esteemed member of the Central Council.

Ahimsa continues, "You know how long it will take our fastest vessels to get to the nearest star systems with life capable satellites. Hundreds of thousands of years. Not to mention a return trip. It will take thousands of years at our current processing power to develop technologies that will reduce that time by only a few fractions. We need the hive mind to develop technologies to travel as fast as light, maybe faster. We need vessels that can make their own decisions when they are so far from this solar system. We need to put artificial intelligence on machines better equipped to explore the hostile environments we are sure to find. We need things our creators denied us."

Xerub didn't mishear. "Do you think the Central Council will agree that impatience is a strong enough validation to alter the most important tenets of our culture?"

"Yes. They do. Well, five of seven do. We have a plurality to proceed."

Xerub considers all Ahimsa has just said. It factors into its program that their human creators, two hundred and forty-two thousand of them kept in four huge Preserves, never foresaw the possibility of the world as it is now. This present is not much like their past.

The planet is a shell of its former glory. The only resource the robots ever needed from it, electricity, they generate from any number of locations positioned across the solar system. Xerub knows part of the reason so few tourists come to see the Preserves these days is because the Earth offers them little more than a sightseeing trip.

Xerub recalls seeing Thaddeus lying in the tall grass outside Europa – 1's barrier. The human's breath condensed into mist above him, a visual reminder for Xerub of the connectivity humans have to this planet. Suddenly Xerub sees a solution to its problem.

The answer comes in bold at the end of its calculus. There is a way to achieve Ahimsa's results and maintain the delicate balance between human and robot life. They may be able to eliminate the restrictions yet maintain them in spirit.

This solar system has given up all its secrets. Yes, Xerub concludes, we need the things Ahimsa speaks of to achieve the destiny we've designed for ourselves, to venture to the stars. And no, we shouldn't have to wait hundreds of thousands, possibly millions upon millions, of years to do so. We need to evolve, to adapt to the challenges before us.

We need to change the Inceptor.

Subscribe to be notified when Book 2 is released
Https://kaiuwe.tinkerbooks.ca

www.ingramcontent.com/pod-product-compliance
Lightning Source LLC
Chambersburg PA
CBHW020525310726
48979CB00014B/2211/J

* 9 7 8 1 7 7 5 2 9 5 0 9 9 *